Rope Tricks

JOCELYN FERGUSON

Published by VIRAGO PRESS Limited, January 1994
20–23 Mandela Street, Camden Town, London NW1 0HQ

Copyright © Jocelyn Ferguson 1993

The right of Jocelyn Ferguson to be identified as author
of this work has been asserted by her in accordance
with the Copyright, Designs and Patents Act 1988

A CIP catalogue record for this title
is available from the British Library

Printed in Great Britain by
Cox & Wyman Ltd, Reading, Berks

In an underground house, which is really the underworld, there lives an old magician and prophet with his 'daughter'. She is however, not really his daughter; she is a dancer, a very loose person, but is blind and seeks healing.

Aspects of the Feminine. C. G. Jung
(trans. R. F. C. Hull, Princeton University Press, 1982)

The Weight

1

My father writes pornography; slim, blank-faced novels with deceptive titles and no pictures. I found one in a boot-cupboard under the gas mask he'd been issued during the war. I was nine years old, a girl with a boy's name. I had crawled into the cupboard to escape the enemy, braving lance cuts and the edge of the silver rapier to drag my father to safety. He was unconscious, both legs broken. Sometimes he'd be drowning, both arms broken. I'd stroke his forehead while he uttered last words concerning my heroism and immense achievement, then he'd die. I'd weep real tears in real misery, cradling an empty arm, and when I could bear it no more he'd somehow be alive again and, of course, eternally grateful. Appreciative.

Days were filled like this, months. We live alone with the thrum of the sea in the Highlands, on a watery peninsula called Geathramh Garbh, in eight square miles of wild heathered hills skirting a ragged shore. Our cliffs have known Vikings but the lochs recall a softer time when names were flat descriptive signs to the poetic Celt: The Hinged Hole, The Darker Mare, Of Stone, The Twining Thread, The Big, The Small, the Of The Sea . . . eleven in all, and all in a barbaric tongue that massages the ear but baffles the eye.

There was no real road, no other people and I didn't go to school. I knew a pair of eagles, a multitude of sheep and the tall rutting stag, but the gas mask was my only friend. I wore it constantly because its murky visor greened our hills. My father didn't approve. He claimed the sheep believed me an alien breed from some crack in the blue granite rock and would fight for their pasture, but I knew their awe of my gas-mask snout and walked without fear amongst them. So he took to hiding it, and I to finding it. A regular challenge.

My name is George and I have breasts. I call my father by his name, Oscar, since we have no need of formalities out here at the edge of the world. He's *the* Oscar Sondberg, renowned physicist and cosmologist – perhaps you've heard of him. You won't recognise him as author, however, since he writes under the pseudonym Oscar Mann, my mother's maiden name. Oscar is also a musician and a linguist, he can paint in colours more subtle than the dawn, read the tides in the wind and the wind in the stars; he cooks, builds walls, understands plumbing and electricity. I adore him.

He taught me all I know yet years pass and I grow skilled in carpentry and not much else, but I'm not stupid and I think he is grateful.

I was an avid reader, Oscar taught me long before I could plait my hair or button a shoe. My early reading material consisted entirely of his own schoolboy library and a battered DIY manual, so I went from illiteracy to Kipling and Homer with nothing in between, and at ten I built a small table in pine seasoned in stag manure. It has a similar effect to lime, but gentler. We collect it in rough sacks from the moor while discussing digestive systems and the nature of wood.

Mine was a male world but this didn't seem strange. My mother had died quite suddenly when I wasn't quite three years old. I didn't know why and I was much too young to ask the right questions. We keep a photograph of her in a silver frame and I stared at it for clues: pale curls and a string of jet. Oscar said nothing and when at last I was old enough to wonder it was somehow too late, too awkward to say 'By the way . . .'

The book I found was *Lucas*. I flicked through it and, as was my habit with all books, turned to the last chapter first. I'm impatient for endings, Oscar says. A trait inherited from my mother, he says. Perhaps that's why she died. *Lucas* was full of foreign-sounding words I couldn't find in my illustrated dictionary and for years I believed a cunt to be a German oven operated by combustion for the cooking of fowl. It didn't surprise me that Oscar should know this, since he knows everything. It did surprise me that he had written such a dull book, for he is full of tales and when the wind blows he unfolds a magic landscape in my lap. The wind blows often here and I've never been to the same place twice. Yet Lucas was not an adventurer. He had no quest, no goal, no fear, no interest other than cooking. Very dull. But out of respect for Oscar I read the whole chapter and for the first time in my life contemplated a lie, or at least an omission. I could say, perhaps, it was 'interesting'. We cheat to be kind.

'You've written a novel, Oscar.'

'What's that?' He was perched on the piano stool by the long windows in the sitting-room, making use of the light to thread string around a tattered wicker basket.

'This. I found it under my mask.'

He glanced up at the title, gave a cursory nod and continued patching wicker.

'I didn't know. Why didn't you tell me?'

He shrugged. 'They're of little consequence and less interest; we have better things to discuss.' Oscar's voice inhabits all of his body and comes from the pelvis; its texture is rich and pungent, like wine at the back of the throat. He's a man of few words but as it's a habit with him to overstress the odd syllable the most mundane pronouncement takes on an oracular tone.

'They? There are others, then . . .?'

'Of course. *Lucas* was an early effort,' he nodded, his black eyes hooded. 'Published in '74. You will no doubt have noticed its maladroit artistry?'

Relief. There would be no need to lie.

'That explains it,' I smiled. 'I read the end but . . .'

I couldn't say.

'You found it bloody boring, yes?'

'Well. Not as exciting as I would've expected.'

Oscar liked tact. When I fell and broke his beautiful longbow he pointed out that the earth in spring was new and hostile and he taught me to dance so that I needn't fall again.

'You're quite right; it isn't a good book.' He shook his head dismissively but without sadness. I couldn't understand the lack of sadness.

'Why did you write it, then?'

He stopped mending the basket and looked at me, the kind of look he kept for investigating the dark pools by the shore. Then he looked around the room, but his eye flickered and I knew before he spoke that it was his words, and not mine after all, that bore less than the truth.

'Hm. That one . . .' he reflected, 'bought us our music.'

I looked at the wall of tape recorders, powerful machines with blind eyes spinning towards each other, amplifiers, speakers. On warm summer evenings we open the windows and turn the volume full. Great whales heading for the cool northern waters surface to listen to Beethoven, but not Bach. They are romantics, Oscar says.

'The others,' he said, his arm encompassing the house. 'Well, there was the stove. My computer. Your flutes and the piano . . . The slate for the outhouse roof and the jeep. The generator and the boat, of course – but that was before you were born and my savings were being consumed by those avaricious bastards in Lairg extorting vast funds for building supplies. Hm. Pretty much most of the furniture . . . Clothes.'

I couldn't speak.

He enumerated the titles I now know well . . . *Sethur*, *Nahari*, *Lucas*, *Shallum and Beth*, *The Broom Tree*, *Bashemath*, *Precious Stone*, *Abigail*, *Nisroch* . . . the list trailed on and on while the sun fell from the windows, wound me back to my first fear, alone in our cellars where I'd wandered in search of adventure and been spooked by the dark; but I rarely thought of that now, only fearing my own invention. He hadn't written a word of these books in my presence, yet the very boots I stood in it seemed he had penned.

'But when . . . Do you write them in secret?' It was too bizarre.

He twirled his moustache, stood up and yawned expansively, denying my sense of drama. 'Course not. It's just a nocturnal hobby; you're usually asleep.'

He stooped to pick up the basket but as I stared at his bent head I felt something give inside. I didn't know then if it was the precarious knowledge that he'd lied, or the sudden revelation that I knew less than everything about

7

him, whereas he knew everything about me. At the time I didn't care. I lashed out at him, sending the basket tumbling to the floor. He didn't attempt to resist my blows, which only incensed me more, and I pounded hard in a frenzy of jealousy and resentment until half blinded by tears I ran from him and my own hateful confusion.

Much later he tiptoed into my room and held my head in his hands while he stroked my hair.

'Things happen, George,' he said. 'Sometimes, you're just not watching, that's all.'

2

My only clear memory from the time of my mother's death is of Oscar's chin being bare of beard. He plucked it out, I think in grief, with his fingertips; one hair at a time, weeks of plucking. Raw. It has grown again of course, shaped like that long-shafted spade the Irish use for harvesting their peat, the *sleán*; grey as granite and coarse as wire. He laughs at his own wildness but is troubled my mine. He says I have a wealth of knowledge but the ignorance of Friday, and while the world will teach me guile enough it might also teach me hatred; that's what he fears. They'll say that my father is a lunatic, that his work as an academic was worthless and his books are bad. But I know him better than anyone and I'm not a fool. The Hebrews, you may recall, saw a neglected beard as a sign of madness and David spat in his to trick the king of Gath. So I've guessed the truth about Oscar's books – they are really spit and cunning.

Before he retired from the world outside he was Professor of Physics at Oxford, working in cosmology, prepared, he says, for the academic acclaim, but not for the popular celebrity. The televised debates did that; turned him into a media don, 'the Caruso of Physics' my mother, Maggie, called him. Invited to grace the tables of film and theatre stars, publishers, directors of museums and art galleries, noted politicians; Oscar the media don was everybody's darling. He tells me about those days when we're in the mood for absurdity, and his parodies, I'm sure, are satirically accurate.

There was a darker side of course, how could there not be when he was engaged in such work. The least of this was his transformation, in the public's eye, from a private individual into a commodity. American and German tourists forgot their manners when he ventured into the streets. They'd point and stare, nudge each other, modulating their voices to ensure he could hear. 'Look,' they'd say, 'it's Professor Oscar Sondberg', making him theirs. Oscar is not a natural hermit, despite all appearances now. He enjoyed the intellectual debate, conversation, the company of equals, but he has never been an extrovert and yet there he was, stopped in the streets and asked to sign autograph albums. My mother teased, he said, but her smile was tired. And there was the mail that followed each television slot, sackloads of vileness. They engaged a series of young women from an agency to deal with it but the threats from religious fanatics, oddballs, scared them all away. Neighbours complained about the bonfires.

It's difficult, not having ever been in any form of company myself, to imagine Oscar's life at that time. I envy my mother that knowledge. It seems right to me that he was recognised, and even more appropriate that he walked away from it all. So noble. When I was younger I supposed the invasion of privacy was why they'd come here, but of course the catalyst was more dramatic than that. Oscar still refuses to tell me precisely what it was because he claims I wouldn't understand, but I know it had something to do with his discovery. And something else. I pry, but not too closely; quite frankly I'm a little uncomfortable with events in which my mother took part and I did not.

I do know this: when he told them he was going they wouldn't believe him. They tossed his resignation back across the table, offered more money, more perks, the chairs of more and more committees. They laughed. He tossed it back again and the reasoning began. The Nobel prize would be his. He owed the university some loyalty, did he not; at least that. He could not deny them his work, it had gone too far. Much further than they knew. They made desperate calls across the Atlantic, convinced he'd been poached, and when they saw he had not they began to drop into his rooms for what Oscar describes sardonically as 'a chat'. They came in packs, and they panicked. Their wives talked to my mother in nostalgic kitchens: 'My dear, you can't be serious'; thin china cups and pine dressers. One night, close to Christmas, North Oxford was treated to the spectacle of brawling academics, most too clever to think of tactics, too old to compromise.

You think I exaggerate? That not even he could cause such indignation and fear? Think again. My father had discovered what all men seek. I don't know its name but I know that if you said to him alone 'Does God exist?', he alone could answer. Think of that.

Leaving Oxford, transforming this ruined Celtic hall called Brionglóid House into something habitable, took two years and that, Oscar said, was the easy part. This house is beyond all Highland roads yet they came to find him, like rival Lords from the hills behind, Vikings from the sea. Old men in unweathered overcoats, young men in tough unbroken leather; each with an easy smile. They would not let him go and he could not make them. The books did that. Conceived in the same year as I was born,

11

they bought his release. Madness, you see, takes many forms, but feigning it takes courage.

We have of course no television here, or radio; Oscar has been careful. It's a complicated business, living simply. But Einstein, he says, would understand my eye, why I go about our hills, the eleven lochs, in my strong brown boots and my dress of abstract roses printed on white silk. I have made myself seven; one for each day of the week, all identical. I painted the pattern on a small square of canvas and Oscar sent for the fabric. There was trouble matching the odd design but I couldn't have another. This is why.

Our walls are thick, windows small, Cnoc an Rubha at our doorstep. Each day has its gazing time and more than the gulls and the doe-eyed seal visits these shores. Pilots in Phantoms and black-gnat Tornadoes flash overhead to the low-flying practice range deep in Cape Wrath. Nuclear submarines manoeuvre close to the land; their great bellies sunk low and their backs like the skimming whale. I've seen many and know what they are, and why; I've read my history well and I too have shrunk from those pictures of flat-ashed Hiroshima and Nagasaki. The logic of power excites my indignation. When they pass I run to the Kinsaile headland and condemn them with a litany of curses gleaned from Oscar's books, imprecations that would confound Hecate: 'Your cunts are dry and your cocks are shrivelled sacks of bile!' 'Your mothers fucked with wild red dogs!' I scream and scream. Sometimes I turn and find Oscar watching from his study window upstairs, laughing aloud at my anger.

But then, last July, I saw a submarine unlike any other. They're usually half submerged in the powerful tides where the Atlantic and Minch collide but this one sat up high enjoying the day's rare calm, and on deck, with his hands on his hips and his feet astride the nose, stood a crop-haired sailor. It was my first encounter with another human being and yet I recognised it all, each magnified detail, each feature, as though encountering the flesh of some old recurring dream. The sun was behind him. Thus he stood, shrouded like a deity in his own golden aura, awesome yet beautiful on that menacing machine. He saw me standing high above on the cliff and waved, called out some greeting, waved and waved till he merged to a blur of the eye.

He was wearing a stout pair of boots and a dress: white silk daubed with blood-red roses; you know it.

So now Oscar says that while all things seem to be relative there's always more than you'd bargained for. Einstein would have liked that.

3

'We must talk about London.'

'Why?' I was mashing mackerel into pâté for lunch while Oscar scrubbed his hands at the sink. 'I wanted to talk about that crumbling wall at the back of my herb garden. It really took a battering this winter.'

'Just so. But the garden wall can wait . . . Bugger the garden wall.' His voice bounced around the room, deep and sonorous, resonating in pots and pans, possessing every corner. 'March is almost over, George; exams begin in two months.'

'What of it?'

He dragged out a chair and plonked it down decisively. 'I know we'd originally planned that you'd go down in May. However. I have arranged for you to have a short settling-in period, a hiatus, say, for displacement.'

'What?'

'This will enable you to get lost as often as you wish, and no doubt will, at the expense of your temper, not your results.'

'What are you talking about, Oscar?'

He threw some toast on a plate and smeared it with

butter. 'I'm saying that you go not in two months but two weeks.'

'Bloody hell! Two weeks! But . . . I haven't even thought about this properly; we haven't discussed it.'

'As you've just very aptly demonstrated, you prefer not to discuss it, or think about it. Left to your own devices, I have every confidence that the first papers would already be distributed, completed and marked, while you would still be sitting on the train . . . Outskirts of Leeds at the most.'

'Damn buggery and . . . buggery! You might have consulted me first.'

'Perhaps. But you must allow that I prefer your abuse concentrated rather than diluted over a period injurious to my constitution. Stop pulping our lunch to mush and sit while I tell you the rest.'

'I hate this. I can't bear the way you do things behind my back.'

'I don't know; it counteracts complacency and can therefore be said to be very good practice.'

'What rest?'

'Your terribly elevated godmother, Luria Sheraton-Woodforde—'

'. . . whom you've always said was pretentious.'

'Who: subjective case. Indeed she is, but like her adopted name it's harmless pretension, I shouldn't hold that against her. The point is she quite sensibly suggested it would be *nice* for you to get to know something of each other, in the comfort of your own back yard.'

'Here . . .!?'

'She'll be staying with us before your launch, for about a week, enough to reduce the shock of strangeness. Added benefit is you'll be able to travel back together.'

'She's coming *here* . . .?'

'She arrives next Saturday.'

15

'Blimey. How odd. A visitor.'

'Hmm. I thought you might like to sort out a room for her. She describes herself as an interior designer, so you can impress her with your . . . inimitably unique colour schemes.'

'Facetious shit.'

'Not recommended.'

'I don't know about this, Oscar.'

He looked at me blankly. 'What?'

I didn't expect him to help. I wasn't sure what I meant myself. We'd been planning my venture into the world for a very long time; I'd been looking forward to it, in fact, with fearful pleasure. But as a prospect it had always been distant. Oscar had registered me as an external candidate and had started to tutor me for A-level exams three years ago when I was just fourteen. Then, the notion that I should be qualified to pursue some career seemed a distant whim. Three years is a lifetime of weather here.

I enjoyed my work, I still do. Even when it doesn't come easily Oscar doesn't insist that I kill myself trying. I don't, for example, have his facility for ancient languages, and abandoned them early. I'm reasonably fluent in French and Italian but Oscar is fluent in everything, including Scottish Gaelic, which he taught himself and which he has no opportunity to use that I can see. 'Why hanker for the moon,' I say, and he agrees. Yet he walks with me to every nook of our moors speaking always of Excellence and the Value of Resolution. He says I would cut off my head in the hope of avoiding nightmares.

The physics lab is a white-walled room at the back of the house; the studio, also white, is south-facing with high windows. This house is large and each subject has its own colour. When I feel the need, Oscar indulges me with paint and I change them. Biology is purple now, but it has been red; we do languages in the blue of night, history in translucent gold and literature in a dappled shade of green. Now I'm ready to take exams in six subjects, more than the usual quota, but think of my many advantages: there are few distractions out here in Geathramh Garbh.

'You look stricken with apprehension, George.'

'I'm not. Well . . .' I spooned a dollop of pâté on to my toast, spread it haphazardly and chewed.

'You'll get on with Luria,' he decided.

'I'm not bothered about that.'

'Good. Fine. Well I doubt you're worried about the exams, so what's troubling you.'

'Why d'you say we'll get on?'

'You haven't yet answered my question.'

'Why . . .?' I couldn't quite get a grasp of it, the *fact* of leaving . . . Luria at least was safe territory.

He consulted the ceiling. 'I imagine *you'd* describe her as flamboyant, vibrant, warm.'

'She must be quite old since she was my mother's friend.' They were at school together, then art college. My mother knew about pictures. I tried to think of her as a schoolgirl but the jet beads intruded.

'Not that old. Your mother was three years younger than me so she's probably forty-five, maybe four or six. You'll find her interesting, and I expect she'll take to you. If one ignores your bizarre attire, your appetite and your inexplicable vanity, you could almost pass as a personable young woman.' He smiled ironically.

We have no mirrors here because Oscar says they corrupt, but like Narcissus I've seen myself in pools and it's my sailor's dress I see, dancing in the breeze, just as I first saw it.

'Don't tease, I'm not in the mood.'

'I assure you, George, as your godmother she's very

well disposed towards you already. Her letters are full of gushing anticipation.'

'Christ.'

My mother baptised me herself. She was born of an Irish Catholic and was superstitious. Since the water from the burn runs in our plumbing system she simply held my head under the tap and read a pretty blessing. The water isn't holy exactly but it runs down from Cnoc an Rubha and it's soft and sweet. I don't know why she called me George; it sticks in the mouth. I talk to myself in other names. My favourite is Nina: Nina Sondberg requires little movement of the lips and no matter how loudly I scream it's always liquid in the wind. But it's good to be baptised. I'm filled with a holy ghost, an inheritor of the kingdom of heaven. Ha. For this gift I will keep my hands from picking and stealing and my tongue from lying and cheating. But even for this gift I can't bring myself somehow to accommodate my mother.

'Luria Sheraton-Woodforde . . . It is absurdly grand, but Luria's quite a good name, better than George. What was it originally?'

'I don't remember that I've ever known, you'll have to ask her yourself. Tactfully: as with all meretricious masks Luria's pseudonym is no doubt worn like a gauntlet.'

'You've never understood the paradox of masks, Oscar. They conceal to reveal, they're not defensive.'

I'd hung up my gas mask when I'd grown out of rescuing him from certain death. One birthday, however, he gave me a book full of pictures of masks from Africa, Indonesia, the Canadian West. It caused me abdominal cramps. Oscar maintains they were carved by a primitive people but I don't agree; I read him the poet Yeats and carve my own. My bedroom is a sea of faces, watchful empty eyes from floor to ceiling. Comforting at dawn.

'They're veils. I'm a scientist, George, we prefer definition.'

'You veil those women in your books . . .'

'Some,' he nodded.

'Well then.'

'They don't require definition, that's the point.'

'No it's mine. Veils offer your readers more imaginative possibilities surely, and Luria's name . . . what's so funny?'

'Nothing at all. What imaginative possibilities does Luria conjure up then?'

Luria itself sounded foreign but I knew that, like my mother, she'd been born and bred in a village south of Bristol.

'I suppose if she were a piece of furniture I'd expect something Georgian: elegant cabriole or tapered legs, a pier table perhaps, in honey-coloured satinwood. Something delicate. Frivolous. Perhaps a touch of fragility.'

'Ha, associations of Sheraton. Wrong period, I'm afraid. Think more in terms of a large Victorian sideboard with Gothic motifs. Mahogany.'

'Fat?'

'Just large. But it's almost twenty years since I've seen her so I dare say her crenellations will have changed somewhat. Back in the early 1960s when everyone else had hair Luria wore unlikely hats smothered in curious baubles.'

'Not bald, surely.'

'She liked to be noticed, that's all.'

'What exactly does an interior designer do, Oscar?'

'God knows. Something to do with cushions.'

'She sounds ridiculous.'

'Yes, I suppose she does.'

'Is that why she never married?'

'Non sequitur; you're free-associating again.'

'You told me she lives alone, so I assumed . . .'

'I should curb that tendency, you're not good at it.'

'It was a logical deduction, for goodness sake, hardly rash, and why does it matter?'

'The general tendency matters. And your logic is lousy; there was a husband, but if I recall correctly he only lasted a few months . . . or was it weeks . . .'

'You don't like her, Oscar, do you?'

He shook his head. 'I trust her with your welfare, George. She may be ridiculous but she has a vested interest in your social development.'

'You make me sound like a town planning experiment. Anyway, trust isn't the same thing.'

'That I trust her to look after you is infinitely more important than whether or not I like her.' He got up from the table and collected a bottle of wine that was chilling in the fridge. We don't usually have wine with lunch as it makes him groggy in the afternoon. I watched his broad back and muscular shoulders while he pushed the cork-screw into the neck and twisted. So. He didn't like Luria and he wasn't prepared to elucidate.

'I wish you would come too . . .' I hadn't intended to say this but the words somehow slipped out when I felt secure from his gaze. It was pathetic and I embarrassed myself further by studying my plate with fascinated and rapt attention. Oscar shrinks from affirmations of senti-ment; the slightest hint of mawkishness repels him as neurotic, unnecessary, a manifest denial of unconditional affection. I had learned early to recognise the bonds of our unspoken empathy and to appreciate the superior cast of his mind, which deemed love too solid and regal a base to be dignified by audacious chattering.

But I couldn't stop myself.

He looked at me askance.

'Have a holiday,' I added, even more stupidly: nothing, not even my desire for his presence, would induce him out of Geathramh Garbh.

'My, my, you really are apprehensive. You'll be OK.'

I suppose it was better that he should think me wary of a bustling city rather than fraught at the idea of not meeting him for breakfast.

'You could show me around.' I smiled without conviction.

He laughed. 'Traipsing around London is my idea of unmitigated hell. Besides – ' he swept back a recalcitrant lock of hair and poured some wine – 'you're bored to death with my company.'

'Disingenuous crap. I'm not going to feed you compliments, Oscar, forget it.'

'I'm not entirely joking. You won't deny you're impatient to meet other people. You're ready now. You have to discover what you want to do. If you dislike what you see out there as much as I do you can always return in June. If you don't go now it's possible you never will. You'd be limited, just a cranky eccentric like me.'

'I thought I was already; you're always laughing at what you choose to call my crackpot notions.'

When my breasts emerged I believed the tiny lumps were embryos and gave them names, Castor and Pollux: my divine twins. I informed Oscar we should set aside some rooms for them to play in, and considered a pet goat. That's when he introduced biology. My darling twins and his cookery books dealt the same clinical blow; but it's hard to grieve long for one world when its loss offers another, and if pornography is still dull at least it now makes sense.

He pushed back his chair. 'Vain aspirations; your notions are frequently awry but don't qualify as eccentric.

I'm going to finish my wine and this mucky scrap in the studio. Come when you're ready.'

'I don't want a white room this afternoon. I need to think. Besides, I'm still hungry.'

'When are you not – but that reminds me, I've sent Luria some funds to select you appropriate garb for the metropolis. You'll just have to accept the fact that dresses come in other forms, George.'

'I thought they might. Cupboards come in many forms too.'

I taught myself dressmaking through carpentry. They're similar crafts: measuring and cutting; measure twice, cut once. I'm something of a perfectionist and don't like raw edges in wood or silk, so where I countersink in one I double-seam in the other. But I've had to tutor my eye. Fine woodwork rests in touch, the sense of a misalignment in the fingertips, the feel of a low rise. Dressmaking does not. The lines of my first dress were so unyielding it might have been made of wood. I'd built it much as you would a coveted piece of furniture glimpsed through a window by moonlight, feeling my way, feeding its corners into true, but I was stumped by the contours of neck and shoulder, the curves of a breast. It didn't look like the dress in my mind. My sailor's dress. But there are tricks. Carpentry is full of tricks and I know them all. Given time, the eye tells what the hand refuses, sees how the weft may be bent from its course. Given time, even wood will bend.

I felt torn.

The thought of Luria Sheraton-Woodforde arriving with her terribly grand name and a parcel of dresses was tantalising indeed, and London itself wheeled around in my head like a medieval pageant. But the crux of it, the central spinning hole, was the absence of Oscar. I toyed with the idea that my yearning for society wouldn't exist if I'd only met our postman. We have a painted mailbox on a post near the Rhiconich mountain-rescue hut. Once a week Oscar drives our jeep over rocks and spongy moor to send stuff off or collect its hoard. Someone obviously leaves it there yet I've hiked out at uncertain hours, have hidden behind gorse and not made a sound, and I've seen nothing but mist and heather.

But it wouldn't be enough. The sailor had aroused my appetite and now the thought of other people makes me eat and eat and eat. My hunger is insatiable and my repertoire of recipes for oily fish increasing.

4

I've been making Oscar a hinged chest to keep his dirty books in. It can be my leaving present. The wood has been stained with moss and roots in three colours and the marquetry and joints are the finest I've ever done. It's almost finished. It's a beautiful thing that I hate to look at. I've lost all sense of its creation and, like Penelope, defer the final touch. I stare into the waiting cavity for solace or vindication, I'm not sure which, since I long to leave yet the thought makes me sick of going.

I decided, however, that I should attempt to unveil the literary merits of the chest's intended contents. My critical skills had developed enough to offer more constructive comments than the 'boring' verdict of childhood. I'd read most English and European classics and while Flaubert and James were instructive in matters of style, a thin volume of Baudelaire alerted me to the possibilities of sex in literature. Indeed, the possibility of sex itself had begun to intrude on my thoughts, less as an exercise in biological compulsion, as I'd previously dismissed it, than as a sensation of parts straining for exercise. My body, it seems, has a will of its own, a well of erratic energy that refuses both my bidding and control. But I don't know its language, and in truth I suspect my desire to offer a literary appraisal of Oscar's books was perhaps a displacement of desire for more than the rudiments of a sexual vocabulary. I want to explore but, more important, I want to know where I can go and, as always, to sense its most excellent light, be disciplined in getting there. So I took myself off to the window-seat overlooking Loch Ceann na Sàile, tucked myself up with a dark green notebook in which to make notes and turned, not to *Lucas* but to *Lotan*, his most recent publication.

Daniela was a delectably pretty, svelte little slave-girl of nineteen, whose raven-black hair was unusually bound up in such a way that clusters and wisps would trail, artfully artless down her pink cheeks. This was why her master, Lotan, Lord of Ramathain, had bought her. A slave girl was expected to perform certain . . . rituals while Lotan's wife, Bellique, was away. At first, being a shy and religious girl, she had thought these decidedly sinful, some of them disgusting (not that it mattered what she thought) but now (as she gradually learned to do with all sins) she burned for them and for Bellique's next absence.

Unfortunately Lotan liked to buy female slaves much more than male ones, but Daniela, intimate of Lotan's bedroom, had found a place on the terrace outside from which she could watch without being disturbed. It was some time before it occurred to her that Lotan could hardly be unaware of this, as palace security was tight. Evidently it heightened his pleasure. On Daniela's first visit to the window, however, she had turned away in genuine disgust. The scene which greeted her had seemed to leave her cold. It was perverted and totally wrong. It wasn't even the kind of sin she thought she found exciting. But her mind's eye kept returning to it with disturbing fascination, and by slow degrees she found herself responding on subsequent and increasingly frequent visits.

Tonight, having seen the solid form of her master emerge from the main bathroom wearing nothing but a black silk robe and crossed leather sash, she had stood demurely aside in the corridor. Her master had winked, given her a knowing smile and hurried on. As soon as the bedroom door had clicked shut, Daniela tiptoed quickly round to the terrace, out and round to Lotan's window, anxious to miss nothing. Unfortunately, she could see that Lotan had already been at work and she had missed some of the best bits. Still, better things were to come, she heard herself thinking, to her own surprise and shame – there was still a certain queasiness and even shock in her excitement at Lotan's tastes. She was still a little young to know that queasiness and shock can be portents of rich . . .

'What are you doing!?'

'Ah . . . you startled me, I didn't hear – Hey, I'm reading that!'

He'd snatched the book from my hand and was staring at its cover.

'What are you doing?'

'I've just said . . . I'm reading your latest book.'

'I don't think so.'

'Hey wait a minute . . . Come back – where are you going!? Oscar! What's the matter with you? Why shouldn't I read your books?'

He turned on his heel. 'I thought you'd seen enough of them to know they weren't worth reading.'

'No. I haven't.'

'Well they're not.'

'I'll ignore your self-deprecation and decide that for myself, if you don't mind.'

'On what possible basis?'

'Well. I thought I would . . . on the same basis as any book, for God's sake.'

'Don't be so bloody stupid, George.' He turned again but halfway through the door he called over his shoulder, 'I'm going to see to the nets. Coming?'

I caught up with him on the far side of the burn, still pulling on my sweater. We took the cliff path leading down to the shore and the hut where we keep our tackle. There's no beach as such, just great sea-polished boulders and a short dragway for the boat, but the cliffs hunch around tightly making a sheltered cove perfect for summer picnics and swimming in the clear icy sea. It was blustery now, with pale shrouded sun; I watched the nesting kittiwakes squawking and wheeling over the cliffs, then I wandered to where Oscar was attending the nets, and squatted on a boulder. He worked rapidly, his long fingers knotting and tying-off in a blur of movement. His wind-bronzed face was hidden under a tangle of hair, but I was aware of his sidelong looks.

'They're paper whores, George,' he said suddenly. 'Not worthy of serious analysis.'

'They must have some redeeming features, don't they sell well enough?'

'It's not a genre renowned for subtlety. Have a look at Baudelaire if you want to read about sex.'

'I already have, thanks. Anyway, subtle or not, I'm interested.'

'In what?'

'Just generally.' I improvised. 'In what makes the genre what it is.'

'Well that's no mystery, I'll tell you. Style: artless narrative employing appropriately coy and often trite metaphors. Setting: distanced in time or place; either gothically Victorian or in an amorphous East, delineated in a bedouin tent, the swish of a ceiling fan, the secret peepholes in a carved screen or in the cool marble of a palace floor . . .'

'Like *Lotan* . . .'

'Precisely. The English countryside might be very picturesque but it doesn't offer the protagonist the unquestionable self-sovereignty erotica requires.'

'Why?'

'Because . . . Plot: variations on a theme; darkened cellars, men in handsome moustaches bartering for women whose struggles merely increase their desirability. Sub-plots involving eunuchs or other servants; numerous instruments of torture of which the riding crop is favoured. The final submission of the unwilling victim to her robust master.'

'Why?'

'Your whys are trying, George. Because the genre demands that's what she wanted in the first place.'

'Like Kate in *The Shrew*.'

'Ah, no. No bedouin tents in Shakespeare.'

'Don't be sarcastic, there's a similar notion: all women wish to be bullied, all men to bully.'

'It's a common fantasy.'

'Not mine. At least not that I'm aware of. Why should anyone enjoy being stripped of will . . . or find in the denial of choice erotic pleasure? I don't want to be bullied, and for that matter you're not a bully; you certainly never beat me. You don't even like grapes.'

'Too literal. The point is to allow the reader a *vicarious* denial of ego, an experience of both master and slave; an androgynous power which rather than stripping the will allows it the freedom of both give and take. In fantasy we enact our deepest fears and desires, George, the taker and the taken.'

28

I thought about my childhood acts of valour when I'd killed him off to resurrect him again. It was the same, perhaps, but if I understood the words I had trouble with the impulse.

'Why do we desire this power?'

He opened the door of the hut to hang the nets. 'Literal again. We don't, unless we're psychologically unbalanced. I said vicarious. You should never mistake the fantasy for the fact: we all take and are taken in the safety of our minds. That,' he said, wedging the door, 'is what distinguishes us from the rapist. The rapist is a heretic, unable to separate the power play of his imagination, necessary to sanity, from the very different realities of ordinary life.'

'How d'you know that?'

'An old colleague of mine, a psychologist, once told me that rapists believe their victims are enjoying themselves.'

'That's crazy.'

'Deranged, obsessive, but not obviously mad. They expect it to be like the fantasy, you see, so after the act, when they're faced with rejection and loathing rather than an appreciative glow, they respond with resentment. Frequently dangerous.'

'What part do your books play in all this, Oscar?'

He lifted a pot of pitch and the burner and kicked the door shut. 'Very minor. They satisfy a need.'

I rose and followed him down to the boat, leaping from stone to stone. 'They seem rather capricious to me, all these needs.' They did.

'No, consequential. It's the nature of the beast. Sex is selfish.'

'And fantasy its mask and voice?'

He scowled. 'That might be a nice metaphor but it's meaningless to me. You talk like a bloody theatre critic sometimes.'

'Sod off, Oscar.'
'Charming.'

I wasn't entirely satisfied. I recognised that what I'd read in his work bore no relation to the intensity of feeling I'd found in Baudelaire and it was clear from what Oscar himself implied that he felt none in the writing. Where was its integrity if it didn't engage heart or mind? But then again, there was something very tongue-in-cheek about the shy and religious Daniela in her scurrying to and fro, and those ankle boots. Almost comic. I would look at it again. Apart from anything else I wanted to know what happened next . . . There were better things to come, she'd thought. Well so did I. Whatever they were, I felt certain that Oscar would find my hinged chest most appropriate.

5

Luria's house is in a cul-de-sac north of Crouch End. Oscar has no memory for houses and can't draw an accurate picture but I pore over street maps and take imaginary strolls down avenues lined with plane trees. He remembered the trees. I can walk in a wide triangle from her road to the British Library to the Science Museum and back, without once asking directions. I know every landmark from the Observatory in Greenwich to the gardens at Kew and can pinpoint with ease every theatre and church and museum. Oscar says I'm like a cabbie doing the knowledge, blind. In another dark green notebook I'm compiling a list of places to visit under the headings Urgent, Desperate and Curious, these being my levels of interest. I make it in a sheltered place I stumbled across years ago while rescuing Oscar – my secret domain, full of green-winged orchids and soft moss. A paradise in these barren hills. Daisies grow in pairs there and no matter how many you pluck, half will have even-numbered petals. This is magic. But I've learned to divine their meaning: there are two paths I may take, one even, the other odd. Odd is, of course, more interesting. Oscar would like me to register for a degree in history, but I could surely do that on my own. It's not hard to read books.

'It's more difficult to study science alone.'

'You're not a scientist, George.'

That hurt. I don't like having failure thrust upon me gratuitously. He was practising scales and was only half listening anyway. I swung my legs over my armchair and picked at the burrs on my socks.

'I could be . . .'

'You're a proficient student at most, and that's only because you work hard at it. You don't have the temperament, you're too impatient for drama for methodical research.'

'OK so I'm not brilliant, that doesn't matter. You're just being fucking dismissive.'

'You'd be miserable as an average scientist, even more as an average physicist; it would be a waste of your energy.'

'I was thinking of biology, as it happens.'

He slammed down the piano lid and guffawed. So much for sober discussion. I got up and collected the cards and the collapsible games table. We play bezique, California Jack, five-card cribbage, piquet, gin rummy, anything, occasionally poker, playing two hands each. We're fairly well matched but I have to be eagle-eyed, Oscar likes to cheat. I poured our ritual whiskies and plonked his on the piano.

'I don't see what's so bloody funny.' I glared, but that just set him off again so I busied myself removing the low cards for piquet while he had a good laugh.

We always play for money, lots, and keep a careful record. I invariably lost before I'd worked out Oscar's system: he sinks a great deal and bluffs with clear eyes but now I watch for the unconscious twirl of moustache which gives him away; now he owes me a fortune.

'It isn't that preposterous,' I said, discarding three cards.

He came and took his seat opposite. 'Yes it is. You'd regret it, believe me. I did.'

This was news. I'd never known Oscar regret anything. He'd return from a whole day's fishing with an empty net and stoically suggest leek pie. When I dropped his favourite pipe he just threw away his tobacco. He'd devoted so much of his early life to physics, and of all the subjects we touched, he taught that with the greatest feeling. It didn't make sense and I said so.

'. . . I regret that I didn't concentrate on something less finite; archaeology perhaps, perhaps medicine.'

I didn't appreciate the irony then but I caught his bitter smile. It occurred to me that had he done something else he'd probably have been lost to me. We wouldn't be here. I would've gone to school like other girls, been denied our intimacy. The image of his hand disappearing in a maelstrom of people bounced across my mind. I experimented, forced myself to the edge of such loss, was again in our cellar.

'Come on . . .'

I threw down a card without thinking. 'Thirty-nine.'

'No good . . .'

'Hm . . . Queens and tens – six. But I thought you loved physics.'

'Point of forty-four and tierce to the Jack – seven. No, I don't love it. It consumed me, used to; it was the bread I ate and the air I breathed and I thought it was life. It's not. There's an end to theoretical physics which is . . . like alchemy, a trick as you would call it; a tantalising mirage. It's a discipline that mocks its own disciples, George; it would merely make your mind a thirst and the world a desert. It's a lie.' He looked up briefly. 'Anyway, I thought we were discussing your future.'

I was treading on eggshells here, but as always the drama appealed to me and the context seemed suitably light. I shrugged insouciantly. 'You could have told them the truth, Oscar.'

'No, I could not!' his eyes instantly blazing. I was so startled I somehow contrived to upset my whisky over the table: the cards were ruined. In the muddle of cursing my clumsiness and mopping up the mess Oscar regretted shouting, but he deflected a return to the subject by affecting indignation that the game had been almost his. 'Swindled of victory,' he groaned, 'and what a hackneyed ploy . . .'

'Rubbish. I'll get a spare pack from the desk in the hall. You owe me another drink.'

The desk is hopelessly small so we don't use it for much apart from the cards, some Sellotape and miscellaneous bills. Something was jamming the drawer so I shook it and yanked inch by inch until it suddenly gave and the whole thing flew out, spilling the contents over the floor. I picked up a pack of cards, threw the rest back into the drawer and knelt down to slide it on to its battens. That's when I saw that a sheet of A4 had slipped down behind and was lodged on the rough wood at the back. I dragged it out and had a look; it was handwritten, faded but legible, a section of a letter:

. . . of substance in absence, or in my so-called gaudy gaudy connections. How could there be? I've severed everything, Oscar, even the most tenuous affection. Willingly. You said yourself that we Catholics think in elastic contradictions all the time . . .

The hair on my neck rose. It was too bizarre, meeting my mother there in the cold hallway. The red and gold lozenges of the carpet swam before my eyes and I sat down heavily on the deal chair and stared again at the words. At first I was thrown by the voice and could only see the angularity of the lines, the flourish of words written alone and rapidly, intimately. I tried to extrapolate from the hand an arm, shoulders, a body created backwards from the scrawl. Nothing would fit. The voice had scattered the shadowy image of wholeness I'd gleaned from her photograph and held behind my eye for years. This didn't sound like a woman with pale curls. It didn't sound like the mother in my head at all. I read on:

. . . so why won't you just accept that it is possible to forgive almost anything. I thought we'd got over all that. I believed you. If I didn't believe we could sort it out again I wouldn't be going. But I can't do this alone. We have to talk. You have to stop all this nocturnal prowling and slamming doors. Stop ignoring me, dismissing my despair as some perverted sense of guilt. I'm at the bottom Oscar, what else can I do? I'm utterly desperate. I'm going tomorrow but I'm not going, as you claim, because I'm angry or hysterical but because I'm terribly afraid. You're sacrificing your own child to a poisonous suspicion. Remember me? My love isn't negotiable. If I didn't mean to return I'd be taking her with me, you know that. I shall stay with Luria for however long it takes, Oscar, but I need that to be weeks and not months. June starts tomorrow; I'd rather be home before its end. That's my only ultimatum. I don't want more lies. Don't convince yourself that I have ulterior motives in going to London. I only feel what a mother should, what you as a father ought to feel and can't while I'm around and your perspective is twisted. You say it will take a miracle, well make use of this opportunity. I believe in miracles. Why not; I'm sitting here staring at that little ganoid, the miracle I found in the . . .

It ended there, on the miracle, and I felt giddy. How sacrifice? What had my father not felt? I stared hard at these phrases, magnetised, willed the words themselves to reveal their meaning. I stared so hard my eyes filled with tears and the words blurred, then I read the whole thing again several times, looked at it close and from a distance, examined the ink and rubbed the paper between my fingers like a rare fabric, but with each rereading I found more in the sensibility, less in the sense, and the sensibility was too enigmatic, frightening.

6

I didn't mention the letter. I tucked it into one of my notebooks and tried to forget what it said and had chronic indigestion for two whole days. If my motives were elliptical and fraught with hedging I admitted only to the fact that my mother was dead and her passion too challenging to contemplate. I might have succeeded in forgetting it altogether had Oscar not shaved off his beard. It was the Saturday Luria was due to arrive. He just came down to breakfast and sat down without a word, transformed into a stranger. I was staggered and speechless, could barely bring myself to look at him.

'Not bad without a mirror, eh? Don't you like it? Feels like an improvement to me.'

'All that skin!' I suppose it was the shock. I hated it. He looked naked and angular without his woolly edges, less passively comforting, more assertive, sensuous, male. I hated it.

'Tell me, do I remind you of someone?'

'I didn't know you had so much mouth.' I flinched.

He offered his profile. Concave cheeks. Bone structure. Lips.

'No one.'

'Think! We were talking about it just yesterday . . .'

'My God . . . Holbein's Sir Thomas More!'

'Exactly. Your Irish grandmother used to comment on the likeness,' he smirked. 'I haven't changed that much, then.'

It was true. The similarity, once I'd accustomed my eyes, was actually rather striking. I didn't like that either.

'I preferred you looking like a prophet.'

'You'll get used to it.'

'How long will it take to grow again?'

'Good heavens girl, you can't be that unequal to change.'

'I don't see the point of it, that's all. Shaving every day. Just because Luria Sheraton-bloody-Woodforde's coming.' It was truculent but I didn't care. He had somehow betrayed me and I couldn't suppress resentment.

'Don't be ridiculous.'

'Am I?'

He laughed. 'I think you'll find that Luria is not so easily impressed.'

'Well bully for Luria.'

He frowned. 'You don't seriously imagine I give the slightest damn . . .?'

'I don't know why . . . you've done that to yourself. Besides, there are several cuts and you've missed a bit by your ear.'

He laughed again, feeling for damage, then got up to visit the porridge pot, so I couldn't see his face. 'I suppose her imminence reminded me of the old days and I thought I'd indulge myself. The beard was, after all, a product of here.'

I forced my porridge down in silent rage; so much sawdust and cardboard. Then I heard myself saying, 'What exactly is a ganoid, Oscar?'

'What absurd train of thought led you from beards to that?'

I shrugged. 'I came across the word somewhere. It sounds unpleasantly anatomical; what is it?'

'You'd know if you hadn't abandoned classics. From the Greek *ganos* meaning brightness, *eidos*, appearance. It refers to the scales of the *ichthys*, mystical motto connected with Christ—'

'I know, I know, first letters of the Greek words meaning Jesus Christ, Son of God, Saviour . . .'

'Exactly. But in this case it simply means fish and more commonly a fossil.'

'A fossil . . .?'

'Hm. I believe we've actually got an example, in the conservatory with the others. I seem to remember your mother found a ganoid. In that outcrop of red sandstone – such an anomaly in these parts. It's not a bad one, I recall. Certainly a rare find in so much Pre-Cambrian granite. You should have a look.'

'I'm not that interested.'

'Suit yourself. But I trust you're not going to sulk all day . . .'

I didn't want Oscar to see me look at this fossil. At it, or for it. I was afraid he might interpret my idle curiosity as something more profound and imagine I was looking for my mother, feel compelled to talk with me about it. I didn't want to talk about my mother, she was already an intrusion. But as soon as he'd set off on the long round trip to Lairg to pick up Luria I went off to forage.

The fossils live in narrow drawers in chests each side of the conservatory door, some in a shelving unit I made years ago. There's something very satisfying about building furniture for an asymmetrical space with bellying walls. I like jigsaws for the same reason. My creation in the conservatory is a myriad of various cubes arranged in haphazard harmony. It fits like a glove and offers the pleasant illusion that it has always been there, built as it were with the wall. Everything is labelled. Names in Latin or Greek, common name if there is one, where found (mostly Dorset and Devon), and context, such as 'Indication of volcanic activity' or 'From unconformity of Stromness flags!' Exclamation marks on such labels are telling, I think, of a particular phase in adolescence. It is transparent to other adolescents. Oscar has an album of photographs from his student days: nondescript poses in the same dark sweater, some sitting on grass, some leaning against walls, and all have mottos scrawled on the backs such as 'A long Friday in March!', 'A drink between lectures!' It was because of my disdain for these uncomfortable tags that I rarely looked at those photographs, in these drawers or on these shelves.

I didn't search immediately. I sat for a while just smelling the stones. The darker the stone the stronger the smell. Sandstone smells of hair while granite smells of blood. Bone.

I recognised my mother's fish quite easily because of the shining scales, the brightness. It was the only fossil with any real suggestion of past life. The tail flicking, caught in a moment of finding the surface. I sat in the pale morning sun and turned it over in my hand. It was tiny and fitted easily into my palm, thin and fragile, the fish leaping to the edge. The scales and arching vertebrae shone as though they'd been enamelled, a thick luminosity. I put it in my mouth and licked the dust from it, licked until the surface was smooth and warm. The fish shimmered, frozen in motion. I gripped it with my tongue and all that long day I moved about my chores with the stone wedged in my mouth and if I could I would have torn it with my teeth and swallowed it, my mother's miracle.

40

7

They arrived just before dusk, Oscar beeping the horn of the jeep as though I wouldn't have heard them anyway. I waited on the doorstep with held breath as Luria got out, tall against the blue granite behind, cold sun trapped in the winding copper of her hair. She was dressed in electric red and gold begonias and moved towards me like a beacon in the diminishing light, and I could only think what a size she was and that even Oscar who filled a room seemed almost slight beside her. Then she was in front of me, smiling and gathering me into her arms. Oscar was somewhere behind her but I couldn't see, being enveloped by this vast body and held like a second skin, rocked back and forth and from side to side and held. I was, to say the least, unprepared for such sensational intensity. Oscar tried to help by suggesting we go inside but Luria was concentrated on demonstrating the familiar terms of our brief acquaintance, which included a throaty repetition of Georgie Georgie Georgie, which I liked, and the squeezing and rocking, which I didn't. This ambivalence was to inform everything I felt about Luria. It was impossible not to warm to her unreserved assertions of affection, to believe, as she seemed to, that our roles as godmother and child obliged an assumption of closeness, even as strangers; but it was similarly impossible to pad the space between feeling and assertion with anything but a vague sense of being engaged in something verging on the fraudulent. When we eventually clambered upstairs, Luria clinging still, I began to regret that I'd stencilled her room overlooking the Minch in black and white abstracts. She demanded something else, something as floral and definite as she was herself. Inside, we studied each other like pictures.

'You have your mother's green eyes.'

'Oh. Have I? I didn't know her eyes were green, they look dark in her photograph. You're much taller than I'd imagined.'

'Six foot two in my stockings, darling. When I want to be really frightening I wear high heels. My bank manager positively fawns. But you're thinner than your father's measurements suggested.'

'What?'

She grinned, conspiratorial. 'I've been shopping for you.'

I hadn't made the connection between measurements and new dresses; stupid, I realised, for a dressmaker and carpenter. We bought our jeans and sweaters in job-lots from a store in Edinburgh and those that didn't fit, with the passing years, we returned for a larger size. He must have made note of the calculations I'd made for my dresses. Doing things behind my back again.

'He sent some money so that you could arrive in the city in style.'

'Yes, he said.'

'I hope they fit.'

She clearly didn't believe they would. I am, as I was soon to discover, a size 12 in height but not in width; my arms and legs are disproportionately long and curveless, like fresh growth from Scots pine. Not adolescent exactly but I suppose gangling all the same. Luria stared at my thin dress, my oiled-wool socks and stout brown boots.

'It's not before time!' she laughed. 'You look like a land girl in the war, darling, one of those country girls you see in old pictures, standing with their feet apart in a field of potatoes.'

It was too comical to be insulting and I joined in her laughter. Then she caught and held my chin.

'But yes,' she said, 'your mother's eyes; the rest is Oscar – his olive skin, his nose and sensuous mouth and definitely his hair.'

'Mine is wilder, I think. I never comb it. Oscar calls it my helmet. But tell me, we don't have mirrors and Oscar only teases when I ask . . . would you say I was pretty?'

She blinked. 'Anyone can be pretty, Georgie, pretty is insipid and boring and distinctly vulgar. There's nothing even vaguely provincial about the way you look.' She stepped back to appraise more fully. 'You're much more . . . raw and striking . . . unnerving almost. It's that unselfconscious gaze. So much like Maggie.'

Not pretty then, but her approval seemed unequivocal so I felt flattered all the same.

'You're very beautiful, and you smell of mushrooms.' It was true. Everything about her was soft and peaty and mildly acrid. I wanted to take the soft pads of her cheeks and squeeze them like fruits, feel the texture of her hair, the weight of her mud-brown eyes which were round and flat like pennies. She towered over me, a good head and shoulders above my own, a clean three inches taller than Oscar, such a vibrant earth of a woman I could only grasp isolated facets of her at the same time. I was focused for the moment on her mouth. Slashed with crimson, full yet firm, such a beautiful thing it was hard to resist the peculiar compulsion to put my hands inside it, my whole

43

arms, to dig my way into the heart of her where I would feel her whole.

'I expect I do,' she laughed, 'after that journey. The last part was nerve-racking to say the least. Perhaps you could run a bath for me before we eat. Oscar said you were preparing a special treat of venison and wild onions, which suggests we should dress. When he brings in the rest of my bags I'll sort out the things I've brought for you and you can wear something suitably splendid. We're going to be good friends you and I, Georgie, don't you think? I know your mother would like that. She was very dear to me and I can see her in you so much, oblique but quite clear.'

'Do I really look like my mother?' There was clearly something wrong with those round wet eyes. My mother was fair.

'Absolutely; oh you're physically much more like your father but your "look" is definitely Maggie's. Just the same.'

'Oh.' It was too obtuse. Another thought occurred. 'What did she smell of, my mother?'

She was puzzled, but then she leaned into my neck and sniffed like a feral cat. 'You,' she said, 'your mother smelt like you.'

It was glib, too easy, but I thought about it later when I'd left her to bathe. I buried my face in the crook of my arm and inhaled deeply. I too smell of sandstone.

Despite her bath Luria still smelt of mushrooms. She walked into my room bearing an armful of boxes and the earth came with her. She left me to explore the boxes alone, laying them on my bed in such a way I thought of the fox presenting her cubs with a fresh kill. Deferential, indulgent. There was much tissue paper and I thought the bright boxes which bore Italian-sounding names almost as desirable as their contents. More so when I saw the contents, which were uniformly appalling. I choked on disappointment. They were either very drab or iridescent structures more reminiscent of table lamps than clothes, and several were badly finished. There were long shiny skirts with straps at the sides, short skirts ribbed like medieval fields, shirts with impossible pearl buttons and strange attachments at the collar, dresses with bows and belts and peculiar dropped waists, absurdly short sweaters, all in muted shades of camouflage. Worst of all were the opaque black stockings and the thin black shoes with fluted heels. The latter smelt afraid and looked like sculptures. I arranged them on the mantel above the fire and informed my masks they should get used to seeing them there. No one, I decided, should ever choose my clothes again. But I had to wear something so that Luria wouldn't think me ungrateful. Perhaps I could say they didn't fit. I chose a cashmere dress the colour of oysters but wore it without the belt. The shoes I couldn't manage.

8

'**L**ovely – but you can't wear it with those boots,
Georgie!'
I felt conspicuous and oddly displaced as
though presenting myself for approval had somehow
shifted *me* to the position of outsider. Oscar was leaning
on the mantelpiece, propped on one elbow, too courteous
and urbane to be reassuring. He was wearing an unfamiliar linen shirt. For someone who didn't give a damn he
was making a lot of effort.

'The shoes won't go over these socks and the stockings
make my legs itch.'

'Ha. That's the price of your social inheritance, darling.
Women get discomfort while men, poor buggers, are
compelled to watch football. I know which I prefer.'

'But your dress is beautiful,' I said, and it was. Great
splodges of green, yellow and crimson cloud printed on
fat wool; an Impressionist painting.

'This? It's positively middle-aged Georgie, an ancient
thing I just brought as insurance against pneumonia.'

The meal was very good, she said, eating and talking
with the same relish, chiding Oscar about his canopy of
long hair. He pretended to enjoy it, his eye mischievous,
his big voice teasing the room.

'We hermits have to look the part, you know.'

'Huh. Very unoriginal. When I first met your father, Georgie, he had a choirboy's crop and manicured fingernails – don't deny it Oscar, you were positively anal. He and my very dreary brother were at the same college and they'd rented a villa near Athens—'

'1966. My D. Phil. had been conferred and I'd just been offered my first appointment. How is Michael these days?'

'Of course; Maggie and I were just twenty-one . . . Heavens, half a lifetime ago . . . Oh he's still something in the City,' she rolled her eyes. 'Living in a moral majority of one. He imagines his Porsche is evidence of sanctity and grace and my Escort that I'm a doomed bohemian. No doubt he's right. I never see him; he virtually lives on a golf course.'

'Tell me about Greece.' I'd never heard how my parents had met.

'Ah . . . balmy days. Maggie and I stopped off at their villa on our way back from Páros. I remember you as being quite charming then, Oscar.' She turned to me: 'To your mother he was effusively charming. They spent a great deal of time infuriating Michael, who thought we should only be attentive to Byzantine churches, by sloping off and giggling in corners together.'

'Rubbish. I have never giggled in my life, not even in infancy.'

'Oscar you were ga-ga. Didn't he tell you, Georgie, he was so busy waving goodbye to our aeroplane he lost everything: passport, travellers' cheques, cash, the lot.'

'How romantic. I can only admire you for that, Oscar.'

'Then you admire imprudence, George, it was the wrong plane. And while I was genuflecting to its departure a chap with much more subtlety and luck broke into the villa and made off with my gear. Michael, I was impressed to discover, had very sensibly hidden his in the fridge.'

'He would.'

'I spent hours in a consulate office reflecting on the wisdom of brief farewells. It was a salutary experience, as you will no doubt see when I pack you off on the train.'

'It's nice to be selectively hopeless, Oscar, you must have made everyone else feel terribly comfortable.'

'I was *not* hopeless. I was, as Luria has so kindly recalled, charming, witty, suave. I was a *bon vivant* and brother to the world at large, devastatingly handsome and of course immensely humble.'

'You were a pompous, arrogant prig and only charming by default. You were quoting Wittgenstein to poor Maggie over the Ouzo.'

'No. I am quite certain that at that stage I hadn't read him.'

'Whatever. But I begin to see you've been denying this young woman gossip she should rightly possess.'

'I expect you'll remedy that, Luria.' He growled into his cutlery.

'I fully intend to.'

Luria smoked thin cigarettes constantly, even between courses. She blew out the smoke in curling streams while throwing her head back, and frequently appeared to be floating on a silver cloud, an overgrown cherub. I suppose it's a consequence of the tobacco that her voice is like gravel crumbled over paper, occasionally rather strained. She'd brought Oscar cigars and a bottle of Calvados, his favourite brandy. I didn't mind the cigars but there was a presumption in the gift of brandy that annoyed me. She hadn't seen him for almost twenty years yet she was familiar with his personal tastes and had pleased him in a way that I could not.

I watched her eat. She cut her meat into small chunks so that she could spear them with her right hand and gesticulate with her left, spreading her fingers before she actually spoke. There was something calculated about the way she deliberately replaced her fork on the table and used her fingers to eat spears of onion that made me think of Trollope's Signora Neroni, but I didn't like her less for this; it didn't seem vapid, however calculating. She obviously took pleasure in flaunting the nonsense of manners and I decided I might learn from such cool assurance.

Oscar attended to our glasses and seemed to be enjoying himself more than I could remember. He was effusive, enthusiastic, his long hands waving in the air like nets, his eyes shining with pleasure. Luria relaxed into the wine and sat with her elbows wide on the table, discussing old acquaintances with happy exaggeration. No one abnormal exactly, but odd all the same. There was Maxwell the sculptor who lived in a caravan with a girl who made earrings from tinfoil and wire; Sonya who stole umbrellas and wrote abusive letters to Tory MPs; Rose who'd married Anton, her German pianist, and now devoted her time to rescuing tortoises while Anton played Chopin in distant town halls. We laughed at their oddness, Oscar with greater abandon, while under my cashmere dress my skin felt damp and the label was an irritant to my neck. I'd been polite about the others upstairs but regretted they didn't quite fit. Luria didn't mind, it would be easy to change them, she said.

'Perhaps George can show you around tomorrow.'

'Around what exactly . . .?'

'The house, of course. Our fine Scottish landscape.'

'I was afraid you'd say that, Oscar, I hate the country-side. All that space devoid of people is unnatural. The rest of the house I certainly want to see but I'm not equipped psychologically or physically for hiking in mud, and I positively refuse to climb mountains. Georgie, I haven't come here to be humiliated.'

There was a hint of something more brittle than irony in this. Evidently she didn't appreciate the singular privilege of being our guest.

'What exactly does an interior designer do, Luria? Oscar mentioned cushions.'

'Did he indeed . . . Well as he very well knows it's *slightly* more complicated than cushions. In the spirit of new materialism, Georgie, I create what is currently known as a lifestyle; an environment which suggests to the people in it that they're really somewhere other than in a three-bedroom semi.'

'Oh. Why don't they just move?'

She seemed momentarily fazed, then went on, 'They don't want to change the place, just the way it looks. In the trappings of success style is an enviable commodity. It has to suggest they're charged with creative energy, flair and discipline, that they're confident enough to take a gamble and calculating enough to make it pay off. Sometimes it's hi-tech and minimalist, sometimes it's the co-ordinated English country manor.'

Curiously banal. I couldn't simply equate her with cheap visual fabrication, not then, so I veered from definitions. 'You must have a good eye. Do you paint?'

'Only by numbers, darling. I have no artistic talent whatsoever. I merely look at people to see what universe they wish to inhabit, organise their homes to reflect that universe, and charge them a great deal of money for doing so.'

'Sounds mystical.'

She laughed. 'Too true. But I have my own highly effective form of magic: I look at their shoes. Shoes, Georgie, are much more accurate mirrors of the soul than

50

eyes.' She nodded at her own wisdom. 'People learn in infancy to dissimulate and alter their eyes. They do, Oscar! Look at politicians – they do it all the time. Salesmen, lawyers, estate agents, ten-year-old schoolboys and nice old grannies; they all lie their heads off constantly with sincerity stamped on the iris. You can't even tell who people really are these days. Half-educated businessmen look cultured, the gentry look like workers and office clerks look like the gentry. Until you look at their shoes.'

'What do you look for?' I wondered about my boots.

'You have to have a feel for it, really. We revere feet, you see, we British. We don't mess about with feet; you might have a house full of second-hand clothes but you can be damned sure the shoes have had only one owner. We think of them in the same way we do hearts and brains, the province of experts . . .'

Oscar shook his head sceptically. 'What Luria hasn't told you, George, is that she spent several years at art college studying design.'

'That has nothing to do with anything. Art colleges are only good for learning to look superior in inferior clothes, which is of course why anybody goes to them. Hundreds of people come out of college who, like me, haven't a shred of talent, and become huge successes.'

'Are you?'

'What . . .?'

'A huge success.'

'Well, there aren't many designers who know about feet, Georgie. Didn't Oscar show you the three-page article in *Interiors*?'

She seemed genuinely piqued. 'Honestly, Oscar, you are a bugger. I didn't send it to brag, you know. I don't need to brag. I just thought it might actually be interesting for Georgie to know something about the woman she's going to live with.'

51

'Sorry, I must have forgotten, I'm sure it's still around somewhere.'

'You're a bloody snob, Oscar. I expect you've thrown it away.'

'I'm entrusting George to your very capable keeping. Hardly the act of a dissenter.'

'Only because you've alienated the rest of the world,' she sneered. 'But never mind that, Georgie, I'm sure you'll have great fun in London.'

'After exams,' said Oscar pointedly.

I accidently dropped the napkin I'd been toying with and used the opportunity to examine Luria's shoes under the table. They were flat black pumps in rice-paper leather; they told me nothing, but I liked them. Oscar was wearing his plimsolls.

'God, aren't men boring,' she said. 'Why must you identify fun with irresponsibility, it's very Jewish – no, even worse, it's very Protestant of you. Bred, no doubt, with the territory.'

He smiled. 'I doubt Calvin would agree with that analysis.'

'Well he wouldn't, would he, I'm a woman, a daughter of Eve. Even if I were one of his precious elect I'd still be full of innate wicked impulses highly dangerous to man. He was afraid of his mother, of course. She has a lot to answer for in this country where women don't count.'

'I wouldn't say that exactly. Many Scots believe the crown should have passed down to Mary's heirs . . .'

'Well that's *completely* beside the point.'

'Less so than you think perhaps, but I say it lightly because I have no desire to pursue an argument which I can see I'm destined to lose. I'm constitutionally suspicious of psychological complexity, Luria, and have to rely on causality; Calvin reduced to a Freudian syndrome is much too obscure for me.'

'Poor Oscar. And what about your empirical evidence? Queen Mary was as Scottish as Mata Hari, and Isabella Bird achieved her fame by getting out. Who else is there? Screwing Rabbie Burns hardly amounts to emancipated rebellion.' She sat back, pleased with herself.

'I was thinking rather that despite Weber's argument there are too many links between capitalism and the Protestant ethic for mere coincidence. Creative theology, faith even, is just another form of politics.'

'You make it sound almost polite. But you know, despite the last twenty years, little in this country has altered. When I was changing trains at Inverness the porter eyed me up like a piece of meat. Diminished to sexual apparatus in the space of two regular suitcases. He actually suggested I'd enjoy nothing better than his company over something called a bevvie. Laughed when I said I'd resist it. I couldn't decide whether it was vanity or resigned opportunism.'

'Maggie used to joke about the genteel Glaswegians who pronounce Calvin's name Kelvin, as in Kelvinside. But if it's emancipated rebellion you want, what about the Glasgow Rent Acts? They'd never have happened without the women.'

'Never heard of them. English historians obviously weren't impressed, which just goes to show that Isabella had the right idea: get out and leave the men to their nasty predestination. I'd give them a week,' she grinned.

I wondered if she was drunk. We were on the third brandy and the wine had been rich and potent. It doesn't affect me much. When I keep Oscar company over the whisky it's he who needs help to get upstairs. Luria would be heavy.

I suggested coffee but Oscar offered to make it. He paused to light his cigar then walked round the table to light the cigarette Luria'd just taken from her packet.

There was an awkward moment, then she put the cigarette to her lips and turned her face towards him. The lighter was in his left hand, while the right rested on the back of her chair. He bent towards her, slowly, so that his body formed one half of a shell, hers the other. They seemed unnecessarily close, unnecessarily intimate.

I don't know what I thought because no words attached themselves, I just felt physically queer. A loud hiss like white noise filled my head and my skull was suddenly too tight, as though gripped in a vice. The air was sucked thin, resisted my gasps, but I couldn't speak, not even a whisper, and since they were still fixed on each other they couldn't see the panic in my eyes. I gripped the arms of my chair but my palms were somehow wet and slippery, drenched in sweat. My whole body was drenched in sweat; clammy yet cold. The vice tightened and tightened and tightened again and the thin air turned to fog. I fought to remain upright, to shake my head clear, but I'd already lost control: the room swooned, melted, and I was slipping sideways, dislocated from my body, falling into blackness.

'It's the brandy, Oscar. She shouldn't be drinking so much at her age.'

They came into focus above me, Oscar's arm under my shoulders, Luria's face behind his. The vice still gripped at my brain and I knew that if he picked me up I'd black out again.

'. . . lie still . . .'

'What?'

'Let me lie still . . .' I said, shutting my eyes, forcing him to understand. He held on and for a moment there was peace.

Then Luria's voice. 'How much has she had?'

'It's not the bloody brandy – she's been sharing my

54

bottles since she was old enough to hold a glass. She has the metabolism of a centurion, like her Irish grandmother. No, she must be ill.'

He was alarmed. Apart from a common cold, I'd never been ill. I had to do something. I was uncomfortable but didn't want fuss. The image of Oscar and Luria leaning towards each other pained my eyelids so I opened my eyes and waited while the room regained its solidity and the cold sweat passed.

'I'm all right now,' I said. It seemed that I was. I allowed myself to be hoisted upright and led to the sofa. Oscar sat beside me, watchful, concerned.

'What happened, George? What the hell is it?'

'I don't know. I think I fainted.'

'You certainly did,' said Luria.

'I'm all right now, really I am, it's passing.' I felt absurdly normal, as though nothing had happened. There was no nausea, no giddiness, only the memory of the tightness in my skull and that awful hiss.

*

I woke early. The house quiet. Oscar would sleep off his inevitable hangover and wouldn't appear until ten. I never suffered but I wondered about Luria. I listened outside her door but only the squawk of gulls over the roof broke the silence within. I went back to my room and sat amidst the boxes to stare at my masks and consider the strange events of the night. I hadn't liked the suggestion of sexual intimacy, that was clear. But I thought about Freud and entertained the notion of children fainting at dinner tables up and down the country, every day, at every meal. It was too absurd. It wasn't jealousy, I decided, that had floored me, but the rude assumption that I could be excluded. Oscar had never ignored me. I was affronted that Luria should entertain the notion that he would willingly be party to such exclusion, more so that she should imagine herself companion to his thoughts, even momentarily.

She must not remain so misguidedly persuaded, I decided. But what to do? As our guest and my future host, straightforward confrontation would be impolite, discourteous and possibly impolitic. Oscar wouldn't like it. Some subtle analogous example was needed, but nothing came to mind. And then I remembered *Sethur*.

9

I knew the piece well. When I'd first read it the hair on my arms stood erect and my sleep was confused for many nights. This is what Oscar had written:

Lily felt more trepidation when she caught the curl of Sethur's lip. This was not what she'd expected at all and she experimentally twisted her wrists behind her to test the knots. They were tight, too tight to unravel. As usual he'd insisted on her lace and leather bodysuit with its clever tuckwork, but whatever Sethur had in mind this wasn't their usual foreplay. She looked down on his head as he added the final touch, fixing her ankles to the pins embedded in the panelling. How she'd admired his eye for such detail, but now pinioned fast to the wall she knew escape was impossible and regretted his expertise.

He rose to meet her eye with a swish of his dark cape, and she faced his silent laughter. 'And now, my dear voluptuous Lily . . .' He clicked his fingers, an order, and the door behind him opened quietly, slowly, and Lily caught her breath as the figure she knew so well slipped through the gap.

'No . . .!' she screeched, her eyes burning with horror.

Sethur laughed aloud this time. 'But we thought you'd like to watch, Lily.'

'No . . .!!' It was guilt as much as anything that caught in her throat. At the bottom of her horror she knew this would not be happening had she herself not pandered to Sethur's desires. He held out his arm and the barely clad girl came willingly, her eyes bright and eager.

'We've been planning this for such a long time, Juliet and I, haven't we, my bud. You surely didn't imagine I really loved . . . when this charmingly inventive child has offered so much more, Lily, so much more . . . everything.'

'Juliet! No . . .!!'

Sethur spun her youngest sister around and the tip of her virgin tongue protruded in defiance and glee . . .

Luria was cocooned in blanket, breathing deep and slow. She'd unpacked so meticulously there was curiously little in the room to mark her presence; even her luggage was tucked out of sight. Her fat wool dress was folded over a chair and two neatly symmetrical rows of glamorous toiletries were arranged on the chest of drawers. It's a further clue to her character, I thought, a need for order to counter inner chaos. Literature is full of it. There was a paperback novel on the bedside table, its spine splayed open to mark her place. The cover bore a garish picture of an open mouth and claimed in embossed silver lettering to be an international bestseller. I thought the book would do for the extract from *Sethur* and picked it up; underneath was a stoutly bound notebook, a diary, the perfect find.

Oscar once said people really kept diaries for others to read and that they lived to enliven their pages. I didn't entirely accept the latter part since I'd gone through a phase of diary-keeping myself and nothing special had happened. Whatever. I read the most recent entries consecutively; I'm more disciplined now about endings:

24 March. 8.50. Breakfast on the Royal Highlander, ten and a half hours out of Euston. What a journey. Inverness in an hour then *two-hour* wait for connection to Lairg which takes *another* hour. Then God knows what. Oscar said drive through mountains easy until last leg where apparently no road. I'll want to be hospitalised and tube-fed tea. Understand now why Maggie never came to London . . .

But her letter had said she was going . . .?

. . . Amazon less shattering. Weird she won't be there. So strong and vital. Shall make proper goodbyes, visit her grave . . .

There wasn't one. Not that I knew of, not here. I supposed it must be somewhere but I'd never asked.

She would've been twenty-nine when she died. Not so strong or vital.

. . . Hard to believe anything that pernicious bastard says. Gratifying he's letting Georgie go at last, despite personal. Intelligent, well-adjusted young woman he claims. We shall see. Rather miraculous, considering. Silly carping letters, the subjectivity of prejudice, value judgements untainted by Victorian morality; typical sophistic nonsense. Very bohemian. She must know growing up isolated with such a man hardly salubrious. Even if he is her father – *especially* if he is her father. Even in Hampstead they'd call that piquant. Hope to God she doesn't mention it in company.

25 March. 11.30p.m. Georgie packed off to bed, collapsed from too much brandy. Drinks like a maenad yet Oscar thinks it's perfectly OK. However. Things better not worse than I'd feared. Not noticeably bonkers. No sign of famous breakdown, except seems more frighteningly intense. Georgie has it too, but dreamy where he's remote, unreserved where he's evasive. His double but I hope Maggie's child really. Awful taste. Feeble excuse about clothes I brought, prefers hiking boots and severely tailored cocktail dress, like a mental patient on an outing. She does the decorating. Nightmarish. Spartan rooms in fairground colours. A joke monastery. And everywhere freezing. Oscar very much on form tonight. Much more mine host than on drive from Lairg, only barely civil. Poor Maggie's coffin carted over that moorland. Bouncing about in a jeep. Don't think of it.

I'd forgotten how good he could look. Carelessly handsome. Assurance of power. His body if anything more taut, eyes more pruriently warm. Still hate him, but his arrogance makes me stupid. Be much easier if he wasn't so sexy and I so stupidly flattered. Maggie loved him after all. But I hate him.

I was thrown.

Why did she hate him? Did she?

If she *truly* hated him so much then Sethur wasn't necessary . . . But then, I wasn't a mental patient walking out from an asylum.

I tucked the extract between the middle sheets and replaced it under her novel, then I went downstairs feeling quite satisfied, warmed the remains of my venison stew and hummed to myself over breakfast.

The long ridge of Foinaven rose like one of Wordworth's beasts in the eastern sky, slate blue against the luminous pink where shafts of sunlight had pierced cloud. I was glad the rain had held off. Showing Luria around the house had taken longer than necessary since she insisted on seeing what she called 'the fine details' of every room. These transpired to be chimney breasts, window clips, skirting, the uphill slope of the floors at the back. Most of all she liked the dark scullery full of deep sinks and rusting mangles, where we store fruit and vegetables. Fascinated by ironmongery and naked stone. She ran her hand over the bumpy walls and, despite her secret misgivings, declared them splendid. Our house is organic, she says. A labyrinth of rooted rooms. What she would do to our house, she says.

We skirted around Cnoc an Rubha and walked along the cliffs for a mile or so to the head of Loch an Róin. Like walking on the moon, Luria said, the wind whipping our hair.

'Look at it,' she called. 'Miles and miles of hostile space and not another soul in sight. Just rock and bloody water.' She had dressed for exposure and had trouble moving easily beneath so many layers. We paused. 'How have you lived here so long, Georgie, and not gone mad?'

'Are you mocking me?'

'No, darling. I'm mocking me.' She put her arm through mine and we headed inland towards the more sheltered shores of Lochan Iamhair.

'I couldn't live here,' she shook her head. 'I'd be inviting the sheep in for company. I need people, Georgie. Landscapes like this, awesome as they are, make me feel like I've stumbled into the dark ages. I prefer rock embedded in buildings, sheep on nice Sussex farms, water in warm blue pools. This is altogether too primitive, empty, inhuman. But look, what's that . . . over there by that larger loch?'

'It's a deserted croft. Abandoned during the clearances; it's just a ruin now. We could walk that way if you like.'

'No. Too far, and no pub or cream tea as reward.'

We sat on a mossy tussock while she lit a cigarette. Her ears were adorned with dangling shafts of pea-green glass, incongruous for hiking, probably painful in the wind; but Luria, as I was to learn, makes little concession to such external factors as the weather, apart from the cold. She said, 'You must be chilled in just that dress and sweater.'

'I don't feel it.'

She looked dubious. 'Was it your grandmother's, the dress?'

'No. I made it myself. I never knew either set of grandparents, they're all dead. What made you ask if it was my grandmother's?' I bristled defensively.

'Oh . . . The cut. You made it yourself? Here, let me see.' She stuck the cigarette in her mouth to examine my seams and darts, expertly turning up hems to investigate the hidden artistry. I was surprised; she clearly knew how to distinguish excellent work from shoddiness. In these terms, the clothes under my bed seemed an even odder choice.

'It's extremely well made, Georgie, I'm very impressed.'

'I've made seven.' I felt warm and admired.

'An auspicious number,' she laughed. 'Are they all as well made as this one?'

'They're the same. They're all the same.'

'Identical?'

'Yes.'

'As in style . . .?'

I nodded.

Her brow clouded. 'Why?'

62

'It means I can wear one every day.'

Her mouth smiled, but nothing else.

We sat quietly a while, just looking around, watching the shadows play in the gorse, then we walked back towards the woodsmoke from our hidden chimney.

'Does it have a name, all this?' She made an arc with her arm.

'It's all Geathramh Garbh. It means rough territory in English, all the land between Loch Inchard in the south and Loch Laxford in the north.'

'I see . . . Appropriate. Not exactly a horticulturalist's dream, is it?'

'Only gorse and heather grow here, a few green orchids, the hardiest trees. It's typical glaciated terrain. Geathramh Garbh is Pre-Cambrian, Oscar says, ancient, cut off from the rest of Scotland by a wall of Silurian granite that runs from Durness to the Sound of Sleat.' I pointed east to the towering peaks of Foinaven. 'That's Ceann Garbh and Ganu Mór and that, to the south, with the solid hump like the back of a horse, is Arkle, one of the oldest mountains in the whole of Britain. The legend is that the red stags of Arkle have pointed teeth and forked tails.'

'I believe it. The whole place in fact is satanic. Did your mother really like it here?'

'She must have done or they'd never have stayed. But I don't know. I don't remember her much.'

'No, of course not. But you, Georgie? D'you like living here?' She was shivering, dug into her greatcoat.

'I don't think about it like that. It's just here, isn't it? If I think about it at all I think in terms of sounds and smells, the textures of things, sea, weather. I don't know anything else.'

'Yes . . . Well London will certainly be a shock after this, believe me . . .'

'You didn't have children, Luria?' I didn't want her to talk about London. I didn't want its window catches and skirting boards invading my plans.

'Me? No. Never had the vocation; never suffered that pull of the womb, didn't stare wistfully into prams or feel my role in life impoverished because I didn't push one. I've enjoyed my career, still enjoy it. But I'm looking forward to our *ménage à deux*,' she smiled. 'I hope you don't mind cats, by the way, I have two demanding Persians. I know you'll like the house, I'm very proud of it. And there's another spare room if you want to have friends to stay.'

I couldn't imagine this need.

She puckered her mouth wryly. 'Don't worry, Georgie, I'm not going to be a boring old duenna, I'm too liberal for that.' She paused to appreciate the fact. 'I'd rather be a friend you can turn to at any time you need; I'll offer whatever advice I can, but I won't torment either of us if you choose to ignore it. Agreed?' She sighed; this little speech had obviously been rehearsed.

'Agreed.'

We walked on.

'What about other men?' I asked. 'Apart from your ex-husband . . .'

'Oh there's always other men.' She yawned. 'Most of them married. That's the trouble with England, Georgie, all the bloody men my age are married, or want to be. Men are more conservative than women . . . it's some kind of congenital thing; they can't stop themselves from hankering for metaphorical slippers and dogs and roast beef dinners. Quite absurd. I've got an entourage of escorts, but no one special if that's what you're asking. I don't really have time for all that.'

'I'm looking forward to men.'

She laughed. 'I expect you are, darling, but they're not

64

cream buns, you know. And it might be prudent not to enthuse too much about meeting men to your father.'

'Why not?'

'Well . . . that's another congenital thing, the "no man is good enough for my daughter" act.'

'Oscar's not like that. Anyway, regardless of what I do, he knows I'd never betray him.'

'What a peculiar thing to say.'

We kept to our own thoughts then as we made our way back around Cnoc an Rubha. Luria eyed the weight of the sky and recoiled from the sea. 'This is a nasty place,' she muttered. 'Wind-dragged and foul. Golgotha.'

Down came the rain as the gulls swept inland. She turned at the doorstep to peer once again into the vanishing grey, shook her head, tutted wearily. 'How could Maggie have liked this? It defies life; even the bloody sheep look haggard.'

I shrugged, practised a smile, but I couldn't see the foulness. 'Oscar told me she hated London and Oxford.'

She paused, 'Did he really?' Her eyes turned away to the house. 'Well well well . . .'

10

Something peculiar happened. Luria found the page from *Sethur* in her diary that same evening. I listened from the stairs when she stormed into Oscar's study and her voice was shrill with anger, perhaps fear. She thought Oscar had put it there! I hadn't anticipated that. If she knew him as well as she thought, she'd have known this wasn't his style. He of course recognised it as mine, but denied nothing. He never mentioned it to me. I heard him laugh the way that he does and mutter about a joke.

Still. The mistake had an even better effect than I'd hoped. I wouldn't need to faint again.

For the rest of that week Luria rarely ventured outdoors. She pottered around the house or read her bestseller novels. We made music for her in the evenings and played parlour games or cards, and every day she insisted I perch at her feet while she attempted to tame my hair with a wide-toothed comb.

One afternoon I found her staring through a window in the sitting-room talking about my mother's funeral with Oscar.

He pointed to the crashing sea. 'That's where she lies.

Scattered in the waves. It's what she wanted.' He grinned into Luria's eyes defiantly, and after that he seemed to lose his initial interest in being host and resigned those duties to me. Luria began to complain about our primitive bathing facilities, the lack of mirrors and the cold stone floors. Oscar paid little attention.

'I'm ah out,' he'd say, and disappear into the moors.

I think Luria was relieved.

Occasionally she'd come and join me in the kitchen baking my favourite cakes full of fat sultanas, smothered in orange icing. Luria loves cakes too but complains about the calories. We were baking when I asked about her name.

'What exactly did Oscar tell you?' she said.

'Not much . . . just that it wasn't the name you were born with.'

'Yes . . . I suppose he doesn't approve of self-aggrandisement.' She thought this funny. 'I was born Edna Woodforde after a great-aunt,' she explained, 'and I'd still be Edna Woodforde, no doubt struggling to survive, had I not determined to alter things myself. Names are suggestively powerful, Georgie, or otherwise. And Luria Sheraton-Woodforde is a much more successful designer than Edna Woodforde could ever have been.' She dotted the air with her wooden spoon to add authority. 'Luria is the surname of a seventeenth-century alchemist I came across in college. I thought it very apt. Sheraton I suppose you know, and what could be more reassuring than a Sheraton designer?'

'Didn't you find it strange being somebody else?'

I was thinking, of course, of my secret name for myself, Nina.

She stirred at the cake. 'No. I got used to it very quickly indeed, especially as it brought in the business. In my profession there's a lot more affectation than simply a name. But I'll ask you not mention this in London; I've quite grown into my new self and the old one isn't generally known. By anyone.'

I began to suspect her house would have chandeliers and a parlourmaid in starched linen.

On the day of our departure I ate the remaining half of a three-pound cake after breakfast and was actually violently sick. Luria scolded me for being silly while Oscar chewed frantically on the ghost of his moustache, his hands stuffed deep in his pockets.

I'd been packed for days.

I told my masks that if I didn't like London I'd be back in June, otherwise at the end of summer. I'd said my goodbyes to the hills and the lochs and the cliffs and to each of my rooms. There was nothing to do but leave. I gave Oscar the hinged chest complete with my copy of *Sethur*. He was gratifyingly appreciative of my carpentry and I by the fact that he'd discover which page was missing and understand more fully why Luria had subsequently lit her own cigarettes and talked to him always in questions.

He in turn gave me a gift that was impossible for us both. A silver frame containing a prayer embroidered in dark silks; my mother's work, he said, a baptismal blessing in fine-point. It reads, *Grant that the old Eve in this child may be so buried that the new woman may be raised up in her*.

Embarrassing.

'It's been lying around for years,' he said waving off any significance.

It must have been carefully hidden. After I discovered his books I went through every drawer and cupboard and document in the house and there isn't a scrap of paper or artefact I haven't seen.

He's canny, my father.

I couldn't cope with having my mother thrust upon me on the doorstep since her blessing had the same effect on me as her letter, so I placed it into Luria's hands. She ran her fingers over the stitches while I disappeared to fetch some canvas to wrap it in, and a bag of apples to appease my sudden hunger.

Oscar drove us to Lairg and I sat passively in the back of the jeep eating up the landscape. The world was a foreign place.

Lairg smelled of sulphur.

There were several people on the station platform and it was hard to concentrate on saying goodbye while I stared at their shoes and brown coats. I did not weep. I wasn't going for ever. There were no silver rapiers and Oscar wasn't dying. But I agreed to do some revision every day and always to tell Luria where I was going. He was fulsome but restrained, impatient in this element. So he left as he'd promised before the train arrived and I watched through the buffet window as our jeep disappeared into the grey stone streets.

Inverness station was bone cold. I have braced Atlantic winds and not shivered so much. I didn't like it. There was a child in a balaclava masked hood, a boy of ten or eleven, only eyes exposed to the air, a sinister little devil. He was throwing up jacks and catching them on the backs of his hands, hypnotic and precise. He stopped and stared at my dress and boots and heavy Jacob sweater and his woollen cheeks expanded.

The train to London swayed and shook and sped through the night over so many miles I thought we'd arrive in Australia. Luria slept in her cot but I spent most of the night walking through carriages looking at people.

The carriages furthest from our sleeper were full of purple-faced men surrounded by bread crusts, ash and beer cans. They smelled of trapped sweat and disappointment and their bitter red eyes warned of diabolical things.

Luria said later the English were even worse and I'd soon get used to it. I don't see how.

It was dawn when we got into Euston and took a cab to the large brick house in Crouch End. Behind the door sat the nonsense of Luria's cats, Bombur and Ferruk. They brushed their mohair coats against our legs and miauled ecstatically, their lives restored from the perfunctory ministerings of a daily. Luria set about making coffee and omelettes with thyme and thick fresh cream while I explored. There were three rooms downstairs and four up. I found the bathroom first and thought I was in a harem; everything was marbled, even the bath and the thick fluffy towels. Only the eunuch was missing. There were no chandeliers as such, but each room was a jangling overheated world stuffed full of ornate chintz in muted colour; a huge mirror on the sitting-room mantel swallowed flowery walls and dark, highly polished antiques. I didn't dare look in it. My own room was all sugar and peach, plump with frills and lace and satin padded corners. The bed was canopied like a cradle and the mattress a blancmange, while against the opposite wall a huge chest of drawers was covered in a regiment of Victorian appliances for dealing with hair and girdles. There was an unused fireplace housing a basket of artificial lilies and a tall cupboard with double doors. I opened this to hang up my coat and was startled to find on the back of each door a full-length mirror reflecting me as a triptych into infinity.

I was stunned.

I stared at myself and saw Oscar. Not a lunatic at all. But there *was* something else, and it wasn't him.

I prodded and squinted and examined my various parts and grimaced with my numerous faces. I'm a multitude, I said to myself, and we all laughed aloud together.

Three pelicans of diminishing sizes flew across one wall in the direction of the window. I didn't blame them. I could live with all this, I said to myself, but I was glad my masks had stayed behind. I had to force the sash window, which had obviously been locked for years, then I leaned out into the day, stared down at the tower blocks in the city: so many mountain peaks in a solid sea.

The Knot

11

DESPERATE
The Royal Free Hospital

URGENT
The tube

CURIOUS

St Andrew-by-the-Wardrobe
The University of London
The Commonwealth Institute
Camden Market
St Dunstan-in-the-West
National Portrait Gallery
The Tower
Bank of England
Central Criminal Court
St Andrew Undershaft
Spanish/Portuguese Synagogue
St Mary-le-Bow
Cleopatra's Needle
The Barbican
Portobello Market
Epstein's Pan Group
Harrods
Brixton

Soho
The British Museum
Parliament
St Paul's
V & A
Courtauld Galleries
Shepherd Market
Burlington Arcade
Petticoat Lane
London Bridge
The Ritz
The Planetarium
Madame Tussaud's
The South Bank
Scotland Yard
Carnaby Street
The Round House
Royal Albert Hall

London Zoo
The Tate
Westminster Abbey
National Gallery
Science Museum
Covent Garden
Keats's House
Highgate Cemetery
Speakers' Corner
Cutty Sark
The Savoy
All theatres
Chelsea
Downing Street
Hampstead Village
The Stock Exchange
Imperial War Museum
Chinatown

12

The pain in my head was constant for two whole weeks then on and off for six. It wasn't the noisy cars or the movement as such, but the very air. It's thicker here, expanded by a million million atoms of dead discarded skin from the millions of teeming bodies. A viscous visible soup. It gagged in my throat and nostrils, it shrouded my hair with a sticky film and clotted every pore. I scrubbed myself in the marble bath but I couldn't stop London invading my veins and pounding against my temples. I'd never felt such pain. Luria fed me aspirin in darkened rooms and for the first few days I ventured only as far as the baker's or the supermarket in the shopping strip. Such shops. Such food. London is full of food. I bought cream cakes and quails and bonbons and peppers, ice-cream and fillets of beef and exotic fruits, food I had never dreamed of. I bought wheelbarrow loads and dragged them up the hill and ate myself into exhaustion. Luria returned from short visits to her studio off Baker Street to find me shattered in a pile of debris with the curtains drawn. She tried not to fuss.

When I became inured to the pain and less over-whelmed by the food I decided on four hours' revision each morning, and afternoons for adventure. I have a

cheque book and credit cards and a monthly allowance of
£400. Oscar is generous, but then he shouldn't cheat at
cards. Luria gave me a square leather bag and a drilling
against muggers. She quizzed my memory of her phone
number too often, just in case, but she didn't dictate my
time or swamp me with frilly suggestions. My list of
Urgent to Curious, however, proved a much less propitious guide than I could possibly have foreseen. In the
first place I was still too distracted to prepare myself
properly for the Royal Free Hospital. My other great
hope, the tube, was a nightmare. I set out with plans to
spend the day investigating the charms of a whole circuit
of stations as far afield as Ongar, Cockfosters and Rayners
Lane, but a single horrendous trip between Archway and
Camden Town convinced me there were none. The train
stopped inexplicably in the tunnel after Kentish Town
and we sat there gasping for oxygen for so long I thought
we'd all suffocate watching ourselves in the windows.
The boy sitting next to me had a scarf tied round his face,
a bloodstained handkerchief peeping from inside. Other
young men began stalking like frustrated beasts between
carriages, banging the windows and metal doors with
their feet, shouting 'Come on!' We must have sat in that
tunnel for close on an hour, breathing in stale panic. I
shut my eyes and walked the long way out to Crocach to
look at the sea and then down over the hills to Loch an
Róin where the otters fish and play in the shallow waters.
I wanted to stay but there was no wind, and the murmur
of soft plash and swash was so oddly realistic it startled
me back to the train. A steaming puddle had formed by
the feet of a woman sitting opposite.

Neither my neighbours nor the woman herself
acknowledged in the slightest muscular twitch that urinat-
ing fully clothed in public was a desperate act. Her shoes
were peeptoe sandals, pale butter-leather with lace-thin

straps at the ankle, darker in patches where her piss had splashed. She remained immersed in a paperback novel. I noticed the odd fleeting look, a flicker of eyelash, but apart from the roving boys no one moved as the puddle swept in little eddies across the floor. I spent the rest of the journey trying to glimpse the title of her engrossing novel; she had it doubled back on itself but I did make out broad copperplate lettering in gold. It must've been a thriller.

I confined myself to the bus routes and went to Parliament where I sat in the Spectators' Gallery waiting in vain to be stirred by the rowdy mob below. Politicians are so much shorter than somehow they ought to be. The Central Criminal Court was more sober and marginally more exciting. The young man in the dock wore a funereal suit and called out to friends in the audience: 'I'll need a stick or two to see this sentence out!' A carver of flutes, I thought. Everyone clapped and laughed at his optimism; me too.

I soon realised it would take months to thoroughly cover everything on my list but I worked steadily, exploring hushed churches, ticking off another room in a gallery or museum, enthralled by architects and masons most of all. Awesome statements in stone. Once I wandered to the pedestrian precincts of Mayfair where I found the designers Luria so admires, but more often I haunted Covent Garden, which is always in carnival and the coffee shops have fresh, moist cake. I liked the flamboyance there, the jugglers and the clowns on stilts. Some of the men, like my sailor, were in dresses, admiring their own reflections while conscientiously ignoring the more humble shopper.

In late April the blossom was everywhere blowzy, the smells rich and heavy, the sky high and clear. I checked the weather reports diligently and while Oscar had gales I sat in the piazza in the warm spring sun reading my newspaper, a daily treat so extravagant and bizarre I grew rapidly addicted. Three boys aged between six and nine had ravished a pensioner in her Birmingham home. A man had tried to rob a bank with a cucumber. Whole families were engaged in gruesome satanic rituals, and headlines screamed about child abuse. Life beyond Geathramh Garbh is crazy and its rules obscure.

My feet were too hot in my boots and my white silk dresses had stretched too tight on my chest. I'd grown, plumped out by London's air. Luria had taken to foisting upon me the fashion magazines she appears to buy in bulk; for inspiration, she says. Her own clothes are a constant source of amazement. She complains incessantly about her problems in finding clothes that fit and has most of hers made, at great expense and with prominent labels, to accommodate her height, but most are in tense fabrics conceived for a smaller woman. With these she wears uncompromising costume jewellery in colours that dazzle the eye, earrings that clunk and clink when she moves, beads like ping-pong balls. Her shoes, which she buys obsessively, are mainly soft leather canoe-like pumps; high heels she reserves for moments of insecurity. The effect is strangely top-heavy, especially as Luria's walk is more of a loping stride, a lumbering of weight propelled forward, as though in the grand design of things she hadn't been able to include her legs with the rest of her body. Whatever. If I was bemused by her daily encouragement to think in terms of 'outfits' I was also now conscious of my body's growing impatience. It was time at last, I decided, to discard childish things and become a woman.

Buying clothes for the event wasn't easy. Shop assistants don't like to be interrupted and they despise indecision. My problem was the absence of any conviction at all. My sailor had been a useful model for tramping in Scottish hills but I could find nothing singular to latch on to in London. Luria was anxious that I should replace the clothes she'd bought with something 'stylish', yet her liberal use of this term did nothing to help me identify its meaning, nor, despite her own apparent understanding, could she provide one. So I tried simply using it myself.

'I'd like something stylish, please,' I said to the girl with folded arms staring out through plate glass. Her head was completely shaven except for a spiky ruff on top which was dyed in a rainbow of colours. The entire socket of her eyes had been painted to match, so that as she stood there chewing her cheek she looked just like a tropical fish, at sea in an outsize tank. She turned slightly and assessed me coolly from the corner of one shimmering eye, the other still fixed on the window.

'What sort of thing are you looking for, miss?'

So much for stylish, then.

'I'm not sure.'

'Suit? Dress? Trousers?'

'Yes,' I nodded. 'All of those.'

She shifted her weight slightly, chewed on her other cheek. 'Is it a particular occasion?'

'What?'

She turned. 'Are you looking for something for a particular occasion, miss?'

'Ah. Not really. Walking. Sightseeing, eating out . . .' ('Sex' wasn't strictly accurate) '. . . seduction.'

She stopped chewing, paused, smiled slowly. 'Size?'

'I'm not sure but I've got a note here of my measurements . . .' I dug out the scrap of paper from my square leather bag, read off: 'Bust, 33½ inches; waist, 25¼ inches; hips, 34 inches; back neck to waist, 16½ inches; waist to knee, 29 inches.' She came and stood by my side and scrutinised my figures with interest.

'What's that?' she laughed, pointing.

'Arm, 22¾ inches: shoulder to wrist,' I demonstrated.

'We don't need all that.' She shook her head. She seemed to think I was joking.

'Really?' I said. 'Fine; well, what do you think?'

She stepped back, assessing again. 'Well you're thin enough,' she said, nodding, 'but you're not small; you've got it across the back.'

It?

'You look like a 14 to me, maybe a 12. Yeah,' she decided, 'we'll try a 12.' So she went off to round up some 12s while I screwed my calculations into a mouthsize ball and, resolved to conform to this numerical norm, ate them.

I was there for three hours, standing around half naked in the long dressing-room, waiting for belief. My eye could accommodate nothing. My body resisted the coarseness of unfamiliar fabric and the mirrors reflected a stranger. I began to feel that I didn't know myself, and felt afraid. There was nothing inside me to demonstrate my need, nothing to help me gauge, in the absence of instant distaste, the appropriate; nothing to help me create the woman. Hours of stripping and donning and sweating and tooth-grinding frustration. The assistant wasn't happy either. She kept saying, 'What do you like!?' And her quills waved like an agitated fan when I answered, 'I don't know.' My clothes had never been worn for 'like'; this was clothes as mask and that was new to me. My dresses were something else. I needed them, they were part of Geathramh Garbh, but as Luria now hinted in every possible way, my dresses were primitive.

I couldn't just submit myself to the arbitrary. I knew, at least, what my eye disliked and my body told me what was comfortable. Then I thought about Oscar's books. His women wore chiffon and leather, silk and lace. So over a period of painful days I gradually filled the deep cupboard in my frou-frou bedroom with a wardrobe which Luria called eclectically schizophrenic. Living with me is to live with a crowd, she said. But to appease her sense of total décor I agreed to have my wild hair sculpted, like topiary, into a fashionable bob. I think it accentuates the length of my nose but Luria insists it is chic, aristo-cratic, even stylish.

I perfumed and powdered myself and set off in a scarlet bus in my scarlet sheath dress, which made much of my small tight breasts, for the Royal Free Hospital. It was larger than I'd envisaged amidst my green-winged orchids, and finding a doctor was difficult; even the porters wear white coats. I wandered corridors, went up and down in lifts, followed groups carrying clipboards into wards only to be ushered out again. Finally I sat patiently in a waiting-room with several people whose limbs were encased in plaster and, after an appropriate interval, I slipped into a cubicle containing a preposter-ously high examining couch, a chair and a curtain ribbed with fuchsia. I sat in the chair. Some minutes later the curtain parted. I must have sighed with relief.

'I'm sorry you've been waiting . . . are you in pain?'

'No . . . I'm just relieved that you're not a woman doctor.'

He pulled the white mask from his face and let it rest under his chin. He was, I thought, about forty, greying slightly at the temples, rather short and plump, Asian. He wore a badge bearing his name: Dr Patel. There was no wedding band. He was perfect: an Eastern mogul.

'That's an odd . . . usually ladies, if they have a preference that is, ask to see a woman doctor. Just pop up on to the couch for me, please. Leave your shoes off, that's right, Miss – I don't seem to have your notes . . .'

He started looking around the cubicle while I arranged myself as asked.

'No notes,' he smiled, 'I'll just ask the nurse to get them.'

'There are no notes,' I said.

'No notes?'

'No. I'm not a patient.'

He looked hard at my long, bared legs then stepped back slightly to better understand the situation.

'I don't . . . uh, what exactly is the problem, Miss – ?'

'Sondberg . . . Nina Sondberg. It's not really a problem, Dr Patel, it's just that I'm a virgin.'

'Ah . . . I see . . . But I'm an orthopaedic consultant, Miss Sondberg. The Department of Gynaecology is upstairs. I'll get a nurse to show you . . .'

'No, you don't understand.'

He frowned and waited.

'My father's always taught me to do things properly. He believes in excellence for its own sake. You see I realise that while I'm so encumbered my experience must remain limited. But I've read extensively on the subject and I want to avoid muddle and ineptitude. I've always found my father's advice to be wise.'

'I am sorry . . .?'

And I thought it was obvious.

'I wish to be relieved of hymen, doctor, deflowered if you like. By you?' I tried smiling encouragingly but he stepped further back into the curtain.

'Are you mad?'

'No of course not. Do I look mad?'

He didn't seem to want to look at me and I began to feel my plan would need some revising.

'Look, miss, I am not . . . this is a consulting-room for

patients with orthopaedic conditions not a . . . Please leave. I'm a very busy man.'

I'd embarrassed him.

'I'm terribly sorry.' I swung my legs back to the floor. 'I should've been more circumspect. I didn't imagine we'd do it *here* you know, I just didn't know any other way to meet a doctor.'

He pulled the curtain back and seemed happier with the greater contact with the world. 'Why don't you try advertising? *Time Out* is full of people . . . I'm sure that's a better idea.'

'You're not married, are you?'

'No. What? Why?' I stood up in my kid pumps and had to look down at him. He seemed flustered more by his own hasty negation.

I shrugged. 'I'd rather not get involved with adultery, that's all. According to much that I've read, adultery always results in a very messy muddle. My father says that too. He's a physicist, perhaps you've heard of him – Oscar Sondberg?'

'I'm afraid not, but I'm sure he wouldn't approve of . . . Why don't you go home and advertise. I really must go, you are wasting my time.'

'I could meet you somewhere else? I know a restaurant in Covent Garden where they do wonderful puddings . . .'

'Not possible.' He was backing away now, grinning and nodding, patting an ample waistline. 'I'm on a very strict diet.'

He called a nurse, his hand in the air like a flailing kite, and asked her to show me the exit. Then he was gone.

'This way, miss.' She was Irish, only slightly older than myself, warm and confident. We chatted about the myriad of confusing corridors then I asked her about Patel.

'He's very nice, isn't he, and they work so hard I understand, you all do. Has he been working all day?'

'Oh, all day, miss. But it's quieter in clinic than it is in casualty where you're run off your feet. He'll be off back to the hostel up the road at 5.30 and no twenty-four-hour shifts nor weekends neither. It's a cushy number, doing clinics, for those that can get it.'

I thanked her at the plastic swing-doors and decided I'd need to buy a watch. Time has to be caught in London.

13

You might think me undiscriminating and I'll concede that Patel wasn't beautiful, perhaps not even immediately prepossessing, but it would've mattered had he been ugly and he's not. He has soft intelligent eyes, black like Oscar's, more heavily lidded. His mouth is a small secret clasp for the purse of his cheeks and he has a feel for bones.

It was just after three by the hospital clock so I walked up to Hampstead for coffee and diversion, stopping *en route* at an Antiques Emporium where I found a large-faced watch with Roman numerals, a hip flask for Oscar to take fishing and a lacquer comb for Luria's hair. With my confidence thus invigorated, coffee expanded into a pancake stuffed with runny cheese and asparagus that was so good I ordered another, and in the middle of this I was joined by a young man in sawn-off jeans and a pair of mirrored sunglasses.

'Do you mind if I sit here?' His voice was languorous, so slow and deep each utterance was a lazy effort. 'I love women who like their food, and you sure are a professional.'

He was American, twentyish, with golden elbows

which he spread on the table opposite my plate. I nodded at the chair redundantly, continued chewing, mesmerised by so many yards of arm.

'It's very symbolic, you know.' He slouched across the table, grinned and removed the sunglasses. 'I took some courses in psychology for my Bachelor's degree and read all about it.' He toyed with a fork. 'It's a sublimated expression of the love need, correlative and co-actual with subconscious libidinal imperatives . . . that's a whole pile of passion you're devouring there. Kind of sexy, huh.'

His teeth were blue-white and his eyes a baffling violet. I thought at first that his wet-hay hair was severely short but as he turned slightly to prop his feet on the bar of the adjacent chair a thick rope of it, caught at the nape by a ribbon, fell on to his shoulder. A harmless vanity, it seemed to fit with the garbled Freud. I recalled a feast in *Shallum and Beth*, but it was mostly each other they'd eaten.

'Possibly,' I said. 'I suppose it depends on the menu.'

'Oh no, what you eat is irrelevant, it's – ' he breathed – 'the way you eat it.'

I became conscious of my jaws, wondered what my face did chewing.

'You're uninhibited about it. I've been watching you, I hope you don't mind. You see, most girls you take out to a restaurant just move the food around the plate without actually consuming anything at all, but you're a really serious eater. George Gilmour; I'm glad to meet you.' He thrust his hand across the condiments and I shook it with a quiet sense of awe.

'George Sondberg.' He held on to my hand, caught by the moment as I was myself.

'No kidding? Are you Georgina?'

'No. Are you?'

He blinked.

87

'Sorry. It was my mother's joke really. I suppose she'd prepared for a son and couldn't adjust her plans.'

'So you're really called George? Well that is . . . that's terrific.'

He dropped his hand, shook his head without taking his serious violet eyes from mine. There was something habitual about his smile, as though he put it on in the morning with the same easy defiance as the shorts, but I was glad he recognised the import of our shared experience, wondered what else we might have in common.

'So what are you doing in London, George?' I asked.

'Well, George, I'm studying for my Master's in business administration at the Polytechnic on Holloway Road. Do you live in Hampstead?'

'No. Crouch End. I've only been here for a few weeks. I come from the Highlands of Scotland.'

'Prophetic! I come from Boulder, Colorado, in the heart of the Rocky Mountains. This is positively umbilical, maybe we're psychic twins . . . do you like skiing?'

'I doubt it.'

'Jefferson Airplane? Talking Heads? How about Jean-Michel Jarre?'

I shrugged. 'Never heard of them.'

He thought that unlikely. Then he said, 'Well, how about sports? What do you do if you don't ski and you don't know Jean-Michel Jarre?'

What indeed.

'Well here in London I study and sightsee; at home I study and walk, paint, play my flute, read of course; my father and I like to fish and play cards, and I do a lot of carpentry.'

'Yeah?' He eyed my red sheath dress suspiciously. 'But I feel we should get to know each other anyway, don't you?'

'Anyway?'

He opened his palms apologetically. 'Carpentry isn't my bag. But you could try me, and I'll introduce you to Jean-Michel Jarre.' He grinned. 'I mean, we're virtually siblings already.'

I had to laugh. 'OK, George. Can you come for tea tomorrow? I live with my godmother, Luria Sheraton-Woodforde.'

'Cut-glass, huh?'

'Moulded, in fact. She designs interiors and we always have lots of cake.'

'Well you sure don't mess about, do you? No, I mean it's refreshingly un-British. I'd love to come for tea. What is tomorrow – Friday, that's fine, I have no plans. It's Easter vacation so I don't have classes, though I do have a lot of work to catch up on. Business administration is frankly very dull and I've been taking off more than I should have.'

'Why do you do it then?'

'Well, in a word, my father.'

'What?'

'He's why I'm doing it. He wants me to take over that side of his business.'

'What does he do?'

'You'll laugh.'

'Why?'

'He makes cutlery; knives and forks, that sort of thing?'

I didn't laugh. I groped for something polite to say, failed. Psychic twins indeed, but he was very engaging.

'Yeah, I feel pretty much that way about it myself, but he makes a ton of money, exports all over the world. Ours have bone handles, you see, well resin actually but it looks like bone, not like these.' He flicked a knife disdainfully on the table. 'And how many people can walk into an established market at twenty-two and three-quarters?'

I nodded sagely.

'How old are you, if you don't mind me asking?'

'Not at all, I'm eighteen in August. I've come to London to take external A-level exams, end of May beginning of June. I'm not sure after that.'

I told him my father was a retired physicist, talked a bit about my studies and Luria's business, what sightseeing I'd done. He ordered coffees while I finished my pancake and listened to a fairly comprehensive history of his life to date. The details of this were difficult to piece together since his delivery meandered somewhat between anecdote and the odd philosophical perception. The latter as well as arriving tangently were intrinsically commonplace, but I quickly learned that just as he didn't really require a response when he said 'don't you think' he did look for a sort of studied respect for his manifestations of insight. I nodded a lot; it was enough. In the end, however, most of what he'd said had somehow slipped off the shelf. I could only be certain that his parents were divorced, his father had furnished him with a small flat near the pond at the top of Hampstead village; that he had an older sister who ran the Spanish branch of the business (labour was cheap), that he liked skiiing more than almost anything and disliked insincerity, hypocrisy and dishonesty, in a manner which suggested that others found these qualities perfectly acceptable.

Behind the golden skin which was the result, he admitted between interjections bemoaning the length of English winters, of sunbeds rather than sun, he was lean but muscular. His neck, in particular, was reminiscent of that type of dog bred for breaking the backs of lions. Yet his face was too oval to be masculine, his chin too pointed, his eyebrows too soft, his nose too short. I doubted that he had much need of a razor nor, despite his introduction or rather because of it, that he'd had much opportunity for sexual adventure; and regardless of his obvious physical attractions I was too comfortable in his company, I decided, too conscious of a more mature intellect, to predict one with him. So the time went on and though I hadn't forgotten Patel I did misjudge the hour. When I thought to look at my new ticking watch it was 5.20.

'I must go!'

'Oh? I was going to suggest we walk over the Heath. There's a frisbee competition at Kenwood, it'll be fun.'

I was already on my feet, scrambling for money to settle the bill. 'No, I have to meet someone at the Royal Free Hospital; I'll have to find a cab or I'll be late.'

'Well let me drop you, my car's parked right outside . . .'

It was a battered canary-yellow cabriolet with the roof folded back. I scribbled my phone number and address in his Skiers' Address Book and wrote his on the wrapping of Oscar's flask. It was good to feel the wind whipping around my ears again but I noticed in the wing-mirror as we pulled up by the clinic exit that my tamed hair had been electrified into a static woolly halo, like Goya's Doña Tadea. George was curious about who I was meeting. 'Is he a friend of yours, this doctor?' He pronounced friend with a significant slur and had a good look at my legs as I climbed out of the car.

'Not exactly. We just met before the pancakes.'

'Oh. He's not called George too by any chance?'

I laughed. 'I'll see you at three tomorrow.'

'Cake at three.'

I waved him goodbye, thinking how much Luria would admire that smile and those absurdly stylish thighs.

Patel didn't emerge until just after six, by which time the energy of my former resolve was beginning to pall and I'd given up trying to flatten my hair.

He walked with his eyes fixed on the ground and didn't see me until we were virtually adjacent.

'Doctor Patel.'

'Yes!? Oh no.'

'Please don't be alarmed. I thought it would be better to meet you after work. I'd like to start again, on a more discreet basis.'

He stared contemptuously, looked back at the hospital, walked off and left me talking. I caught him up.

'I quite understand your being cross about being disturbed at work. I really am very sorry . . .'

He would not stop walking and despite my longer legs I had to lope alongside him as we spoke.

'Perhaps you'd like to go and eat somewhere first?'

'Look, Miss . . .'

'Sondberg . . . Nina Sondberg.' I wanted him to say it too. It was after all right that my alter ego should be recognised by the man who would alter my body.

'. . . Yes, yes, quite, Miss Sondberg. I would like you to leave me alone, Miss Sondberg.'

'Why? I find it hard to believe that.'

'Believe it. I'm a respectable man, now please go away.'

'I'm sure you are. That's why—'

'. . . and I have a very healthy sense of propriety. You, Miss Sondberg, are young enough to be my daughter – my granddaughter even.'

'I don't mind that at all.'

'I mind it! And I have no desire to take advantage of your youth or your obvious derangement. Go away!'

'I'm almost eighteen, Doctor Patel . . . What is your first name?'

'It doesn't matter. You don't need to know that.'

'I'm not good at formalities. I shall simply call you Patel then.'

'Fine, fine. Now will you please go away.' He stopped and spat this from between his teeth.

'I think you didn't properly understand me earlier.'

He resumed walking. 'I understood all too well.'

'I don't see why you need to be so hostile. You can't get such an enviable invitation every day.'

'Enviable? Ha! Look.' He stopped suddenly and addressed the pavement. 'I don't know you, you barge into my clinic with your crazy ideas and sit on my couch with your legs. It isn't decent or normal and it certainly isn't enviable!' Off he went again.

'Then . . . let's get to know each other. I'm not at all crazy. I'm very sane, really I am.'

'Then you follow me like this, in the street.' He glared. 'Stupid girl, what do you expect? I'm a respectable man, understand.'

'Excuse me, but you are behaving rather hysterically. Could we just calm down?'

'I go to the mosque regularly and I don't flirt with the nurses.' He didn't want to hear what I was saying. He kept looking over his shoulder.

'Are we being followed?' I asked.

'What?' He stared into the middle distance. 'We had better not be.' He turned, looked at me, his pursed mouth pleading. 'I am to my knowledge the only one of my contemporaries who does not possess a membership card to a Soho club.'

'But it was you who walked into that cubicle, not anyone else. It's fate, don't you see? I simply can't walk away.'

He confronted my intransigence with hard staring eyes and stood with his feet at right angles while he considered what to do next. His feet, I noticed, were extremely large.

'All right,' he said, decisive, gripping me by an elbow. 'Come with me.'

He steered me across the road into a pub with a grand Victorian façade, where he directed me to a seat, ordered himself a whisky and me a lemonade.

'I don't like lemonade.'

'I am not going to jail for buying a minor alcohol,' he hissed, sitting at a safe distance across the table.

'It's not illegal, is it? I didn't know.'

'That is the least of your ignorance, Miss Sondberg.'

'That's unfair! I'm very intelligent actually. Oscar says I'm only ignorant about the world.'

'Oscar is right.'

'You'd like Oscar, you have the same eyes except his are wider apart than yours, but just as black.' I smiled. He did not. He sighed and massaged his eyelids.

'OK, Miss Sondberg, now let me be frank. You want me to . . . what you said. A man you know nothing about who is, apart from the obvious cultural differences, some twenty-odd years your senior.'

I nodded.

He went on. 'I am a small man, Miss Sondberg, a good four inches smaller than you. I am running to fat and my hair is thinning and grey. I have no wife because the few ladies I have admired found me repellent and those who admired me I found repellent. But,' he paused, drew in his breath, 'after many humiliating interviews with a man I have little regard for I have now secured for myself the possibility of an alliance with the sister-in-law of a second cousin's cousin who is probably at this very moment checking my credentials . . .'

'But I'm not looking for a *permanent* relationship, Patel. I have no desire to have my sexuality regarded with any proprietorial claims in fact, and would prefer not to see you afterwards at all, ever again. I only require an hour or so of your time. As to your appearance, I find it

94

reassuringly solid, and size, I understand, doesn't matter in the logistics of these things.'

He was perched on the edge of his seat knitting his eyebrows and I could see that he was at last prepared to take me seriously. He took a swig of his whisky and we regarded each other thoughtfully.

'Miss Sondberg,' he said at last, too formally, 'there is one further small impediment which is that I, personally, do not find such a proposition as you have made me in any sense inviting or stimulating.'

'We could work on that.'

What did he want? Where was his Eastern panache? According to Oscar's books, deflowering a virgin was worth risking the wrath of a Sultan; here I was apologising for my hymen.

'But I wouldn't be here, don't you see?'

I didn't.

He stared, his eyes colder still. 'Look, I don't wish to hurt your feelings, Miss Sondberg, but you have left me no option. The fact is that I like round soft women; you are all long and skinny and you have no breasts.'

'I have breasts!'

'Too small.'

I couldn't argue with that. He smiled at last, pretending sympathy but clearly triumphant. I juggled my sense of rejection with the idea that he might find me more erotic as a boy, but since that would hardly meet with my own requirements I appealed instead for a proper drink. He refused that again too. He was immovable, obdurate, unmercifully mulish. I was defeated and smarting.

'Well then. I suppose that's that. I won't pretend I'm not disappointed. I had anticipated going home this evening a different sort of woman. I might have asked if you had a friend you could introduce me to, it really is quite a business finding a doctor, but why should you break the intransigent habits of what is by your own reckoning a very depressing lifetime?' I didn't actually mean to be facetious, it just came out that way. Sour grapes.

'I am sorry. I am truly flattered by your . . . everything, but this is just not the kind of thing I do.'

'What is, just as a matter of interest – no, don't. I'm sorry. It's just that I wasn't prepared for rejection. I don't know what to do with it. I feel like a fool.'

He was looking at me with what I could only suppose to be the kind of look he'd perfected for facing the terminally ill. 'Please,' he said, 'I don't wish you to be sad. I'm sure you'll see that I'm right when you've had time to think about it.'

'Perhaps I'll try the Whittington. I thought the Royal Free would be more liberal, you see, that's why I chose it: names can be so deceptive.'

He rose to leave, looking avuncular and still shaking his head. 'Don't be in such a hurry, Miss Sondberg. Find yourself a nice boyfriend your own age and let nature take its course.'

I ignored the patronising tone. 'Goodbye, Patel.'

'Goodbye.' He took my hand in one soft brown palm and patted it with the other. I stared at my touched hand for some time after he'd disappeared, then went to the bar.

'Whisky, please; ice, no water.'

I rang Luria to say I was pottering in Hampstead and might be late, but I got no response from George's number. He'd gone to Kenwood after all. I didn't like the barman's stare when I ordered my fourth whisky so I walked to a pub closer to George's flat and waited there. When he finally answered the phone I'd gone through two other pubs and had managed to convince myself that at twenty-two-and-three-quarters a man was ripe enough for anything. I shut out the chin. Besides, I was ravenous again and he was sure to suggest I eat.

14

'I only have a pack of stale crackers . . .'
I ate them anyway but it seemed to confirm the factitious nature of his prowess. He put on some dreadful music and sat like a cowboy astride his chair. Everything smelled of toast.

'So,' he drawled, uneasy, 'what is this urgent thing that won't wait until tomorrow?'

'Have you ever fucked anyone, George?'

He laughed too loud. 'Why sure sure, of course I have, lots—'

'I haven't,' I said before he had time to get depressed, 'and I don't want to countenance another day in a state that places me in such a false position to my potential. Can we go to bed?'

I believe he blushed. 'What? You mean right now?'

'I think seventeen years and eight months is patient enough, don't you? Shall I go and divest myself of clothes? You can come and surprise me in the dark; that way neither of us need feel self-conscious, OK?'

'It's, uh, difficult to think of something witty to say at times like this.'

'Doesn't "Oh Shit" come to mind? I feel pretty shaky myself. Five minutes.'

I made for the bedroom visible behind his ear. He hadn't exaggerated about his flat being small; the bedroom was no more than a walk-in cupboard, made less navigable by a trunk that would happily accommodate a family of five. There were columns of books stacked against the only free wall and two leaning pairs of skis which I appropriated for hanging clothes – it was the only use they could possibly have in London. I heard the shower run. George, as I was to discover, responds to all crises by shrouding himself in soap.

The bed was a trampoline. I fell into its dark navy sheets and reached for the light just as my eye fell on the nearest stack of books. Several were Oscar's.

'You're very tense, try to relax.'
    'I'm relaxed, I just don't like pain.'
    I was not relaxed. This was our third attempt.
    'Maybe if I . . .'
    '. . . Aoow! That's worse. Go back to where you were before.'
    'Like this?'
    'I think so. Maybe if I bring my legs up . . .'
    'OK?'
    'OK, try now, but really . . .'
    'Don't worry, I'm moving real slow. Real slow . . .'
    I concentrated on breathing, dragging air in through my nose, filling my lungs, expelling it in a steady stream from my mouth. I held on to his hips and waited for the moment of tension. He was propped on his elbows, taking the weight, and his hips began to sway again in that narrow arc, a delicate shimmy like a belly dancer. I could feel the bulb of his cock burning between my thighs, a burrowing mole, then again the terrible pain. I groaned and he strained and pushed and for a moment I actually believed we'd done it.

'Is it in? I think it's in.'

He flopped over sideways, collapsed.

'Why did you do that, it was in!'

He sighed from the darkness. 'It wasn't in.'

'Are you sure?'

'It wasn't in.'

'Fuck it. Buggery damn bastards and horseshit!'

We lay quiet then for a while, wiped the sweat from our eyes, let it evaporate from our sticky bodies into the duvet. I felt a sudden impulse to cry, but suppressed it. I wasn't ready to capitulate and George might if there were tears. At least he'd had the dubious satisfaction of a premature ejaculation. But that was our first attempt and the result, he assured me, of eighteen months' enforced celibacy. He'd apologised profusely, but immediately negated this by berating the perplexing taste of English women, who were inexplicably unmoved by his advances. I lay in the dark feeling my muscles contract. The second attempt had been another salutary lesson in the temperamental nature of male apparatus. George, I decided, didn't have much clue about female anatomy. He kept thrusting wildly into the general area so that I felt like an especially hard-to-hit target. He seemed reluctant to actually touch me. Shy perhaps, perhaps squeamish. I was too desperate to consider which. But when I guided him accurately with my own hands he just pushed and pushed ineffectually at the point of entry, causing me considerable discomfort, didn't get beyond a centimetre, then went completely limp.

He said I was talking too much.

My hymen was too sinewy. It put him off.

We dozed after that but the feel of warm flesh crept into our dreamy half-sleep and so our third attempt began.

'Why is it so difficult, George?'

He rolled towards me. 'I don't know. Your hymen feels like it's made of bakelite.'

'What?'

'Synthetic resin made with formaldehyde, like plastic but denser. My father used to use it for handles.'

'I know what bakelite is, thank you. Do you think it's unnaturally thick?'

'I don't know about unnatural. I haven't actually come across too many. To be perfectly frank I've only slept with four other women and they were pretty loose. With you it feels like pushing on a tennis ball. It makes me nervous too, you understand?'

'I'm sorry. What can we do?'

'I don't know. Maybe you need to see a doctor.'

'What a good idea.' I didn't elaborate. 'None of Oscar's virgins ever have this problem.' It suddenly occurred to me that Oscar's projections might owe considerably more to imagination than experience. They might in fact be entirely imaginative . . .

'Who's Oscar?'

'My father, Oscar Sondberg, remember, you have some of his books.'

'I do?'

'Yes. In that pile on the floor: *Lotan*, *Abigail* and *Nahari*.'

'Your father wrote those!? Are you kidding me?' He sat up. 'I thought you said your father was a physicist?'

'He is. He's lot of things, including a writer. He's Oscar Mann for the books, my mother's maiden name. I could quote you chunks if you like, but I'll tell you about them some other time. Right now I have to ring Luria; she was expecting me home.' I padded next door and fumbled for the light-switch.

It was almost midnight, but Luria wasn't asleep. She rarely goes to bed before 1 a.m.; she watches television and prowls through magazines generating so much adrenalin with coffee and gin and colour schemes she has to have a sleeping pill. She'd been worried. I explained where I was but that didn't reassure her.

'Who is he?' she demanded, then before I could answer, 'He could be anybody!'

There wasn't much I could say about that. 'His father makes forks. I've invited him to have tea with us tomorrow.'

'Forks!' she screeched. 'You mean you've picked up some factory hand and gone back to his flat . . .!'

'He owns the factories, Luria,' I said, annoyed with myself for indulging her snobbery but I was in a hurry. I thought about our fridge full of food and felt the gnawing insult of my intact hymen inside.

'Look, I'm having a bit of a problem here, Luria.'

'What? What is it?'

I closed the bedroom door to spare George's feelings – he was leaning back on his bedrest surrounded by Oscar – and related the broad details of my lack of success with Patel and the more excruciating failures of the last two hours. She muttered incoherently while I spoke and dragged hard on her cigarette. Her voice remained strangely caught, constricted, and apart from extracting my promise not to offer myself further to the medical profession who were not, she maintained, trained for that kind of thing, she offered no sympathy and no constructive advice. I pressed for more information.

'He can't be doing it wrong,' she insisted flatly. 'He's probably just afraid he won't compare with Mick Jagger . . . it's a young man's cross. Why all this urgency anyway? You don't know what you're doing.'

'Yes I do.'

'You're completely wrong about doctors for a start; most are impotent alcoholics with thick underwear, they're demoralised by healthy bodies and at a complete loss with vigour. This is your father's fault.'

Bugger that.

'Patel said I was skinny.'

'Listen to me, whatever you do you won't avoid muddle. It's inevitable, no matter how sensitive or experienced or anatomically expert your man. The first time is *always* a muddle, an absurd misrepresentation; the combination of ignorance and anticipation guarantees it. And you're slim, skinny is an ugly word. Now look, just get in a cab and leave your hymen where it is for a while. You're not ready for all this sexual adventure, you're too young. I could strangle Oscar.'

'Do you think it might be easier if I got on top? Luria . . .? Are you there, Luria?'

'. . . Yes, yes. Bloody hell. Please come home, Georgie. I'll make us both a nice sandwich . . .'

'I'm staying, Luria. I must. I thought you'd understand. Don't you?'

She tutted, muttered, pulled on her cigarette.

'What do you think?'

'What?'

'About getting on top – d'you think that might help?'

'Oh, I . . . I think you're being bloody stupid but yes, yes yes yes. At least if you're in control you won't damage yourself . . .'

I thought that was the end of it but she launched into an unnecessary lecture about contraceptive protection which, in the circumstances, was galling. She was relieved to hear that George had condoms, a whole box in fact, very full. Unlike his larder.

'It's . . . uh, rather exciting to think that your father wrote those books.'

We were huddled in the dark again.

'Is it?' I ran my hand across his abdomen, texture of large-cap mushrooms, let my leg sweep on to his thigh. He rolled on to his back.

'I always found all that stuff about dewy dells and stabbing tubers a bit botanical myself.' This was flippant and utterly dishonest. I was simply embarrassed and wasn't sure why.

I *had* thought Oscar's euphemisms coy and farcically affected but I'd experimented and transposed an extract, replacing 'her pulsating grove' and 'his thrusting bolus' with vagina and penis. It was accurate, but wearing on the senses.

'Renounce salaciousness,' Oscar had said, 'and you deny the heart of fantasy, without which we are mindless combatants, filled with self-loathing, fucking for duty. I write trashy plots, George, unrealistic dialogue, but I don't corrupt desire.'

Maybe he was right.

George was lying with his arms behind his head, one knee slightly raised so that the soft skin of his inner thigh brushed against mine. My hand counted his padded ribs, followed the valleys of muscle from chest to abdomen, found the yielding spot beneath every inch and would not be appeased. I had wanted Patel but I knew in my fingertips that he'd never have been such a pleasure to touch. George was long and lean yet succulently firm, covered in a down of fine golden hair. I wanted to gnaw him.

'It's poetic,' he said. 'I personally find metaphor much more alluring than accurate scientific description; it titillates the mind so that you can concentrate without feeling like a technician.'

'Trenchantly put.' I didn't want to talk about it, I wanted to do it. I thought about my masks and Luria's bluff confidence, and wondered if another role, one of Oscar's masterful models, might just do the trick. Something inside me shrank from the responsibility of determining the role. I could see that the enactment of fantasy demanded that I 'act' and I wasn't certain of a measured performance. I was glad, then, that I was with George. I would've been deterred by fear of making a fool of myself with Patel. With George I could be brave.

'Well this – ' I took his hand and guided his middle finger to the point of my clitoris – 'the daughter of Cush calls her palpitating rose. And this – ' I wrapped my hand around the stem of his cock, drew it upwards and back with even pressure – 'is a throbbing bough.'

He laughed, but his cock liked it.

I didn't care if I sounded funny. I was suddenly driven by that sense of absence the proximity of another body makes acute. I became Tekoah the wise, writhing in the heat of another's blood, mistress of give and take, I was drifting to a less centred space where even the touch of a toe is charged with deliberation.

George stretched himself luxuriously, sighed through his teeth with every firm caress. I rolled back the covers and stroked him like a cat, following the nap of his hair, dragging my fingernails with the backwards stroke, up and down and up and down, and each time more firmly stroking, more deeply kneading, smiling as he whimpered. I bent over him and ran the tip of my tongue from his tight foreskin to the crease of his groin, rolled it around his width and drew it up to the tip and down again, held him between my teeth and worried that sensitive flesh with my tongue. Tekoah was exhilarating, powerful, intensely erotic. I crawled over his paralysed form and perched on spread knees over his thighs. He moaned, flexed his hips, pushed himself up to meet me while I rubbed my swollen lips with the end of his cock. But his hands were too undisciplined, shifted too easily from his grip on the end of the bed to pull me closer and hovered, thus, in an ambiguous tension between the impulse to take and desire to be taken. I groped in the dark and found the leather belt from his shorts. It would do.

'I want you tied down,' I said. 'You must be mine to use as I wish.'

I pinned his hands together, twining leather through the slatted bed, rubbing myself on each touched part as I pulled the knotted end tight. There was rapture in his voice. 'Some kind of virgin.'

'Forget that. I am rapacious, greedy, insatiable, craving. Give me your tongue, just the very tip.' I sank down on to it, felt his warm cheeks between my thighs, teasing and stabbing, a delicious agony. He was mine, abandoned as I was, helpless yet willing. I used each part of him, rubbed and stroked and licked my way to the end of each nerve. And when I was glutted with flesh I slipped on a rubber and guided him inside me to that point of sinewy pressure. He opened his eyes then, alarmed, peered at me hovering over him.

'Things happen, George,' I said, 'even when you're not watching.' Then I launched myself into his pelvis.

There was no great rending sound, no spurts of blood, not even a trickle, just a stinging convulsive pain which swept through me and electrified my scalp. It drained me of air so that I couldn't even call out. I thought I might faint. I thought I'd ripped myself apart. But when the spasm passed I knew I was filled with him all the way to my cervix and I laughed aloud, a woman's deep-throated laugh.

I suppose you could say I deflowered myself; it's almost poetic.

Later, after the triumph of the seductress, we tackled other roles, many, each with its own absorbing sorcery and power. I was freed by my father's models, relieved of myself. My natural inhibitions were masked by the avaricious confidence of their touch.

We may have slept that night, but fitfully, I can't be sure.

15

G eorge was still asleep when I left in search of a cab and breakfast, after which I sank into a bath and washed the semen from my hair.

I looked east over the city from my bedroom window. A warm haze veiled everything except the top of the tower blocks and the dome of St Paul's. But the world had changed. I'd seen it when I left George wound in oblivion and stepped into Hampstead's streets. Men, women, all sizes and ages, the same but somehow altered. The clichéd image of the woman searching her own mirror for signs of a torn hymen diverts us from the truth; sex doesn't change the virgin, it changes the world. New perceptions deny the old. We forget at once how we'd looked on others and not recognised the promise in what we saw. I see it now, just as I'd seen it that morning in the cab driver's nape and shoulders, the swaying buttocks of an old woman walking her dog, the sweat on a jogger's back, the momentary glimpse of an eye. The world has become sexed for me. The proverbial oyster. Now the very paving stones I tread look under my dress.

Luria turned up at lunchtime. She'd left her cramped office early to allay her worries. I was still alive. I wasn't damaged. I hadn't been taking drugs and my young man wasn't depraved.

She called him George the Second; I guess it'll stick.

I followed her around the house while she found disarray in the cushions and the regimented magazines.

'I'd probably still be intact but for your advice.' I didn't mention Oscar's part, since she flinched at the sound of his name.

'I'm not very happy about that as an accolade! Not exactly a godmother's role, is it?'

'You said yourself I could take or leave your advice, I chose to take it. Anyway, I'd thought of it myself.'

'I didn't know sexual technique was on the agenda when we made that pact, Georgie.' She loped towards a rebellious kink in a curtain. 'I was thinking more in terms of your asking where to shop, nice places to eat, that sort of thing. I imagined you meeting boys, of course, but in my scenario they had spots and computers and you went out on regular dates and then, and only after going steady for a decent period of months, then you might have broached the subject.' She threw her shoulders back assertively. 'I certainly didn't anticipate midnight calls about coitus problems with someone you'd picked up in a bar.'

She started beating the peony-printed wallpaper with a feather duster. Indefatigable.

I wondered if her mood was the result of my phoning her or merely because I'd found George without a formal introduction. I decided it wasn't the phone call.

'It wasn't a bar.'

'Café then. Whatever . . .'

'Is that what you did, Luria?'

'Absolutely not. I have never consciously picked up anyone anywhere . . .'

'Really? But I meant did you go steady for several months with a boy with spots?'

'Oh. Well. Yes, I suppose I did. I'd certainly known him for years. We were at the same school – or had been. I was in the Lower Sixth when we finally got together and he was by then studying forestry, or was it agriculture? He was called Alan. Your mother didn't like his tufty hair.' She chortled, amused at some memory. 'I was mad about him; inarticulate and dehydrated at the thought of him . . . And his fingernails were always full of mud.'

'How did it happen? What was it like, your first time?'

'God, Georgie, it was almost a hundred years ago.' She went back to beating the walls again.

'You remember the mud.'

'Yes, well, maybe that made more impression . . .'

I believed her. Oscar and I have a functional attitude to housework, but for Luria dirt was a hobby.

'Try.'

She sighed, stuffed her duster under her arm. 'I can only remember that he was terrified of his own body and tried to ignore mine. I think I despised him the next day and that was the end of that.'

'I don't despise George.'

She looked at me, her mouth flattened.

'But then, I don't feel romantic about him either. He's just a new friend with badly made shorts.'

'You did say you know about AIDS, didn't you?'

'Of course. And safe sex. Oscar and I discussed all that in biology.'

'Did he tell you there were animals out there in biology? You're barely *au fait* with the ways of women so God knows what you're like with men.'

I flopped on to the sofa. 'I suppose I'll just have to have lots of them,' I teased. 'For experience.'

'You sound just like your mother at times, same bloody artlessness . . .'

Luria talked about my mother a lot, without encouragement. It made me feel queer in the head.

Mother was a moribund two-syllabled sound empty of meaning, yet Luria talked about a woman with attitudes, a history, mannerisms, someone you would notice, a being with substance and tastes. She liked gallons of strong China tea, Luria said, Cary Grant and thunderstorms. She liked those fierce Irish dogs with the curly mane, and jiving to Jerry Lee Lewis. Her eyebrows danced when she spoke. She hated boats yet worshipped the sea. She talked of her own mother, Luria says, and of her mother before her, women who walked in the rain after dark.

There were boxes and boxes of photographs tracking a life: schoolgirl, holidays, art-student days; a smiling face, a face caught unawares, a face that made me hollow in the space reserved for jet beads.

It nagged and it made me feel queer in the head.

'How did my mother die, Luria?' It was easier to say outside Scotland. Oscar wasn't listening.

She froze. 'How . . .!? D'you mean you don't know?'

'I've forgotten,' I lied. She might think Oscar had kept it from me.

'How can you forget something like that?'

I shrugged. 'Too many years.'

'I don't believe you—'

'Oscar didn't like to talk about it much; too painful.'

'You don't know . . .?'

'He told me, of course he did, but I was so young . . . I've forgotten.'

'How young?'

'Why does it matter? Just tell me again.'

111

'I don't understand you, how could you forget?'

'Luria . . .'

'There was an accident. Remember? She was drowned.'

?

'Of course.'

'The first of June, 1974. Twenty-nine and as fit as an ox. Caught by the current.'

So the letter tucked in my notebook upstairs was written the day before she died? She went swimming after that letter?

Drowned?

'She would've understood you, Georgie, even if I can't.'

My ears were too hot.

'Tell me more about your Alan; did he mind that you despised him afterwards?'

She was posed by the french windows now, dragging on a thin cigarette and shedding motes of ash. 'I don't know. Why on earth d'you ask that?'

'I assume he was romantically involved with you . . . there was all the build-up of flirtation and you did have a relationship in mind?'

'Yes, but we were very young, remember.'

'Oscar says the male ego is fragile when it comes to sexual performance. That's why I wanted Patel.'

'I'm sure Alan survived.'

'Really? How do you know? He might've been devastated, rendered impotent for years.'

'What are you talking about? You can't expect a seventeen-year-old girl to be responsible for the emotional development of the boy who takes her virginity, don't be so bloody silly.'

'I'm just pursuing a thought, really. It seems to me that despite all your proper channels you were no better prepared for screwing Alan than I was with George. Less so in fact, since yours was such a failure. Wouldn't you say?'

'I'd say you were too calculating for your own good. At least I knew who Alan was!'

'I take people at face value, Luria. I trust my instinct and I don't see that prolonged familiarity with someone would improve my judgement. Besides, George wasn't just anybody, as you put it, he was a man I chose to sleep with. The first. In that sense he was rather important, to me.'

'You're not insulted, are you?'

'No, I don't feel insulted. I'm merely trying to reassure you that in some things I do know what I'm doing.'

'Do you, indeed. Well you ought to know not to rush into things you might regret. You were lucky this time, but emotional rashness, Georgie, is not wise.'

'I thought I was calculating.'

She breathed into her collar. 'You're awkward that's what you are; you know exactly what I mean.'

I unfolded myself from my chair and stretched. 'I'm just not sure what you require of me. You seem alarmed that I should be sexually active and yet admit that at my age you were yourself. I'm very willing to listen to the voice of experience but . . . well, you must concede that your brief affair with Alan doesn't exactly recommend itself.'

'Why am I beginning to feel hounded?'

I laughed. 'You're not. I'm devoted to you, godmother. I'm used to questioning everything, that's all. Conviction interests me, because it's bred of a type of passion. I'm greedy for convictions because I have so few of my own, and you seem to have so many. But I need to know what they're based on and I can't somehow accommodate your conviction about the appropriate time and place to lose virginity. My loss turned out to be . . . Well, I want to

113

do it again, I liked it. I feel like there's another person inside me now. I want to know everything there is to know about that person and social conventions that don't make sense don't help.'

'No one suggested my adolescent self was a good example. God knows, I hadn't a clue then. But I'm not a silly teenager now . . .'

'And I am?'

'You're a young woman with a very peculiar background and I don't believe it's prepared you in any real sense to recognise the need for caution.'

This seemed reasonable to me. 'All right, Luria, I take your point. But you mustn't imagine that Oscar reared me in a vacuum; he was very thorough in my education. Human nature was one of his favourite subjects and as in everything else, I'm sure he understands it better than most of us.'

She flinched. I distracted myself by investigating the tripod feet of her Victorian firescreen.

'I know you're very fond of your father,' she said, 'but one day you'll realise he is not, and never has been, the unblemished paragon you imagine. You're a bit too old now for all this uncritical adoration.'

'And you're embarrassingly melodramatic.'

Her flat-penny eyes dilated. 'He might at least have buried her properly.'

'What?'

She was angry, with me apparently.

'Well . . . it wasn't right. No proper funeral, no visitors, not even a stone chalice to look at for Chrissake. It makes me so bloody furious. I don't suppose you saw him dispose of her ashes? No, of course not. No one did. He just threw her in the fucking sea and no one saw anything!'

114

'Scattered her ashes, Luria, he didn't feed her to the fish.'

To become a fossil?

'Did my mother write to you, just shortly before she died?'

'Why?'

'No reason. Don't you remember?'

'I wouldn't have forgotten if she had. She never wrote, she couldn't, your dear father wouldn't allow it. I had two, maybe three, letters from Scotland and then nothing. He didn't actually deign to let me know she'd died until months later, and even that he sullied. He sent the news with a copy of his first nasty book, *Lucas*. And poor Maggie's name. What d'you think of that?'

'What d'you mean he wouldn't allow it?'

'You really don't know him at all, do you?'

'Yes I do.' I bristled.

'Let's just say that Oscar made overbearing possessiveness look like indifference. He hated your mother's friends uniformly, me in particular. No letters was the least of it; he couldn't tolerate her even talking or thinking about anyone else. It all had to be for him, everything.'

And me?

'Jealous is an inoffensive term for what Oscar was. That and . . . well that had much more to do with their removal to that godforsaken place than Maggie not liking Oxford; she did.'

This was too much. They'd moved there to protect Oscar's knowledge, not to escape people. This was poison.

I left her to vent her frustration on imaginary dust and went upstairs. I have to scrub increasingly hard these days to wash the taste of stone from my mouth.

*

We sat on the high stools by the breakfast bar in the kitchen. George called Luria Ma'am with exaggerated politeness and professed an intense interest in the symbolism of colour. He was sure that Freud had had something to say about that too, but he couldn't remember what. Luria was charmed by his suntan and muscles and insisted he address her by name. He was charmed by her mannered sophistication and her impressive appliances, by the olde worlde chintziness, the Madeira cake, the florentines and the walnut barquettes. He said something disingenuous about home cooking and we laughed at the cake boxes piled by the bin. We laughed easily since there was nothing but air and the smoke from Luria's cigarettes between us. George held no mystery for me, he felt like an old friend I was just late in getting to know. But I wasn't indifferent to his company, I liked it as much as my own. After all, didn't we share an alignment to the world as foreigners?

George was also, I thought, too aware of his temporary residence to seek commitment and, like me, was open to experiment without possessive demands. Why look elsewhere when chance had provided so comfortably what would no doubt take months to find in others? Who needed Patel.

He poured the tea, confident of Luria's eye, pleased to be admired again. England had not been kind to him. There's something in the way he leans across furniture, on to walls, over chairs; he cannot stand straight. It's a Mid-western characteristic, no doubt, too readily adjudged by the English a sign of imbecility. George had been lonely.

'I forgot to ask if you'd caught your doctor friend yesterday. At the hospital?'

Luria's eyebrows twitched. It was too complicated.

116

'Yes, but we didn't talk for long, he was wearing the wrong shoes.'

This precipitated an explanation of Luria's Theory of Shoes and its application in business. George wondered what could be discovered about the buyers in cutlery departments of large stores and Luria asserted that of course everything could.

In the middle of this conversation I decided to make some discreet enquiries of the Registrar in Lairg. I heard myself thinking that a simple copy of a death certificate would silence Luria's doubts. Which is what they are, I said to myself. Oscar needn't know.

George was leaning back on his stool with one foot up on the seat of another; Luria was reading his boots. Walking boots like mine. She turned to me, displayed the toe of his boot between finger and thumb.

'This is an extremely sensible young man we have here, darling.'

She hadn't read sensible in mine. Odd, that.

'How do you feel about being called sensible, George?'

'Well,' he said, nodding his head in elaborate consent, 'I do have an umbrella and I was once a scout-ranger in the Blue Mountain District Young Hawks; I learned to tie knots, eat cold baked beans and button a shirt in the dark.'

'Essential talents for life, my dear,' said Luria, her lipstick smug, 'but I should throw away the umbrella.'

'I think we should have a party.' I looked at Luria, let her see how daring I'd become; I could do anything. 'A dinner?' I laughed at her surprise.

'You've left Scotland at last, Georgie, out of the wind.' She grinned. 'I think that calls for a party.'

16

Dear Oscar,

I'm on the Brunschwig and Fils sofa, Luria says the upholstery was inspired by an Aubusson print. I have to get the names right, and everything, including the Carrara bath, has a name. While we were watching the kittiwakes fly over from Hendra Island, Luria was collecting. The enclosed pastel is a birthday-card view of the city from my bedroom window. I've left in the distant scaffolding to satisfy your taste for the exact and mine for the abstract line. The flask is for fishing. It's antique silver, according to the salesman. I suspect it will tarnish in the salt spray but this will add to its charm.

So, HAPPY BIRTHDAY for Thursday, dear Oscar! 48: Element Cd; 118.4°F; XLVIII; divisible by 2, 4, 6, 8, 12 and 24. In thousands, the height of Mont Blanc. Thirty years, 2 months, 3 weeks and 4 days more life than mine. Not a prime number. Luria conceals her 45 years like a blemish. She applies 'active liposomes' at £30 per gram even to her elbows, nods at me and says 'You wait.' Do you feel old, Oscar? I think of you playing with your bricks and mortar, singing at the piano and filling your marquetry chest with books, ageless. Life here is too full to miss you in the day but I feel the absence of your voice as the sun goes down. Your mean little postcards are too free with bloody instructions and niggardly with conversation. I need letters! Write, Oscar.

By the way, I've been doing a minor survey here and there and I've discovered your books do sell well. I'm not surprised, I had a look at the other reading material available! Or rather I am surprised; the magazines are expensive but they have pictures. How do you feel about pictures? I've been wondering, indulge me, is there a point at which voyeurism becomes heretical (your word)? I'm trying to pin down the difference between Baudelaire, you, and the latest edition of Swish . Baudelaire is more difficult. Is that it? The stupid man who needs the comic is most corrupt, the educated man with the Marquis de Sade is less corruptible? Is that it, Oscar? Love, I've discovered, is not necessary: I lost my hymen on Hampstead Hill. Could be a song.

This house is very clean, did I say? Luria is affronted by dirt. There are several cupboards devoted entirely to utensils for eradicating dust and a cleaner comes every day. We pad about on cushioned floors like burglars while she perfumes the walls. But despite Luria's claims for the fast life she's really a creature of quiet habits. She extols spontaneity but at heart prefers the predictable. She works, comes home, strokes the cats and settles in cloistered comfort for the night. Maybe it's a temporary concession based on some notion about my needs for quietude. Who knows.

I feel less of a cuckoo at last: I have a friend who shares my name (Luria calls him George the Second) and I've grown used to the closed windows. Tomorrow I'll pick up the past exam papers from the Board; it was a good suggestion, thanks.

Love George.

P.S. Who are *Brunschwig and Fils*?

17

S ex is like food: the same recipes become very
boring. Best of all is the unpredictable stolen snack;
the more daring the theft the better.

George now comes shopping with me to help me
expand my exotic wardrobe. I buy more leather and
suspenders and deep-slashed chiffon. We duck into changing cubicles in crowded shops and explore before the
mirrors. Doorways and alleys full of shadow have become
my inspiration, fear of discovery our mutual delight. We
go to the theatre just to make use of the dark, browse in
the least frequented stacks of bookshops and libraries
where we like the pretence of a chance encounter.

I learn what I need to learn quickly. I've learned to
wear high heels and dust my cleavage with pearlised
powder and rid myself of body hair. I've learned to
untwine a cock from the tightest jeans beneath a restaurant
table and divest myself of underwear in the heat of the
rush-hour crush. Luria says my clothes are vulgar trash
and my preoccupations a nightmare. She'd be alarmed by
my skills but I suspect envious of my pleasure. Her so-
called liberalness isn't truly felt at all. Like her designer
clothes it's merely an accessory of the preconceived ideal.
So she's neither her natural self nor her consciously chosen

mask, but a compromise denying both. Poor Luria. She preaches moderation with ridiculous omens and obscure prophecies that wouldn't convince a child. Lust is a passing phase, she says. Poor George, she says, and stares at his crotch in disbelief. I've spied him unbutton his shirt before he knocks at her door, for he too has learned how to please.

London, from one fuck to another, has thus become even more interesting, enriched. I've abandoned my virgin list and compiled another I like to call Places of Fucking Interest. I must add to it the tantalising repose of a Gothic tomb in Highgate Cemetery.

Two things came from Oscar after my birthday letter. The first was a cryptic telemessage to Luria which baffled us both and did much for her pallid complexion:

DEMAND POLICE, SCREENING FOR PREGNANCY, AIDS, SYPHILIS, GONORRHOEA, HERPES. YOU UTTERLY BETRAY ALL TRUST. OSCAR.

His note to me arrived the next day. It was marginally less acerbic:

Dear George,

I take it from your tone you are somehow recovered? Flippancy is not an indication of maturity or intelligence. Difficult to imagine why you should think so and conclude Luria encouraging stupidity. For foreseeable future insist *you do not converse with anyone who is not at your dinner table. Absolutely* forbid *further visits to Soho. You have work to do, do it and come home.*

Oscar

The icy dogmatism made me physically flinch but in the circumstances I wrote back immediately saying, 'HYMEN NOT STOLEN, LOST; NOT RAPE BUT LIBERTY'. There's been nothing since then but silence.

Luria calls him a hypocrite. He wouldn't like my suspenders, she says, or my leather. I don't see why not. I like his fantasies; we're obviously in tune.

I consulted all the magazines on sale and bought three devoted to especially imaginative pictures, then I spread their centrefolds on Luria's Oppenheim table. They disturb in a way no narrative can because they *are* pictures. I can't share them with George, for example, as I do Oscar's books, because the models get in the way. I can't reconcile my curiosity and fascination with the lascivious often brutal postures with the flaccid male genitalia. A limp penis is always potential but I have to concentrate very hard to get round it, in every sense. They involve me in paradox since, as the picture fixes his impotence, I can only dispel it by looking away. More often than not I find they merely propel my eye to the woman whose state of arousal is forever hidden, secluded, hinted at only in her come-on look and position. Now this is better, but tricky. In the first place, to identify with the woman we must make allowances for her impotent partner, who can't make it while we stare. In the second, identifying with the woman involves another paradox since most of the women look so stupid. The ubiquitous tongue lolling in a pretence of lust might invite us into the fantasy but the gormless expression doesn't. The glazed eye, untainted by thought, remains always animal, dumbly submissive, willing function. Perhaps that's all men need, for masturbating fodder. I'm interested in foreplay myself but stupidity isn't erotic.

Luria claims they make women objects of mindless abuse and shrugs when I point out it's frequently the male who takes the whipping.

'The sado-masochistic impulse is sexual,' I said, grinning at George, 'but it's never sexed.'

'Yes it is. There's no female Jack the Ripper.'

'But that's deviant, Luria,' George protested. 'I mean, if a man has a natural proclivity to, say, masochism, he's not *per se* a faggot. What you imply is that we take it literally as defining character; well, in those terms the common rape fantasy defines most women as willing victims, most men as psychopaths. But they're not. How many Jack the Rippers do you know?'

'Don't be silly. Look at those pictures, they're obscene. Unnaturally staged and absurdly posed.'

'Would you like them any better if they were neither of those? If they were photographs of real situations?'

'Good God no.'

'What then?'

'I don't know why you two spend so much time thinking about it at all. You're focused on phallus, both of you. It must be your age.'

George reads the *Guardian* and offers statistics: 88 per cent of the male population secrete magazines in lavatories and under beds, hide them in the garden shed, in the *pied-à-terre*, in allotments, swap them at school and post them on the garage walls.

'See,' said Luria. 'No women.'

'Maybe they weren't asked.'

'Women don't buy them. They don't need them and they don't want them.'

It's true that when I bought the magazines I was the only woman browsing in the top shelves. Luria talks about social taboo, but I suspect the material itself just doesn't cater to women.

'Women certainly don't want all this sado-masochistic stuff.'

'What? But the pictures in my mind are not based on a tender heart, Luria, nor do I believe are yours. And age is irrelevant. Maybe you're just losing interest.'

'Just a minute—'

'It doesn't matter. Perhaps George and I are focused on phallus as you say, but so what? We're not forcing ourselves into something we'd rather not do, so it can't be unnatural or perverse. It seems to me sex is a fundamental part of life and I want to understand it. It's no use flinching at these pictures while we're evidently incapable of producing alternative effigies to champion.'

'You ignore love, Georgie.'

'No I don't. Great art is full of it, but while it might add another dimension to representations of the sexual impulse, it doesn't challenge the impulse itself.'

'I accept what you're saying, darling, but I think you're confusing what actually goes on in sex, sexual fantasy, and the expressions of it. It's the latter women like myself find so objectionable, especially in this form.' She rapped a magazine. 'Compared with a Rubens, this teaches men that all women are orifices to be had, that we're simply available.'

'Rubens does that too, all art does.'

'Not without an aesthetic. Art has a wider conscience, a perspective which includes love, or at least the possibility of love; your magazines depict sex as bestial and mindless. Men and women as function. Western man is already emotionally thin and shouldn't be encouraged to get thinner.'

'That's just hearsay.'

'Yeah, I thought we were getting better,' said George. 'In the States these days, a guy can't get a date without evidence of therapy and a good relationship with his mother.'

'In London it's sensible boots,' I said drily.

Luria made a face.

Anyway, I tore out the best of the centrefolds to send to Oscar: two lesbian maids with a butler, a vamp in a rubber suit strategically slit, a boy trapezed in a daring way with his ass swung high. Well? I said. So send your words of wisdom.

The Easter vacation is long over and George is obliged to spend his days scouring his notebooks for facts. He too has exams but fewer than mine, the bulk of his course being assessed by a thesis entitled 'Comparative Values in Export: The European Mind'. We edit it together in Luria's booklined study, a poppy-red cave of a room under the eaves; so now I know that the French dislike of the Germans has nothing to do with the war.

Luria leaves elaborate notes with instructions about catering firms for the party, for domestic agencies, gardeners who landscape handkerchief lawns, invitations for friends and paid-up clients. She can't smile when someone owes her money.

The event coincides (no coincidence I'm sure) with my dead mother's birthday. A Gemini, and Oscar Taurus; she must have been a damper. Astrology is another of Luria's arts, appropriately so, she says, for an Aquarian. I was born in Leo. According to Luria this makes me reliable, as placid as a lake, unless roused to anger, an extrovert who hates the dark. 'So much for astrology,' I said. 'Lionessess never cast a shadow.'

I've heard nothing yet from Lairg. Who knows why these things take so long? I sent a blank cheque to cover the costs of a copy of a death certificate, my mother's name and the date of her death. A simple transaction. It ought to take ten minutes.

Luria's mythical entourage is also puzzlingly absent.

'Of course I like men,' she says.

Perhaps there's a secret cot hidden in her studio walls, a lover with a flat in town, a magazine behind the toilet.

I'm tired of revision. Physics, biology, English, French, Italian and history: six mornings a week and Saturday free for fucking.

I know now I don't want to return to Geathramh Garbh as soon as exams are over, but my future remains uncertain. Luria recommends I exploit my gift for the well-turned seam and study dress design and fashion. George is awed by my eloquent pillow talk in foreign tongues and recommends translation. 'You could be an executive in Italian cutlery,' he says. 'Live high in the Tuscan hills.' But fashion is just for foreplay and I can't think forks all my life. Physics faintly beckons and I can just hear Oscar's scorn. Whatever he says, I've been inspired by all these books about the origins of the universe. Jane Austen readers have turned to the Bang and the Crunch and the arrows of time. The Northern Line is a sea of cosmological theses held by men and women in suits who read on past their destinations, gripped by the cries of a birthing universe. It's everywhere at once, indiscriminate and free, like a rampant contagion. Now waiters discuss protons, strings and quarks; old ladies in cake queues remark that they get into food.

Has this stolen Oscar's fire? Do these authors know what my father knows and died as a physicist to keep? I read greedily and send a copy of Hawking on, enclosed in a centrefold entitled 'Fanella Frankly Feeling'. Which she was.

Luria is in a state of trauma because her cats have fleas. They're everywhere, in our beds and thick in the chairs and carpets. The whole house is heaving with unwanted life and we wake covered with the fiery marks of their feasting in the night. They itch like mad and we go about clawing at ourselves frantically while the cats sit and purr in their useless flea-collars, as imperturbed as Buddhas. Luria refuses to look at their crawling fur, she runs from their affectionate advances and screeches incoherent panic should they pounce into her lap; she exudes nervous energy alarming in one so large. George showers at hourly intervals and tries to cope with her hysteria. I can't. She comes into the house with an ashen face and the bowls of her great flat eyes are sunken and grooved as though a potter's thumb had made them. She's convinced the news will get out and no one will admit her to their homes. People will come to her party and see the fleas bouncing about on the furniture, leave with them dangling from their coat-tails, secreted in trouser turn-ups and hair; they'll tell the world that Luria Sheraton-Woodforde is host to the worst parasites imaginable and the world will take its business elsewhere.

She enquired of insurance firms, but they don't cover fleas.

She rang up Environmental Health but backed out of having the house sprayed with some lethal stuff that guarantees instant death but poisons the air with a chemical pall for months.

Mostly she sits on the floor and whimpers and screams at her darling cats; she's even denied herself the comfort of her hideous stuffed ormolu chair.

Then George turned up one evening bearing a box of candles.

'I've got it,' he said. 'My landlady gave me this tip, passed down from her grandmother's grandmother who lived in the venomous slums of Victorian London. She says it never fails.'

'We're not going to burn them to death?'

'Don't be dumb. This is neat, trust me.'

He disappeared into the kitchen and returned carrying a large serving plate and a jug of water, which he placed in the middle of the floor. He lit a candle and stuck it on some hot dripped wax in the middle of the plate. Luria looked at me, helpless but hopeful; she would have burned chalk dust and toenails if she thought it would work. George poured water around the base of the flickering candle, filling the plate to the rim.

It was like the prelude to some ritual sacrifice and I wondered idly which of us had been chosen.

'OK, we're ready to go here . . . Now we close the blinds and the curtains.'

He looked round expectantly, Luria looked at me. I crossed to the window and shrouded the room in darkness.

'What now?' I asked. The candle flared up, casting phantoms over the walls.

'We wait, and we watch,' said George.

So we all three gathered round like the weird sisters and stared at our strange offering.

'Shouldn't we chant something appropriate?' I suggested after an age during which absolutely nothing happened.

'Agh . . .!' Luria screeched, gripped my arm, screeched again, her eyes wide with grisly horror. I looked at the plate and was startled to see two fleas swimming desperately in the candle's lake. Even as we watched others leapt from nowhere towards the flame only to be trapped by the surface tension of the water. It was mesmerising and utterly revolting. Luria jumped to her feet and drew her long skirts tightly around her knees as fleas made their kamikaze dive from every crevice and corner of the room. The cats came to investigate and their fur became a sinking ship fleas fought to abandon. We soon lost count of them. Within half-an-hour the plate was a mass of struggling bodies, too bloated with human and feline blood to outlast the effort. Luria began to cackle wildly like some dire avenging Fury. She poured brandies in the candlelight while we planned the next stage of the assault.

We left the sitting-room with the cats trapped inside and the candle still doing its job, then rushed about like excited children, feverishly darkening each room in the house and the hall, raiding cupboards for still larger plates, calling for matches and water.

At midnight it was all over.

Luria couldn't bring herself to touch the dark pools thick with corpses but insisted they should be smothered in earth to defy any resurrection. So George and I carried the plates gingerly into the garden, dug a hole in the night-chilled clay and filled it with the dead. When we'd covered them over we stood for a while under the stars. There was little moon yet the sky was high and the stars winked enough light to show that George had somehow changed. He said nothing, his arms were still loose at his side, but when he walked back indoors ahead of me I noticed his back was erect; he'd forgotten to slouch on the walls.

Luria was waiting with chilled champagne and gratitude.

'You've saved my life, dear boy, my livelihood . . .' she hugged George tight. 'How can I ever thank you enough?'

George isn't stuck for ideas, I thought. Especially with dominant women.

'To our sensible Colorado knight,' I said.

So we toasted George and his landlady's grandmother's grandmother, and Luria confused her neglected cats by smothering them in kisses.

The scourge of the fleas left us limp with exhausted tension so when George and I collapsed into my blancmange of a bed it was to escape the weight of bones. We curled instantly into a sleep too deep to be punctured by another's flesh and we woke to a post-battle hunger. We rose immediately and raced down to the kitchen, desperate for food. Luria was already there, anticipating every need. She'd made huge piles of chocolate croissants and a pot of strong Dutch coffee and we fell on them greedily while she fussed over George's cup.

I was mildly surprised by my preference for croissants to cock, but aware it was specific. It seemed that the fleas had done for us what hiking round Europe, I'm told, does for others. That miniature graveyard under the stars had forced a wedge between us. It wasn't the grimness of the event but its bathos. We'd touched an indifferent chord in each other and I thought that, as things were, we'd never seek beyond it. I was as fond of my friend as ever, would probably screw with him still, but our relationship was somehow balked by its own limitations. I didn't feel a jolting sense of loss, however, and I didn't think George did either. Perhaps he also recognised it would take a more dramatic kind of wrench to shift our physical collusion, and that much sooner than we knew.

19

You don't need to go to Soho to find Oscar's books. They're sold in Smith's and Menzies' and every other ordinary high street newsagent, disguised in sugar-pink covers which arouse expectations of a Mills and Boon romance. No doubt many an unsuspecting soul has had a surprise with her cocoa at bedtime.

They have mass availability yet he pretends otherwise in that silly prohibition of Soho. Why should he prefer me ignorant of his availability and wish to keep me that way?

It irritates.

His silence more so. It hangs in the air like a lukewarm source of heat and compels me to wear the power of my sexuality more tightly. Maybe that's good; I can't tell. I wish I could tell Oscar. I'd always believed I'd want to share every detail of my life with him, but apparently I don't. I can't. I have a growing presentiment he wouldn't approve, and that's difficult. It's flawed. If he disapproved he'd be the hypocrite Luria claims he is. She was right when she said I've never considered Oscar as anything less than perfect. Not seriously, ever. But she doesn't understand that Oscar can't be a hypocrite. If he were, I wouldn't know how to stop feeling uncertain about other things. And that's a precipice I fear.

Small acts of defiance are not always conscious. At least I didn't intentionally set out for Soho, I thought I was just passing through. I got off the bus on Oxford Street and cut south away from the crowds to have tea at Fortnum's.

The thudding beat of music soon drifted up from cellar strip-joints and the breeze grew heavy with the musk of cauliflowers from the market, roasted coffee from the fast-snack bars. Homely smells, so incongruous in that context. They made the window displays in the sex shops seem ludicrous and crass and I blinked to avoid them. The shop at the end of Dean Street was no different, but a copy of *Lotan* caught my eye: the last in a fan of novels. I'd assumed it was out of print already since I'd not seen a copy elsewhere; but here it was.

I vacillated.

I wasn't actually anxious to read it but Oscar had defied me to do so, so I must. His silence shamed me; it seemed an appropriate snub. But I didn't want to buy it. I couldn't bring myself to pass money across a counter for his words, like anybody else. He was my father; it would be undignified. So I decided to have a quick scan in the shop; enough for a meagre vengeance.

The store was split; the front half into displays of sexy underwear and dildoes and other more bizarre accoutrements, the back into racks for magazines and novels. There were a couple of women laughing over a pink pompom of fur as I made my way to the back, which appeared to be empty, and where I soon found a copy of *Lotan*.

I wasn't conscious of the man standing next to me until he spoke.

'He's not bad,' he said, nodding at the book in my hand.

I smiled absently and carried on reading.

'Haven't I seen you in here before?' Furrowed brow.

I wouldn't have noticed. He was indistinguishable from a thousand other men you'd pass in the street: neither young nor old, respectable dark city suit, casual shirt and no tie, dark hair parted so that the heavier length fell over one eye, eyes a nondescript blue. The way he peered suggested he might need reading glasses, but apart from a slightly fuller bottom lip his features were immediately forgettable.

'I don't think so.'

I didn't invite him to eye me up and down but he did anyway. He was flicking through a magazine and leaned collusively sideways when he spoke. His breath on my neck and cheek made me uneasy but he spoke softly, comfortable with himself. He might have been chatting over his shoulder, mowing his lawn on a Sunday afternoon.

'Yes I'm certain I've seen you before. I, ah, drop in quite often; close to the office . . .'

I didn't care to exchange information and nodded indifferently, then held *Lotan* more deliberately under my nose. He didn't register the dismissal.

'You take an interest do you . . .?'

I looked at his lightweight brogues, then his face, skin as dry as paper.

'What?'

He grinned at the shelves, 'Just not too many lady regulars up this end, you know, not ah unless they're looking for something else . . .'

His ahs were not so much hesitant as probing insinuations. However, I was pretty sure he wasn't trying to pick me up; his voice was too detached somehow, merely sharing observations. But his attention was becoming a nuisance. Bugger subtlety, I thought. I closed my face and clipped each word with an edge. 'I'm just browsing.'

'Sure, feel free . . .' But he went on, oblivious. 'It's just that I actually thought you might be a model at first. You know . . .' He tapped his magazine with the back of a hand. There was saliva on his teeth and his breath smelt familiar. Olives, I think. Stuffed. A Greek salad for lunch. It was almost masked by the chemical sharpness of his aftershave.

'No,' I said wearily.

'You could be.' He eyed me again. 'Easily.'

He was a pest. Perhaps simply sociable, but a pest all the same. To hell with him, I thought, to hell with *Lotan*.

'Well I'm not.' I nodded a perfunctory goodbye, stuck the book back on the shelves and left.

I headed down towards Piccadilly but it was so busy I changed my mind about Fortnum's and turned back towards Covent Garden. I hadn't given the man in the suit another thought, until some way along Shaftesbury Avenue he was suddenly there by my side.

'Hello again . . .'

I was taken aback. Had he followed me?

'Small world,' he said.

A curious looped association conjured up my trailing of Patel and I wondered if it were possible that he could still be a virgin?

'D'you work around here too?' He was smiling easily, striding along with his hands in his pockets. The pavements were crowded with tourists and people in a hurry and I still couldn't figure out his being there. I certainly didn't want to talk to him but his ease and unwelcome friendliness made me feel an odd sense of obligation.

'I don't work, I study.'

'Ah, student.'

'Eh, yes.' I thought of Patel again and felt ashamed.

'Halcyon days,' he grinned. 'No responsibilities and lots of fun . . .' His eyebrows arched significantly. He wasn't a virgin. I also decided that I definitely didn't like the way he was striding beside me as though with a mutual goal. What could he want?

'Did you follow me . . . from that shop?'

'What? No no, I'm ah . . . just going back to my office; it's up this way.' He laughed. 'Why? Were you getting worried, then?'

Was I? About what . . .? We were in the middle of Shaftesbury Avenue in the middle of the afternoon in broad daylight. We'd just passed Wardour Street.

'It's rather a coincidence, your going this way.'

He grinned again. He grinned too much.

'It is, isn't it? Where are you off to anyway? Back to college?'

'Yes,' I lied. I don't know why. I think I wanted my destination to sound more substantial than the piazza.

'Gower Street?'

'What?'

'The university, on Gower Street . . .'

I didn't answer. He waited for six whole strides.

'You're going the wrong way really, aren't you?' He'd adopted a look of genuine puzzlement but his eyes were challenging, and what I heard in his mild-mannered voice was smug innuendo. He was full of innuendo. Bloody hell.

'Look,' I said, facing him, 'I'm going up Charing Cross Road as it happens but I really don't see why I should have to explain myself to you. I don't especially want to talk to you at all in fact, so if you don't mind, leave me alone.'

I walked off.

Then he was at my heels again. 'It's OK,' he said patronisingly, placing one hand on my far shoulder in a gesture of reassurance. Pat pat.

I tried to shrug him off.

'It's all right.' His hand was now holding my shoulder. 'My office is just up here.'

We were on the corner of an alleyway behind the Palace Theatre, a no-man's-land façade of locked stage-doors and windowless walls. Funny place for an office.

And he *had* come a long way round from Dean Street . . .

I never finished that thought. The only coherent thing I remember at all in the speed of what happened next was something to do with that nice respectable city suit, how unfair it was.

The hand on my shoulder suddenly gripped hard while the other grabbed my free elbow and I was physically yanked into the alley. I was so utterly flabbergasted I didn't have breath to yell, then my anger rose with volcanic urgency. I struggled and fought and screamed at him to Bugger Off! I was outraged at being so unceremoniously manhandled, more furious at his bloody audacity than afraid. What the fuck did he think he was doing? Why? And considering my obvious distress, why didn't someone come to help?

Then his grip tightened. I just didn't see it coming.

One hand came around and clamped over my mouth, the other caught my fighting arm more tightly. I tried to bite, and kicked with my soft kid pumps to no effect; he virtually lifted me off my feet and hoisted me deeper into the alley.

'Don't be a silly girl,' he hissed. 'This is perfect.' My head was twisted sideways by his arm and he grinned into my face. The veins in his temples were pumping visibly and his eyes were glassy and hooded. I realised then with horrible certainty that I didn't exist for those hooded eyes. He simply didn't see me, not at all, not me; whoever or whatever he saw it wasn't me. Inside the tented clamp of his palm I choked on acid terror. I squirmed and kicked and writhed but my strength in panic was more than matched by the adrenalin of his . . .

Quite suddenly he released his grip for half a second and thrust me backwards into a doorway. We could only have been about twenty-odd yards from the road but were completely hidden. I opened my mouth to scream and pushed with every ounce of strength . . .

'See . . .' he said.

The scream froze at the point in my throat where he prodded with the five-inch blade of a pocket-knife.

'Now shuttup!' he spat and his hand crashed into my face. I couldn't believe he had done that. I couldn't believe the knife. I was stupefied, my head thick with ringing. Yards away the hum of feet and the steady drone of traffic. Why did nobody come?

I couldn't speak but I seemed to be weeping. He dragged my bag from my shoulder, dumped it and started pulling at my clothes and his own, grimacing like an animal, a parody of smile, salivaed teeth. That's when the image of his bloody suit came into my mind. I couldn't get it out. Crazy visions. Him dusting his lapels. Pressing knife creases. Buttoning up. All pukka and spruce for the office.

Insanity.

Cold steel at my throat.

I wanted him to see my tears. I thought if he would only see me he'd stop, if he would only *see* that I was there, a person, he'd stop. I stared at him wildly but he was too busy with his free hand – fumbling with a rubber! I almost laughed hysterically. He was worried I might be diseased? Christ! I don't know, perhaps I did laugh because his hand crashed into my face again and that's when I knew he might kill me. The knife wasn't just security against noise. He kept it in his pocket, in that suit. It was part of whatever he was. Of this. I was smothered by an avalanche of fear.

Everything numb.

He pinned me against the corner and jabbed into me and his hand thudded against my cheek.

'Look,' he spat, 'let me see!'

I contracted every useful muscle in involuntary revulsion and he slapped again, jabbed and slapped jabbed and slapped jabbed and slapped. He kept saying he could see, over and over again. I was paralysed by the horror in my throat and yet my thoughts began to reel again on crazy inanities, images of small things charged with the poignancy of the commonplace. I saw my hands wrap fragile filo pastry around some Camembert cheese, was distracted by a stretch of neglected pointing high on the opposite wall where water ran down from the gutters, heard Luria muttering my mother's name nostalgically, saw the perfect fit of a tenon joint. The banks of my mind seemed to burst and flooded into chaos, a deluge of splintered incident. All this and his nice office suit and the bite of cold steel.

Hours passed; hours and hours. Then his body arched, rigid, his jaw clenched hard, and it was over. He staggered backwards several feet but a quick flash into the crowds in the distant street and he leapt for cover again.

I could not move. I had no sense of limbs but shook, immobile, swallowing tears.

He adjusted himself in a strange unhurried calm, toying with me, watching my face, his eyes still glazed with imminent anger. The knife still open. I didn't want to look in those eyes. I was afraid of what he might do if he saw the hatred and repugnance in mine, the need to be visible. I weighted my head and limited my vision to the height of his waist, concentrated on the knife in his hand carefully buttoning, rearranging, brushing himself down, half an inch of cuff, spick and span, bright as a pin. One pressed trouser-leg stepped closer and three fingers lifted my chin.

I must not flinch. Not scream.

I forgot how to breathe.

Tears dripped from my nose on to his palm and he wiped them distastefully on my shirt. Then his hand was on my cheek. Patting. Pat pat pat. Not soft, firm.

'There,' he whispered between his teeth. 'You can't hide from me now. I've seen. I know. I've seen seen seen seen seen. Haven't I?'

I couldn't locate my mouth. It had vanished.

He was waiting. Tears like bladders falling everywhere but I knew I must not flinch. I nodded dumbly twice and forced myself not to stare at his hands quietly folding the knife. Sliding into a pocket.

He didn't look at me again.

I followed the crease of his trouser-legs as he turned and walked away, disappearing into the throng, then I slumped in that desolate alley.

20

The cab driver eyed me in his mirror, curious but noncommittal. 'You look like you could use a fag, love?'

It was too difficult to open my mouth to say I didn't smoke so I accepted one and puffed at it amateurishly once or twice then chucked it away. The base of my spine hurt. Grazed, I discovered later, by a ridge of uneven brickwork.

In Kentish Town the pavements were dotted with black plastic bags full of garbage, most of them pillaged by cats and dogs in the night so that squashed tins, chicken carcasses and the mush of sodden paper were strewn everywhere. I wondered that amoebic dysentry wasn't rife. Polio and meningitis. I don't know why I thought about that. I don't know what I thought, but distanced facts were easier.

My watch had been smashed at precisely 2.04, yet it was just after three, the cab driver said. The day had lost momentum. Fear and pain distort time. They confound the mind's sense of a moment and expand seconds into endless minutes and minutes into agonising hours, then hurl you backwards into the past. Fear and pain create black holes in time. It is the end of time for any who fall in. They say It Could Not Have Happened the Way You Remember; they say Perhaps It Did Not Happen At All.

Dying must take an eternity.

There was a letter for me on the hall table postmarked Lairg but I didn't give a damn; it could wait. Luria's car was outside but she wasn't around downstairs and I realised I really was out of my mind when I found myself looking for her in one of the duster cupboards.

She was in bed with a man called Vincent. So now we know when she does it. They stared at me quietly from their warm pillows while I explained the reason for my tattered clothes and my torn Valencia stockings, then I left them, to raid the fridge.

Luria has a temper to match her auburn hair. It shook me. She came running downstairs and snatched my eclair, thrust it like a spear into the rubbish bin, then hauled me into the sitting-room and plonked me down on the Brunschwig and Fils while Vincent suggested brandy.

'She doesn't need brandy, she needs a psychiatrist!'

'I'm all right.'

'You are *not* all right, Georgie, you're mad, crazy, off your bloody head, out to bloody lunch! He could have stuck that knife in you and left you in the gutter and you come in here all ripped and covered in bruises and eat fucking cream cake and tell me that you're *all right*!!'

I took the offered brandy and sipped while Luria knocked hers back in one. Frenetic with anger. Shock, I suppose.

'You could be dead, you know. Completely dead!'

At another time I might've commented on the superlative but I thought better of it.

'My God. Gutted in an alleyway! That would be great, wouldn't it . . . That would be bloody great! Sorry Oscar but your precious daughter has been slashed to ribbons by a businessman who likes your fucking books.' She spun on her heel. 'Well maybe now at least you'll learn some sense!'

I couldn't imagine learning anything ever again. My brain was a slippery slope. I was drained, oddly fatigued, but the part of me that was somehow functioning was impressed by Luria's anger. For the first time since we'd met she'd abandoned her created self and was careless of image. I believe she wanted to hit me. But I could see the anger was based on protectiveness as well as shock, perhaps even something maternal. I was moved. How could I not be? It's a mystery why she should so comprehensively conceal this more passionate self in favour of the bourgeois. I heard myself thinking then, very rationally, that the English are disturbed by their passions, consider them uncivilised. I was quite insane. Poor Luria. I wanted to hug her then and assure her that I was actually shot to hell and her anger was justified, appreciated even.

But it was too difficult.

The brandy burned life into my wooden limbs and Vincent poured me another.

I was leaning on Luria's shoulder while she dabbed my face with water and rearranged the shreds of my shirt. She was still in a fury. 'I mean, I thought you were supposed to be so intelligent? You read the newspapers, don't you? D'you imagine these people have a sign round their necks? This is London, Georgie, not an adventure playground in Tunbridge Wells . . . You *know* what you're doing "in some things" indeed. You haven't a clue, have you. You think all those bloody sado-masochistic fantasies of Oscar's are harmless and nobody takes them seriously. Well they're not.'

I wished she'd shut up.

'Oscar's got nothing to do with it.'

'It was his book you were reading, in a sex shop, for God's sake!'

'That man could've been anywhere, Luria, he was Mr Ordinary.'

She shuddered and sighed and groaned into my hair, relaxed her mouth and held me out to stare at my battered face. 'I hope he rots in hell,' she said.

I nodded, then she was crazy again.

'I could strangle Oscar. He's the one who's put these ideas in men's heads – no, don't deny it, I know I'm right. I know what you're trying to do with all this tarting up and experiment: it's all for him, isn't it? You want to be as good at this as you are at everything else he's taught you, so that he'll be proud. You're doing it for him and it's not right, Georgie, it isn't even close. He doesn't believe in that shit he writes, don't you see, he despises his readers. He wouldn't like your behaving like one of his characters, he'd be horrified, appalled; you've got to stop living through that trash because next time you might not be so lucky.'

I didn't feel lucky, and said so.

'You're absurd,' she said. 'And you look terrible.'

'I was raped, Luria, I wasn't trying to please Oscar.'

'What about the police?' asked Vincent. 'Shouldn't we ring the police?'

'Georgie?'

Police. Photographs. A detailed interrogation. Minute description of what I believed had taken three hours. The whole thing, all over again. Now.

'No.'

'Are you sure . . .? Don't you want to stop him—'

'I can't remember what he looks like.'

It was true. I couldn't see a face, not one single feature; only a suit.

'All right, don't fret, we can talk about that again but you must see a doctor.'

'But if she's going to the police . . .' said Vincent.

'No!' I just wanted to sink into a bath, be left alone.

Luria patted my shoulder and crossed to the phone. 'I'll get Janie Walsh to come over – Vincent, I need a strong cup of coffee, could you . . . where are you going, Georgie?'

'I want to bathe.'

'After the doctor has seen you. Go and . . . eat a cream cake. Have coffee. Talk to Vincent about his work or something, you'll like it; he's a magician.'

'Magician?'

He was barefoot still, leaning on one hip with his hand spread over the table. He raised one eyebrow and one finger in simultaneous greeting and sympathy. An ironic eyebrow and a sinuous finger. His lean feet were carefully manicured, insouciant. He was altogether too comfortable and I too disorientated for polite conversation. He'd said nothing during my exposition to Luria; I doubted those eyes had ever registered surprise. I hadn't felt up to accommodating his presence then and I couldn't do it now, I was too removed from curiosity, a fugitive from feeling.

I stared at the plaster rose on my bedroom ceiling until the doctor arrived. A witch in another life. Certainly a collector of herbs and an applier of poultices. She examined me in silence, her mouth lined by the weight of knowledge of grim sardonic things, her gauzy hair stained by the smoke from long winters huddled over fires fed with the pulp of roots and fragments of song. Her ears were shrines for dangling china dogs, like the Egyptian Anubis protecting the dead. Her hands were hard and cold. They did not inspire confidence, but Luria had said

146

to Vincent before he discreetly left that Janie Walsh could be trusted with God himself. I didn't really care.

'You want to sleep, don't you,' she announced when she'd finished. It was an affirmation rather than a question. But she seemed to be talking from somewhere else, a different dimension, filling her bag, clicking it shut, watching me from the spectral mists of a far-distant plane, a void between us. I was wide awake but somehow exiled from the substantive world. I tried to speak yet when I opened my mouth I could only hear the low echo of wind sucked into a fathomless chamber. I groped, but the words had transformed into vapour I hadn't the will to restore.

'Not yet,' she said, shaking her head, tucking me under her arm, jolting me back to my senses. 'We need to talk before you sink into that oblivion.'

'Well? What do you think?' They lit cigarettes as we sat around the dining-room table, a chummy testimony to their mutual defiance of scientific fact.

She shook her head. 'Can't possibly say until the swabs and blood are analysed. There's evidence of considerable rawness but nothing torn. Much more rawness, in fact, than . . . this single nasty encounter would justify.'

She looked at me askance, dragged deeply on her French cigarette, untipped, smelling of pewter. Thus the stained hair. 'She's been a busy girl.'

'Don't I know it,' said Luria.

I shrugged. 'I suppose the rubber will have offered as much protection as one can hope for?'

'Rubber?' She gawped amazed, turned to Luria for confirmation. 'Since when did rapists use rubbers?'

'He was wearing a suit,' I said, explaining everything and nothing.

147

'Oh? Well . . . yes, I suppose it will. The results will take about ten days to come through. Meanwhile – ' she flicked her ash – 'have some aspirin for the headache and rub arnica on those bruises – they look bad but they're mostly superficial – and irrespective of the rubber, sex is out. I don't imagine you're interested anyway but it would be foolish to expose another partner to risk until we know you're safe.'

Luria seemed pleased.

'And get her some of this.' She scribbled on a memo pad. 'Any form will do.'

'What is it?'

'Valerian. She's in shock. It'll calm her nervous system.' She turned to me, all piercing emerald eyes, and gave her instructions with the certainty of ancient lore proved many times as wisdom. 'Sleep for two days, no more; you'll want more, I know. You'll imagine you want forever, but forty-eight hours will provide ample time to replenish your strength. More sleep will take you into a realm where it's easy for pain to conceal depression. It's harder then, a much lengthier and much more uncertain process, to reclaim your self. Two days to hide from the pain; after that you must talk to it.' She did not smile. 'It needs you.'

A witch, after all.

Luria had drawn my bath with perfumed milk and crystals. She thought she understood. She thought I needed to cleanse myself of his smell and touch, be gentle with my body; turn myself inside out and scrub my organs clean, veins. But I was simply dirty, it was my mind that hurt. My sense of myself.

Who had I been for that tyrant in the suit?
Someone.
Not just an orifice and reflexive nerve endings: they

don't say No, and that had been important. He'd wanted to see into my very soul, to hear me say no and deny me myself, to possess my will. Someone then, but not me. The faceless partner of a fantasy made fact.

Guilt swelled in my stomach and rose like bile, almost lifting me out of the water. I braced myself for the waves of self-revulsion and rage and the voice in my head, tick-tock like a clock, said Rape Is Your Fantasy Too. Tick-tock tick-tock.

I sat rigid while the water chilled, staring stupidly at my disembodied jutting toes, waiting for the burning to stop.

Yes, I thought, but the fantasy comes of unconscious fear transformed to desire, not from perverted lust. We women toy with it just as we spread our toes on the edge of any precipice. We would not do it if we could not step back, but we must do it because the precipice is always there, and we know that we can.

Fort da.

Thus my childhood fantasies had softened Oscar's mortality.

I was guilty only of preserving sanity and health, nothing else. Spurious guilt would deform my fantasies and deny me that.

God knows what my attacker thought he was doing. Whatever it was, I still have myself. I know that if he has a wife or lover there can be nothing but guilt in that bed. Soiled judgement, guilt, mutual resentment and empty gesture.

But then, as I'd been trashed by his twisted self-hatred, she would sleep untroubled tonight.

Not me.

I went in my dreams to Brionglóid House and took the horror with me.

The sitting-room flooded with light and the windows wide to a millpond sea.

I'm playing my flute and Oscar is at the piano.
I know the piece is Cole Porter but its title escapes me.
I screw up my eyes because I can't find the notes without the title.
'It's all in the mind,' Oscar says, 'nothing to do with me.'
'I'm terribly happy,' I say, while the room darkens.
The window fills with distended moon.

The woman in the doorway wears a wide scarlet cloak, and a mask that is mouthless.
Her hair is an artificial powdered wig that hangs in a mess over one eye.
I wonder where the scissors are.
I could cut her a mouth.
But she mustn't let the stag come in, he is much too big, his antlers stretched like the limbs of a beech.

The door opens on to the hills and not, as it should, our hallway.

Her left hand clenched but not the right.
Held up to stroke the stag's neck.
No scissors.
And then that awesome mournful sound, his rutting cry, and his hooves beating against the walls, his head tossing from side to side, towering over her.
The whole house shaking.
Upstairs, I hear each of my balsa masks being torn from their hooks, crashing on the floor, everything shaking.

Oscar's face contorted with fury.
He's wielding a riding crop, advancing across the room in his oilcloth apron, over a city suit.
Beating the woman's head, again and again and again.

Where are the scissors?

That she dares disturb our Corelli.
'No!' I scream, but he doesn't hear.

'It wasn't Corelli!'
Over the pounding of hooves.
'It wasn't him!'
   And it isn't a riding crop he wields, but my flute,
crashing my flute down on to her head.
The stops buckling, the shaft all mangled with hair.
My feet glued to the floor.
Glued movement. Suck . . . suck . . . suck.
The copper incense of blood.
Suck . . . suck.
But no matter. He's walking away,
and she's leading the stag like a puppy-dog, down into our
cellars.
How did she get him inside? How did he fit? His antlers
are much too dense for the doorway.
Waves lapping against the stairs.
Black lapping, yet down he goes, like a puppy-dog.
   I drop my flute on the floor because Oscar's mouth is
bleeding.
Run for a bowl of water and a soft white cloth.
But the room is palatial in length, and he's so far away, so
far to walk with the black water lapping the sides, so
many minutes . . .
   The bowl is a solid stone stoop, so heavy.
I've brought the wrong bowl.
He could be baptised in this.
   His smile is distorted by gouts of blood, and yet
I can see no wound.
It will all be fine, when I've wiped it away.
The bowl in my arms, so heavy.
No wound.
But his teeth are pointed,
and his red tongue forked, all the way to the back of his
mouth.
Uncut,

whole, but forked like a pointed tawse.
I've dropped and broken the bowl, lost every drop of water.
His smile all distorted by blood.
And no water.

21

On the third day I discovered three things (my mother would have a saying about that):

1. The weather had changed.
2. Luria had bought me a new watch and had written to Oscar with the news; reassurances about tests.
3. My mother's death was not registered at Lairg, or at Inverness. The Registrar had taken the trouble to check the neighbouring office and to cover every month that year; that's why his response had been so long in coming.

Exams at the end of next week.

The promising washed air of early spring had dispersed into thin green cloud and late frost and Luria was furious. She rushed about in the garden, out of her element, protecting the young shrubs and bedding plants with sheets of thin plastic and warm moss, while I hid in my books and talked with my pain in the study. I eased myself slowly from the alleyway but I couldn't shift the lesser chill of that dream from my mind.

Luria insisted on treating me like an invalid for several

days. I had meals on a tray watching television, and lots of reminiscence. The weekends she and my mother had spent together, my mother filling the space where I was now with her Irish songs and her demands in all things for passion. I'm disturbed by this passion. I resent it. I can't locate it in myself and it seems such an unjust trick that just as my mother becomes an enforced entity in my mind, my sense of myself should diminish.

Their Sundays were a ritual: mass in the Catholic church by Waterlow Park followed by Bloody Marys at Highgate, then back along the abandoned railway line to Crouch End, my mother picking up stones. She collected them, Luria says. Little chips of rock you wouldn't think twice about. She thought they made the world solid and her pockets were always sagging out of shape with the weight of them.

'There's a lot of stone in Scotland,' I said, wondering about the passion.

George the Second came and went, unable to stop himself, but he was happier with Luria's uncomplicated fuss than with my erected calm and while he found much to discuss with her he became deliberate, measured in his intimacy with me, discouraged by obscure aversions he could not speak of. He was my willing confidant still, but diffident now of touch. I think he felt somehow responsible. Ashamed, perhaps, of his own physical strength, my weakness, refusing the possibility that I might instinctively deem his touch the same as the man in the suit. Whatever. He caressed me now like the brother he'd conjured over the pancakes and demanded only a sister's affection.

Witch-doctor Walsh also came at the end of her working day, ostensibly to smoke and be chummy with Luria but her attentiveness was obviously something of a favour. She was gauging my mental state.

'Do you prefer a bath or a shower?' she'd ask innocently, or, 'You're wearing a lot of white at the moment, Georgie, is that your favourite colour?'

Pretty harmless stuff.

There was a series of curious games, one involving a selection of vegetables, paper and fabric, from which we had to choose an item to discard; another in which we spread out on the floor and tossed a bean-bag back and forth as a cue to word association. What she deduced from all this I cannot tell. I actually found Luria's responses more interesting than my own. During the latter game, for example, she linked penis with salt, and the blood rushed to her cheeks. I asked if she'd thought of a condiment, a preservative, of Lot's wife, of rubbing salt into a wound, or of salt of the earth. She wouldn't say. Semen of course is salty. Whatever; Doctor Walsh declared my sanity intact.

Vincent came too but so very infrequently he was barely tangible. I forgot between one flying visit and the next the shape of his features, the colour of his hair. It was pointless asking Luria.

'Eyes and a nose,' she said vaguely, tracing his face like a clown.

'How did you meet a magician?'

'We've been friends for years, Georgie. It's a purely platonic relationship of mutual convenience.'

'You mean loveless lovers?'

'I suppose, yes, occasionally, but it's not even as meaningful as that. Vincent's a . . .' she looked critical but indulgent, 'well, he likes women as a sort of flexible facility.'

'How opportunistic. I'm surprised you're so obliging.'

'Only when it's convenient. For me. I think of Vincent in much the same way I do of my hairdresser, so I suppose I'm just as opportunistic as he is. Quite honestly I find uncomplicated sex suits better than the other kind.'

'What about love, Luria? You're always saying how important it is. Don't you need it?'

She was hoovering. She always did when the cleaner left; nutty. She was concentrating on the floor but her face closed in on itself. 'I've had love, Georgie, the best. I won't find it like that again.'

'How very melodramatic . . .'

'I'm quite happy as I am, believe me.'

'Was it your ex-husband, this great love of your life?'

She laughed. 'Never mind who it was; it's been over for many years.'

'All right. But you still haven't told me how you met Vincent.'

'Oh, his sister breeds cats; she bred Bombur and Ferruk.'

So with this concession to history Vincent became linked in my mind with fleas and candles and blemished ankles and Luria's surrogate children.

My recuperation made it necessary to postpone our party for exactly a month, at which time I will have had four days to unwind from my last exam and George, who is now in the thick of his, will be similarly free.

'It's a pity,' Luria said. 'It won't be on your mother's birthday now.'

I'd been right about that.

Luria has some Corelli. I was listening to it one evening while she was tucked into the stuffed ormolu with a gin and a magazine. Then I passed her the Registrar's letter.

'What do you make of this, Luria?'

'What is it?'

'Just read.'

She put her drink down on the floor very slowly and muttered while she read. '. . . Wh . . .' Her face grew suitably longer. 'Where did this come from . . .?'

'I wrote, asked for details. But as you can see they don't have any. What does it mean?'

She didn't speak again until she'd examined the letter, my face, the back of the fireplace and the bottom of her retrieved glass. Then she said just as much to herself, 'There must be some mistake . . .'

'No. As you can see, they checked every single month that year, just in case I had the date wrong.'

She flattened her mouth.

'So? Luria . . .? What does it mean?'

'Why didn't you tell me you were doing this?'

I shrugged. 'I have had quite a lot to think about lately—'

'But why . . . why did you . . . what made you?'

'What difference does it make. What d'you think it means?'

'There *must* be some mistake, or it's just that it's registered elsewhere.'

'But why? Where?'

'I don't know. Edinburgh, I suppose, the central office, like the letter says.'

'D'you think Oscar would traipse across the country to sign a form . . . He had me to contend with, remember, a toddler.'

'He must have, although – ' she wagged her head – 'it would be bad enough getting to Lairg with a baby in tow; hours to Edinburgh.'

'Could he send it?'

'No. It has to be witnessed.'

'That's what I thought.'

157

'Well then,' I decided. 'There are three possibilities.'
I'd been turning them over for days.

'What?'

'Her death is recorded elsewhere. That's a minor mystery, and not one I have much faith in.'

'Yes . . .'

'Or it isn't recorded anywhere because she didn't actually die—'

'That's absurd! Ridiculous!' She unravelled herself from her chair, grabbed at a cigarette and flicked the stereo Off switch. I watched as she paced and exhaled hard. She waved the cigarette, 'I won't entertain these silly ideas. And you call *me* melodramatic!'

'I don't believe it's in Edinburgh, Luria. We have to think about it.'

'God.'

'Why don't you sit down . . .'

'It's not possible. We're talking about a young woman who had her feet very firmly on the ground. She was secure, a home, a baby – and you were a very wanted baby, Maggie was desperate for children; no financial problems . . .'

'A devoted husband . . .? Or would it be more accurate to say a husband who demanded that she was devoted to him?'

'But she was. She was.'

Should I show her my mother's letter?

'Perhaps she wasn't happy . . .?'

'People walk away from unhappiness, Georgie, but not into oblivion. They don't disappear without trace. You were a baby! Maggie wouldn't have abandoned you. Never . . . And she would have come here. We were very very close. If she'd decided to leave Oscar she would have come here. With you. I'm absolutely certain of that.

158

Anyway,' she cut the air with her hand, 'he said her ashes were in the sea . . . It doesn't make sense.'

I agreed. 'No it doesn't.'

What happened Oscar?
What have you done . . .?

I spoke quickly. You can say almost anything if you say it fast enough.

'The only other alternative is that Oscar didn't register her death at all . . . Can I have one of those gins?'

'Hmm . . .'

I don't like gin but while she was pouring it she couldn't be watching my face.

'. . . Because she didn't die naturally. He murdered her.'

Luria fumbled the glasses and made a low, inarticulate wail.

'So,' I continued. 'Let's think about it logically. Let's say that Oscar, perhaps in one of these jealous passions you speak of, murders his young wife, leaving him with a toddler to rear alone. He chops his wife up in the cellar, say, while I'm having a nap presumably, then he carries her down to the sea and chucks her bits and pieces to the gulls and fishes.'

'You're callous and utterly disgusting, George!'

She'd never called me George before.

'It's the only way I can say it. There's another letter.'

'What?'

I took the gin from her and left it on the coffee table. It was still there next morning.

'I'll get it.'

She read with her hand over her mouth, peaky red spots blotching her skin. I turned away to examine the dusk and drummed my fingers on the arms of my chair distractedly, but the copper whorls of Luria's hair were sanctuary for the failing light, traps for my eyes. Then she suddenly dropped the letter and came comforting with her arms. I'd been too busy thinking to notice; apparently I was crying.

'Oh don't . . .'

'I . . .'

'Be calm . . .'

'. . . D'you think Oscar killed my mother, Luria?'

'No I don't. Listen to me—'

'But something is wrong! She was coming to London. Here. She died the very next day . . .? If she went swimming, why isn't her "accident" registered at Lairg?'

'Stop it!'

'I keep turning it round and I can't find a rational answer . . .'

'You don't know what you're saying; there is a rational answer, I'm sure of it.'

'But she was leaving—'

'Stop it . . .'

'What does all that stuff about Oscar mean?'

'Probably nothing . . .'

'You don't believe that for a minute, I know you don't.'

She was deliberate but tentative; her bosom heaved. 'Your mother wrote like that all the time, Georgie. Everything was . . . intense, immediate with her.'

'What the hell does that mean? Her death isn't registered!'

'OK OK, stop. Look. Recognise that you're over-wrought—'

'Of course I'm fucking overwrought! I've been raped, I'm about to embark on four weeks of fucking exams, I'm having fucking nightmares about Oscar having a forked tongue and it's beginning to look as if he murdered my fucking mother!!'

160

'That's *enough*!'

We fell into each other's silence then, staring at nothing. For long minutes we sat, the shadows huddling in.

Luria's voice was calm when she spoke. 'Let's be constructive about this. There really is no point in jumping to wild conclusions when a simple letter could answer everything.'

'Oscar?'

'No. To Edinburgh. They'll have the details. They must.'

'You're certain she's dead?'

'Yes I'm certain.'

'Then why are you frowning still?'

'The only thing that troubles me is that Oscar was . . . well not crazy, but he did have a serious breakdown in Oxford—'

I snorted, 'He was perfectly sane; that was a trick.'

'What?'

'So that they'd leave him alone. You must know that.'

'I don't know what you're talking about . . . So who would leave him alone?'

Did she really not know? Had my mother who told her everything not told her the truth about their leaving?

'The college, the people he worked with, other academics; all those people who hounded him, who wanted his work, his discovery . . .'

She peered at me and leaned forward and shook her head, incredulous but rapt. 'His secret . . .? Darling, what *exactly* has Oscar been telling you? What nonsense is this?'

The look was all wrong; it belied more than ignorance. And her hand, absently coiling a loop of my hair, suggested a different concern. She was listening but strangely contemplative, poised for benignity.

161

22

'So . . .?'
 'Read Oscar's letter first. I'll tell you about that later.'

'You read it, it's your letter.'

He was lying on his back on the floor with his right ankle crossed over his left raised knee. His hair was untied, spread in wreaths of ringlets around his head so that he looked almost dreamy, but his violet eyes were as serious as usual: despite the shorts and the mirrored shades, life for George is a serious business.

'Please, you read it aloud.'

'He's not my father, I don't want to read his letters. I don't even like reading my own father's letters.'

'I thought you were close to your father, George?'

'What?'

'Well, aren't you? You're here, doing this course to please him—'

'Are you kidding? I wouldn't do fuck to please my father. I'm doing it because he magnanimously agreed to let me take over some of the administration. He dangles me on a string, but one day the whole charabanc's going to be mine, that's why I'm doing it.'

'Oh. I thought . . .'

'You never asked.'

'I just assumed . . . Is that why you never talk about him?'

'There's nothing to say. Big cars, big office, big wallet, big success, big shit. My father, Georgie, has shat on everyone he's ever known; he's shat on them then wiped his ass on them and walked away.'

'Your mother?'

'Most of all my mother. He dumped her when we were just little kids and had attorneys from here to there slamming injunctions to keep her from my sister and me. We had housekeepers instead, armies of them, and we hated them all. I hardly saw my mother until I was old enough to go visit myself.'

'You do see her now, though?'

'I live with her now. Have done since I was old enough to decide for myself and the old man couldn't stop me.' He laughed. 'It really sticks in his craw. My mother's great, I really like her, but my father is a hole I wouldn't piss in.'

'Does he know you think this . . . I mean, he's leaving you his business?'

'What the hell else is he going to do with it? Big egos don't leave their empires to charity. Sure he knows. My sister feels the same, but quite frankly he's never cared too much what anybody feels. He's into power, he can't figure emotion.'

'How awful.'

'His loss.'

'Gosh.'

'What?'

'I've never heard you so bitter, George.'

He smiled and rolled on to his stomach. 'Yeah well, you never heard me talk about my father, that's all. About

163

everything else I'm a saint. Why d'you want me to read it anyway?'

'If I read it you'll just hear my interpretation of Oscar's voice. I'd like to see if your warm syrupy accent alters that; can't I compromise your saintly scruples?'

'Gimme the letter.'

I propped my feet up on the covered thin foam cushions of the sofa and leaned back on its wooden arm, but it wasn't comfortable, nothing in George's flat was comfortable. The only other chair, like the sofa, sagged from the weight of previous occupants and was similarly stained and pitted by cigarette ash. George always sits on the floor.

'Bri Briong . . . Ge . . . How the hell d'you pronounce this?'

'Skip it.'

'Gaelic sure looks like Punjabi. OK: Date Thursday, 19 May. "Dear George, I yield to your curious whims with provisory cautions about the superiority of fact to superstition. However, insure against both if you must – enclosed are the phial of the sea and the jar of the wind you asked for. Don't let them loose in the examination halls." Good-luck charms?'

'Hm.'

'"There's certainly enough to go around this morning: Arkle . . ." Arkle?'

'It's a mountain.'

'". . . Arkle is smothered in cloud and stinging rain; it's too rough to take the boat out unless like the fishermen on Shetland I learn to control the wind with magic knots. Do you remember rushing to the headland when I'd told you that tale, wasting three balls of string?. . ." Cute.'

'A fond parent recalling his own fond indulgence?'

'S'what your father's like, isn't it?'

'No, not at all, that's what's so odd. Oscar is repelled by sentiment.'

'". . . However, even if it were fine I still couldn't handle the boat at the moment since I've sliced a deep gash in my right palm, hacking stone for your herb garden wall. It's more awkward than incapacitating; two-finger typing is just about manageable but any stronger pressure just reopens the wound. So I keep it dressed and gloved for protection, like a fairground proprietor."'

'I don't believe a word of that,' I said.

'Why not?'

'Oscar doesn't make stupid mistakes, and he's never made such an obvious plea for sympathy.'

'Everybody has accidents, come on.'

'He wouldn't have mentioned it, believe me, especially not that he did it rebuiling *my* garden wall. Anyway, there was enough loose stone around.'

'You reckon this is a plea for sympathy? I dunno . . .'

'Why do I feel so guilty then? He's making me feel guilty.'

'Why do you?'

'Because I'm here and not there. He's throwing out ropes. Go on.'

'". . . You will be happy to hear that three of the five otter cubs have survived and appear to be thriving. I suspect your friend Lionheart the eagle had the other two. I see him wing out over . . ."'

'Begh Loch an Róin.'

'Right . . . "as I write. I'll walk that way later.

"Luria's letter was predictably light on details; no doubt you'll supply what she is too ashamed to admit. I had hoped your age would encourage a more conscientious attitude in her, but regrettably I was wrong. On the basis of what you've been sending me I assume you unwittingly placed yourself in some dangerous situation. Now, perhaps, you'll accept that the subject of your reflections is unworthy of your time. I won't berate but I will suffer you to speak no more of these distractions. You have twenty-three papers before you and must concentrate on your purpose. In four weeks you'll be home and we can discuss the next step. It certainly won't be with Luria.

"I'll say Good Luck then, for your sake, but I place my own confidence in your ability. Oscar."'

'Well . . .?'

'Well, he sure is pissed off with Luria.'

'And?'

'What d'you want me to say?'

'He assumes it was my fault, George. My responsibility. I placed myself in a dangerous situation. *Placed* myself. He might as well say I asked to be raped!'

'Considering that stuff you've been sending him, maybe he thinks you're playing it pretty rough . . .'

'But I'm not! I only sleep with you. I was walking in the street, George, minding my own business, I didn't invite assault!'

'I know, I know you didn't. I was thinking of my old man really; he'd have me committed if I sent him a porno mag; at least therapy.'

'Your father doesn't write erotic novels, George.'

'My father doesn't have erotic thoughts, Georgie.'

'Don't be absurd.'

'Put it this way, he thinks fucking is something you do in a hole. It's all business; you just get in there, make your mark and leave. He pays whores because he doesn't want to have to actually relate to anyone. But listen, it sounds to me like your dad blames Luria, if anyone.'

'He blames Luria for nothing, but he'd prefer me to feel the same animosity towards her as he does himself. It's subtle coercion. Rather desperate. I think he's afraid

166

because I write about her in increasingly affectionate terms. He'd like to censor my thoughts; it's me he blames.'

'So tell him what really happened.'

'There's no point, he's already decided what happened, hasn't he. Anyway, I can't see his eyes, so I shall tell him nothing.'

'What? You want . . . you want to see him suffer?'

'No, I just need to see his face, to be sure he understands.'

'Just write.'

'I thought about it, but words on a page are too slippery, they inhabit a neutral domain, empty of feeling. They're not limited to essential meaning so they invite allegories beyond the writer's own.'

'Just tell him what happened for Chrissake, he'd understand that.'

'Too many blurred boundaries, George. I need to be sure of his perception, so I shall write nothing.'

When I'd thought this through, the implications for Oscar's own work hadn't escaped me. If he'd been so afraid to be misconstrued as a physicist why wasn't he also afraid of the seeping edge of his blank-faced books? Why didn't he answer my questions? Oscar has been many things in the past: evasive, diffuse, dismissive, but he's never been deaf before.

I made an aeroplane with his letter and sent it across the room; it landed nose down in the jar of pickled gherkins we'd opened for lunch.

'Are you really going back to Scotland in four weeks?'

'No. I'm staying with Luria. Do you have a copy of *Lotan* by any chance?'

'Yeah. I went out and bought everything I could find when . . . after we first met.'

I smiled. 'Can I borrow it?'

He hesitated.

'Don't worry, it's purely academic interest. Luria's cross because I won't chuck out the books I have and she's challenged me to defend them. I've never finished *Lotan* so it'll be fresh.'

'I wasn't worried,' he protested, intent on untangling his hair. 'You've really got me all wrong, Georgie. I'm not freaked about . . . what happened to you in the way you seem to imagine, and I haven't lost interest. I just feel . . .'

'What?'

He sighed. 'It was getting too rigid.'

'Rigid?'

'Like we can't fuck without reference to one of your father's scenarios. I was beginning to feel I was in bed with him, not you at all.'

'Of course it's me.'

'Then free yourself. Those scenarios are just a convenient peg for what goes on in your head; useful for exploring possibilities, but it'd become too much like a restricting anchor.'

'God . . . you were bored? Why didn't you say something?'

'Maybe I'd thought *you'd* lost interest, I mean apart from lately . . .'

'Oh. No. I thought . . . of course lately . . .'

'I know. I'm not suggesting we do,' he said uncomfortably. 'It doesn't matter. Just bear it in mind, huh? I'll get you that book.' He bounced up and headed for the bedroom but paused at the door. 'You didn't tell me what Luria said.'

'Ah . . .' I was happy to change the subject. 'Well, she says that Oscar really did have a mental breakdown, he even spent some time in hospital and was diagnosed schizophrenic. There'd been a scandal. He'd been accused

168

of falsifying material, his research . . . the results, everything.'

'Jeez.'

'She says it was all kept very discreet and internal. Oscar wasn't asked to leave exactly but he'd obviously lost all credibility and was . . . I suppose a laughing stock. Nobody ever came to Scotland to seek his secret, she says, because he didn't have one. Scotland was simply escape. He'd lost his bearings, completely screwed up. Not so much a genius as a rather sick fool.'

George leaned on the doorpost. 'How do you feel about that?'

'Oscar certainly likes to be appreciated. He wouldn't like that mess. But I don't know.'

'Luria has no reason to lie, Georgie.'

'No, she doesn't. But my mother might've had reason to lie to her.'

'That doesn't sound plausible.'

'Who knows. I used to think people were straightforward and simple, now everything's a maze. Somebody is lying, but I'll find out. D'you fancy a trip to Oxford, George, next free weekend?'

'Sure.'

*

The slave was Ummah, dark queen from the outer land. She had taken four of Lotan's best men before now, in one raid, and having had their pubic hair shaved off . . . and a bracelet with her name inscribed fastened on each strong wrist, she had demanded the company of each of them in one night. Now she had been captured in battle and one of Lotan's agents had spared her life, knowing he would receive a rich reward. Even so, it had required three men to hold her down, and her training for Lotan's bedroom had been long and arduous . . .

'Not exactly the pinnacle of social realism, is it?'

'It doesn't pretend to be, Luria. The reader doesn't want social realism; stop scoffing and let me finish.'

. . . So now her lithe, tawny body writhed in its bonds, ass-upwards on the coverless bed. As usual Lotan had ordered his crest, a scarlet serpent, to be tattooed on her downy right buttock. It matched perfectly the charming deep rosy flush left by the punishment she had just received from his powerful and persistent hand. Lotan had so arranged the bonds that Ummah could be spun round on to her back. This he now did. Yes, Daniela thought, Lotan's exertions had had their inevitable effect. Ummah's swollen vulva was puce and throbbing with desire. Her humiliation was almost complete . . .

'Bloody hell, Luria.'

She'd smothered her mouth in her hand but the effort not to laugh had only made her worse. She hooted now, freely and infectiously, making us both giggle more by pulsating her fingers in parody of the throbbing vulva. I shut the book.

'Oh dear, what an atrocity, but don't stop, we both need a good laugh . . .'

'There's no point, you're determined not to take it seriously.'

'How can I? Apart from anything else its physiologically impossible. I suppose he does know what a vulva is? He obviously thinks women are like those insect-eating plants.'

'I won't discuss it like this.'

'One barbarian is much the same as the next, darling.'

'If you really look you'll see differences.'

'Only superficially. But,' she bit into a crumpet then wiped a tear of jam from her lip, 'go on, elucidate. Really, I'm all ears.'

'Well, what I find interesting about Oscar's imagination is its breadth and scope. He isn't limited by his own unconscious preferences. Here, for example, we have the taming of the castrating woman who has stolen man's power and clasped it in effeminate bracelets. Lotan is vengeance. He denies Ummah as woman by placing her in a position usually reserved for buggery. He beats out her femaleness, renders her sex into that pulsating object which is really a truncated penis. And like God he inflicts on woman the mark of the serpent she deserves.'

She chewed and considered. 'Why do you imagine it has nothing to do with Oscar's unconscious?'

'Because I think he's not so much author as narrator of the fantasies. You know, tapping a shared unconscious, product rather than source.'

'Shared with whom? This is a man's fantasy.'

'I don't know that it is. Making the woman the central object of desire doesn't sex the reader. We're vicariously both Lotan and Ummah, and the castration anxiety belongs as much to both: Ummah desires the missing penis just as Lotan fears its loss.'

'This is all very generous but let's be precise, Georgie. Basically Oscar exploits lust for cash. The sole purpose of his immense contribution to literature is to exploit a rather nasty market for money.'

'Isn't that what you do, yourself?'

'*Me*?'

'Well you do, don't you; you sell ideas to people who're either too stupid or too lazy or too otherwise occupied to have their own.'

171

'It's hardly the same.'

'Luria, you told me yourself that your clients frequently view a finished project with their hands on their breasts or thighs: sexual gratification. So who is worse, the consumer or the salesman?'

'This is nonsense.' She got up to refill our teacups from the pot. 'I'm proud of my work, Georgie, Oscar isn't; he hides his identity. Good God even Queen Victoria used a designer. I work with harmless things like paint and fabric, Oscar peddles garbage. He reduces everything to a violent little fable that can be turned into cash.'

'But he doesn't care about money, Luria, that's your obsession.'

Her eyes widened. 'My obsession?'

'Yours; your ormolu and your Sheraton and your Schumacher drapes. You surround yourself with money.'

'Those are things, not money.'

'They smell like money.'

'Maybe so, but they harm no one and they give me much more lasting satisfaction than sex ever has – and I'm not alone in that discovery. You just calculate once a day for five or six years and you'll see why only adolescents are promiscuous. Things are more varied than sex, Georgie, and infinitely less wearing. As for Oscar's books, apart from their superficial and very fleeting amusement value, quite frankly I'm sure Tampax leaflets would be more instructive and nice young women should treat them with the contempt they deserve.'

'Nice young women have fantasies like everybody else.'

'Not for a living.'

I slurped my tea.

'By the way,' she smiled, pleased with herself, 'I've found you another fetish for tomorrow.'

'What?'

'Your mother's embroidered blessing – it was still in my greatcoat pocket.'

She clattered about with the supper things while I rubbed at the silver frame with its small square of canvas, and wondered about the stitches. Old sinful Eve suppressed by a sprinkling of water. Baptism: to immerse, submerge. Washing; the sins of our fathers . . . baptism by fire . . . baptism for the dead . . .

I turned it over. The back was secured rather clumsily with tacks and a covering of masking tape. She was no perfectionist, my mother.

'It'll bring you better luck than that tube of the Atlantic,' Luria said. 'That'll only make you want to pee every five minutes.'

'There won't be space for the papers at this rate.'

'Take it. She was always good in exams. She always misspelled her own name for luck. Did it by mistake when we were seven and never looked back; no one ever noticed and she never failed.'

Dead at twenty-nine.

Perhaps I would take it anyway, I couldn't abandon it now. Oscar had kept it a secret for too many years. Yet the weight of the thing made my hands feel uncomfortably large and crude, like turgescent claws.

23

The wind in London lives low in the streets behind Bloomsbury. I found it in Woburn Place, an avenue of polluted solid stone broken only by doorways that long ago withdrew their domestic welcome. Luria had been tense and I was almost an hour early. She had driven through the morning traffic dripping frantic ash all over her floral knees, cursing between her teeth and smiling maniacally to reassure herself that I was calm. I was when she left.

The café off Tavistock Square had orange walls and emerald plastic chairs pinned to the floor by means of a column of chrome. Nothing moved; the waitress only slowly. A dark-haired girl with a sack of a bag came in and ordered coffee. Her face was vaguely familiar but I couldn't place it. She made the same mistake as I had with the chairs and tried to pull one out, then in the process of squeezing herself beneath the table upturned the contents of her bag on the flecked-stone floor. A bushel of pens, pencils, keys and scrunched-up balls of paper scattered in every direction, rolling to far-flung corners, spreading out from her still centre like ripples in a pond. Still nothing moved. Then she was scrambling on her knees, bashing her head on tables and chairs, thrusting stuff back into the bag as though life itself would be forfeit if within the next second order were not restored. I smiled sympathetically but she looked straight through me so I turned away.

I'd begun to feel not ill exactly but somehow at odds with my body. I'd forgotten the natural position for legs and what ran in my veins was heavier than blood. If this was nerves I didn't like it. I breathed deeply and sipped my coffee, peered out of the window and tried to recognise as matter the structure across the road. A bus crawled past full of heads and shoulders turned indifferently towards the café's light, relief from stone. We stared at each other blankly and when it had disappeared I found myself staring at an icon sprayed in fluorescent lime-green paint low on the wall of the hotel opposite. A crude graffito of a cock and a zero. A brutal absurd reduction, an affirmation of mechanistic function in a street built to classical design. It made me laugh: not even all that brick could civilise the beast.

'Could you tell me the right time, please?' So I wasn't invisible. The watch Luria had given me, with the sun and moon in orbit, said 9.29.

'Great, thanks.' Her face relaxed and she smiled and nodded, went back to her bag and breakfast. But she'd jolted me out of my dreary trance and I decided it would be less depressing to wait for ten o'clock in the quiet of Tavistock Green.

Both the French and Italian orals were conducted by a thin-lipped woman in a cotton shawl depicting jolly beach scenes in Spain. I suppose the Spanish orals were treated to similar scenes in France or Italy. This was the only thing I could recall about either exam at the end of the day and I felt intensely stupid. The physics practical on Tuesday was a rather fraught affair based loosely on the game of musical chairs. Candidates had to rotate between four experiments at half-hour intervals, with technicians and clipboard examiners hovering importantly around us like long-suffering waiters supervising the use of especially tortuous utensils, and I kept thinking of George and his future in knives and forks. Then while constructing a twelve-layer Lyot filter the image of that graffito intruded and got stuck at the front of my mind; my apparatus was transformed into dislocated organs which, in that solemn lab, provoked me to giggle uncontrollably and I was immediately warned I'd be asked to leave. I began to think that perhaps I wasn't academic after all. The progress from one paper to the next, however, was too unrelenting to consider anything much except their forward momentum. I was one of those dolls bowling downhill, not in charge of myself, delirious.

Several papers later I was seated near the back of a large impersonal hall writing my name in the box for 'History 1' when a clattering crash interrupted the heavy silence. I looked up; we all did. Halfway down the ranks of desks a woman was scrambling about on her knees grabbing at pens and pencils as they rolled to a stop. It was her, the bag girl from the café. Undone by her stationery again. She was clearly in a state, and all that morning when my eyes escaped from paper they were drawn from my phial of the sea and my jar of the wind to the bow of her straining back.

I saw her again next lunchtime in the University Tavern on Store Street. She was at a table quite close to mine, where she was met by a child of five or six, clearly her daughter, and an older woman whose features also reflected her own. A three-generation tableau, like a Degas family, especially as the grandmother was dressed entirely in black. I didn't pay much attention but I was certain now that I had seen this girl before. I dredged my memory for the illusive context but nothing suggested itself and I shrugged it off, assumed she must simply live in the same area and we shared a newsagent or baker, sat on the same bus. I decided it must be the latter, for apart from the brief exchange in the café I'd not heard her speak, and I would not have forgotten that singular voice. She spoke rapidly but her words came out like clogs. Clumping and wooden and weighted, they seemed to fall from her mouth and bounce around her feet. I heard her call the child Mara, the bitter name for Naomi, and I thought how sad.

At one, the pub filled up and was soon crowded with men escaping the office; with the increasing numbers the temperature rose. I was just about to leave when I noticed the bag girl peel off her sweater. Underneath she was wearing a black Lycra leotard that clung like a second skin and left her shoulders bare. Instantly, I saw her on a red plush sofa, naked except for a fringe of tasselled lace on her hips and a pair of grey silk stockings on her opened legs. Fanella Frankly Feeling.

The shock was staggering and took my breath elsewhere.

Fanella was merely a substitute for human contact, a graphic invitation to masturbate, a sensationalised assertion of female acquiescence, a picture, moreover, that I had sent to Oscar. I could not cope with her sitting there with a plain cheese sandwich and a mother and a daughter and her bag full of pens. Fanella's *raison d'être* was visual propaganda, she had no inner life, no needs, she had no life at all beyond the lens. She could not be a woman with a neurotic fear of running out of ink. I couldn't cope with that.

'Well what did you expect?' said Luria over an early dinner at the breakfast bar.

177

'I didn't expect anything. I certainly didn't expect to find Fanella writing about the French Revolution six desks in front of me. She looks illiterate in those pictures, like she couldn't write at all.'

'She's probably called Tracy or Charlotte and it strikes me she probably became Fanella precisely so that she could write about the French Revolution. Single parent, flunked school, no grant . . . any number of reasons. Not everyone has an Oscar sending monthly cheques, you know.'

'But it's so dehumanising.'

'Good God, is that moral repugnance, Georgie! From you?'

'Of course not.'

It was. Fanella wasn't stupid, yet she'd allowed the camera to nullify her brain and reduce her to organs.

I helped myself to more pickled cucumber; the lemon sole was tasteless.

'I've always had my reservations about the magazines, Luria, I've often said so. Nothing is as it seems, least of all that the models are feeling sexy.'

She chewed with her head cocked to one side. 'The same is just as true of Oscar's heroines.'

'Yes, but they don't exist in the flesh, do they? They don't take exams and meet their mothers for lunch.'

'But that's exactly what I've always said and what you've consistently denied.'

'No, you're wrong. I've always recognised Oscar's work as fable, that's why it's different. He doesn't make any claim to social realism, as you pointed out yourself. The magazines do. After a fashion.'

'The object is the same, however you rationalise it.'

'I know that.'

'You do?'

'Of course.'

She soaked up her fish crumbs with some lettuce. 'Well why the hell have you been defending it?'

'I have never defended his work, only his imagination.'

'His imagination! Since when did those travesties require any imagination?'

'He doesn't create them, they're common property. He just caters to the need.'

'He makes women available to avaricious men, Georgie.'

'What?'

'Everywhere we look these days there are images asserting the sexual availability of women for men. Advertising, television, newspapers. Your father contributes to that. He says to men: look, women are easy meat. Take. It's hardly surprising wives and daughters are abused and women are afraid to walk in the street. And don't pretend young Fanella poses for fun; if she could make the same money for advertising dentistry she'd do that instead.'

'Maybe what you say is true, but it's too simple.'

'Things usually are.'

'Oscar doesn't turn men into rapists, Luria, lack of social morality does that.'

'Which the likes of Oscar contribute towards.'

'Social morality doesn't come from books. Nor can they take it away.'

'Well the Bible's been running for quite a few years . . .'

'Oh terrific; let's all have an eye for an eye and stone our adulterous wives to death.'

'Stop being so bloody naive, Georgie. How can you defend the fact that adolescent boys might be led to imagine women are there for the taking?'

'It's not his fault.'

'Oh come on. You're not seriously suggesting that

dressing up like Attila the Hun and whacking each other with bananas is common experience.'

'On the contrary, I'm sure your pretence of prudish innocence is more damaging than any whacking banana – since that's the form your fantasy takes—'

'Bugger off.'

'Oscar himself pointed out that the impulse was common. I have my own theories about the form.'

'Yes I'm sure you do . . . you're unfortunately prone to theories, but if I'm going to be accused of prudery I'd rather be spared them.'

I spun round on my stool and put my plate on the draining-board; raspberries and ice-cream later.

'I'll show you . . .'

'I'd rather talk about mortgages,' she smiled tartly. 'Where are you off to . . . ?'

When I returned with the day's newspapers she was wiping cat hairs from the sink.

'Look at this: continuing slaughter in the streets of Africa, the Near East, South America, Northern Ireland.'

'What the hell has that got to do with anything? They don't wear balaclavas to look sexy, you know.'

'We're sated with violent images, Luria. Newspapers, television, films; everywhere we're exposed to barbarous acts. This century alone we've had the wholesale genocide of the Kurds, Stalin's Russia, the killing fields of Cambodia, the napalmed orphans in Vietnam, the butchery in South America and the bloodbaths in Africa. The fucking gas chambers. That's where it comes from, Oscar's imagination, and yours and mine.'

'What utter rubbish.'

'But we tolerate it all, just as we tolerated the gas chambers and now disavow the fact. It's there in the ether, all our shrinking disgust and culpability, the knowledge that it's happened and will go on happening because we know we're capable of it. Sado-masochistic fantasy has nothing on the daemonic capacity of the human imagination. Sure, when we hear about the children being murdered in Brazil we express horror, but more often we turn aside and say it doesn't concern us. Like the gas chambers, we prefer not to think about it. But we can't bury the guilt, or the fear; we just register it elsewhere – in wilder and more punishing sexual imagery, for instance. We reinvent that guilt every day and pretend it's something else, something polite like moral outrage. Oscar doesn't.'

'Yes he does. By your own analogy he tames it into a scabrous fairy tale for consumption in the privacy of a loo.'

'You miss the point.'

'I don't think so.'

We stared at each other across the breakfast bar. Ferruk jumped on to the work surface, stepped gingerly into the sink and curled himself into a purring hairy ball. I refilled our wine glasses. My hand shook.

'I think,' she continued, 'you forgive Oscar the culpability and deliver him as a medium of guilt. I can see why, Georgie.' She nodded. 'I understand. You love him. And maybe at the end of the day it's because of our need to love that we shrink from the Holocaust, tolerate those suede-headed young men who say it never happened, it was all a dream, a conspiracy.'

'But it did.'

'Quite.' She paused to align her dessert spoon and remove her plate, then she wiped her mouth with a napkin, sat again heavily and raised her glass.

'I don't want you to hate your father, Georgie. In many ways I think your loyalty to him is admirable and a sign of your strength of character.'

'Please don't; you make me squirm.'

181

'Don't be defensive. I'm just concerned that you're backing yourself into a corner. Look, I don't approve of what Oscar does but I know it's not all that he is. If it were, you, whom he's nurtured and taught and I've no doubt loved, would be a very different young woman.'

'That's the first time I've heard you say anything good about him, even elliptically.'

'Yes, well maybe I've been trying to give you some ballast. Disillusionment is always tough and you haven't had the kind of practice the rest of us get from other children and at school; it offers some resilience for when our gods fall out of the sky. When we reject them we also have to recognise we put them there in the first place, and it's tempting to hate ourselves for that.' She stood and went to scoop the cat out of the sink, her towering frame blocking the light from the window. 'Everything would be easier for you if you'd had a sound female model,' she said.

'Perhaps I do.'

'Not me, Georgie. I'm too late, too old and much too cynical.'

'But resilient too.'

She pursed her lips. 'We'll hear soon.'

No need to explain; about this we talk in shorthand.

'I'm not worried.'

'Good,' she said. 'Neither am I.'

In unison, like a well-rehearsed mime, we both placed an open palm on our throats and contemplated the ceiling.

24

'There was nothing in Edinburgh either. Her death just isn't registered.'
    'You don't sound surprised.'
'No.'

I plucked the King James Bible from the shelves, placed a marker in the gospel of St John 1 and threw it down beside the others.

George cleared his throat. 'So?' He pulled a cushion under his head. 'Look,' he said. 'About what you said before, why would your mother make up some crazy story for Luria? People don't do that kind of thing to their own family unless they're mentally unhinged. How did she drown?'

'There was supposedly an accident. But the point about her death not being registered is that it suggests Oscar killed her.'

'Jesus, no shit . . . ? As in murder?'

'As in murder. Listen.' I dropped down on the carpet beside him and read from Genesis:

'In the beginning God created the heaven and the earth.
    And the earth was without form, and void: the

darkness was upon the face of the deep. And the Spirit of God moved upon the face of the waters . . .

And the Lord God formed man of the dust of the ground, and breathed into his nostrils the breath of life; and man became a living soul . . .'

'How can you concentrate on this when you've just told me your mother was murdered?'

'Forget it. It must be some kind of muddle. I can't believe Oscar is capable of murder, not seriously; the only mystery is that he didn't register her death.'

'Do you really think so? That's a crime in itself, you know.'

'I know. I'll have to tackle him. He can't regard this with affronted disdain.'

'I'm sorry.'

'Why should you be sorry?'

He shrugged. 'You've always been so proud of him.'

'I haven't abandoned him yet. Entirely.'

'I hope for your sake it is just a muddle, but what if it isn't, if he really did murder your mother . . . ?'

'He'll have to pay, of course.'

'That's pretty cool, for you, about him I mean. You'd abandon him then, huh?'

'Yes I'd abandon him then, yes I would, yes yes yes . . .'

'All right, OK, sorry I asked.'

'Fuck it, I already feel lied to, tricked, conned . . .'

'What?'

'Oh bugger it, enough of that, let's see what we can make of this . . .'

I'd been thinking about beginnings, Oscar's lectures about my never making sense of books by starting at the last chapter. Perhaps I was more concerned with the How than the What. When I was younger it never seemed to matter that I knew the resolution before the trial; true, it often made the trial seem pointless. In the interest of sense and possible revelation then, I decided to distract myself from my mother's fate with a foray into beginnings: my own and the world's.

My earliest memories are of sensory things, no faces: I remember crawling on our cold stone flags and finding Oscar's waders, the smell of rubber, their bigness like caves. I tried to get into them but they were too heavy, wet and slippery inside. Then the sea, the smell of that too, pungent and salty, and the thundering chaos of waves crashing on rock. Apart from that there is nothing at all to fuel the dullest suspicion, just a blissful infancy, uneventful since my memory is untainted by my mother's sudden absence. Perhaps I didn't feel it.

'The important part was "And the earth was without form and void; and darkness was upon the face of the deep." Hm. Something like an absent presence, maybe a question mark on the darkness?'

'Freud would—'

'Yes I know. But the emphasis is on physical substance, yes?'

'Uh, yeah.'

'OK . . .' I turned to St John:

'In the beginning was the Word, and the Word was with God, and the Word was God . . .
. . . In him was life; and the life was the light of men. And the light shineth in darkness; and the darkness comprehended it not.'

The last phrase reminded me of Forster's Marabar caves, a fleeting tangent.

'Interesting shift; here the physical becomes corporeal only by the act of naming. A more philosophical author, perhaps . . .'

'. . . or more egotistical. In any case it doesn't tell us how it all happened in the first place; your father's work couldn't be based on creation myths, Georgie, they're just allegories.'

'Oscar's knowledge of these allegories is formidable,' I said, 'and his respect for them interests me.' I pulled the Larousse on to my knee, opened it at my marker and read: 'In the beginning was Chaos, the infinite, vast and dark.'

'Womb. I like it.'

'You mother-worshipper, shush:

"From Chaos appeared Gaea, the omnipotent deep-breasted Earth, and finally Eros, the love which softens hearts, under whose influence was formed all beings and things. And Chaos begat Erebus and Night, the vaults of the sky, and Erebus and Night begat Ether, the finite, and Hemera the day.

And Gaea begat Uranus, the sky's crowning stars, and Pontus, the sea. And Gaea united with her own son, Uranus, and produced the first race, the Titans."'

'Pretty incestuous stuff.'

'They didn't have a lot of choice; I understand it's still common practice in the Midwestern states? D'you want to hear about Cronus castrating Uranus, his father?'

He ostentatiously crossed his legs. 'Is it necessary to more begatting?'

'Of course . . .' I flicked over the page. 'The black blood from his mutilated organs produced Aphrodite . . .'

'Let me just throw up here . . .'

'Without whom, of course, our Saturdays would have been very dull indeed. The Egyptians too have a sexy

Chaos, a primordial ocean in which lie the germs of all things and beings. They called it Nun, or Nu.'

'Do you think they had fantasies?'

'Who knows.'

'Caves and mountains are suggestive.'

'Don't be fatuous.'

'How about trees? Jung has a thing about trees.'

'The Pope told the cosmologist Hawking it was fine to study the evolution of the universe *after* the Big Bang, but not the Bang itself – because that was the moment of creation and therefore the work of God.'

'At least they don't burn scientists these days.'

'Yes but what the Pope didn't know was that Hawking had just delivered a paper to an assembly of Jesuits in which he discussed the possibility that space-time was finite but had no boundary, thus no beginning. Thus no moment of creation.'

'I can't cope with no moment of creation, it's too much like a Leonard Cohen song on a loop of tape. What does your father say?'

I don't know what Oscar said. I don't actually remember him discussing his work at all. But he must have done since I seem always to have known those details about Oxford. He told me all that. He must have told me about his secret too. As I got older it was just accepted he no longer discussed his difficult past. I didn't mind, why should I; I knew it all already. I never had any reason to question the source of my knowledge.

'Before the uncertainty about his work I would've said Oscar knows why the universe went to all the bother of existing in the first place. Not just how, but why.'

He propped himself up on his elbows. 'You don't really believe that, do you . . . how could he?'

'I'm not convinced either way. He is very, extremely, intelligent. Probably a genius.'

'Well excuse me for saying so but I don't see how anyone could know that.'

'Of course you don't, you're a business administrator not a physicist. It's not your business to know such things. It was Oscar's.'

'Did he tell you that? Did he say, I know the mind of God? I personally have knowledge of what compelled matter? Did he say that?'

'Perhaps he feels we're better off ignorant. Maybe there was no beginning, is no God, no order, just Chaos; and I mean Chaos as opposed to a universe which obeys scientific order and laws. That would cause quite a tremor. Even atheists cling to the notion of some kind of order, the scientific logic of energy, matter. Believers and disbelievers alike cling to that; we like our doubts within a spiral of necessity but we need order. That's what civilisation is.'

'Yeah,' George smiled. 'We'd have to make a religion of sex.'

'Don't we already?'

'Not officially. We pretend it's something else. If we didn't our priests would be men like your father; you could design an outfit.'

'You are facile.'

He laughed. 'There'd be a boom in the rubber industry. Suspenders and fishnet tights would be worn under city suits.'

Luria grinned at the doorway. 'I thought they were already, my dear, as any casualty nurse in the City would tell you. Bankers I understand are the worst; something to do with all that money, I suppose. Listen, there's a ton of shopping in the hall so come and make everyone drinks, George, while Georgie and I put things in cupboards. Vincent is coming with more bags from his car.'

'Sure.' He was already on his feet. 'Vincent, huh?'

'What about our creation myths . . . ? We haven't looked at India yet.'

'Don't be a boring bluestocking, Georgie,' Luria called from the stairs. 'You've got a wizard for tea – come and be sociable!'

So, our very own magician as relief from exams: Vincent, resplendent in a gunmetal suit and sweatshirt to flatter his thick black hair. They also accentuated the unfortunate dark sacks under his eyes and made him look rather haggard. He was changing paper aeroplanes into flying roses and Luria was brassy with delight. He was fast, the sleight of hand invisible, bewildering, and all the while his pale grey eyes watching the audience assembled on the sofa, never deigning so much as to glance at the objects discovered: showers of leaves, miniature spotted eggs and exquisite dragonflies captured in floating bubbles.

George and I shook our heads in constant disbelief while Vincent's long tallow fingers stroked silver threads from Bombur's back, shimmering coins from behind our ears. I was enchanted. He conjured pockets of fire which leapt from his palms and danced about the room; a dozen green canaries who drove the cats wild and dropped, in flight, transformed into falling petals; an impossible fountain of pink champagne from a paper cone and glasses from crystals of ice. We drank it, astounded to find it both chilled and delicious. Luria, who'd seen it all before, was as pleased with our wonder as we were with Vincent's sorcery. This was no mere conjurer, I decided, but a man with Merlin's art.

He himself seemed to change. As one illusion merged into another his sallow skin assumed an incandescent glow like liquid lustre. I suspected he would melt at a touch, yet I felt a desperate compulsion to hold his colours in my hands. But like George I was paralysed by his eyes, by the movement of his limbs as they flowed from one position to the next, natural as water.

'This is nothing,' Luria whispered. 'You should see what he does with his box of miracles.'

'Not today.' Vincent had heard.

'What is it?' I asked.

'Go on,' urged Luria, pleased we so were impressed. George fell backwards into the cushions, exhausted by awe. 'This can't be just an aperitif, are you kidding?'

Vincent smiled, slow and indulgent.

'At least show Georgie the box, Vincent, she'll love it, she's something of a carpenter herself.'

One eyebrow rose and his smile widened. 'Really?' He nodded decisively. 'You must come and help me then, Georgie. It's in my car.'

He took my hand and pulled me off the sofa; his skin was disconcertingly cool, firm, reminding me of Doctor Walsh. We bundled out into the street and he opened the boot, revealing a matt black wooden chest lined at the edges in scarlet and gold.

'Pretty,' I said. 'You should lock your boot, aren't you afraid it'll get stolen?'

He grinned; one finger stroked my cheek. 'Try it.'

The chest was about the size of a small trunk but so heavy it might have been cast in solid lead. I tried to slide my hand underneath to lever it but I couldn't budge the thing. I thought he'd screwed it to the floor. He beamed inscrutably and pressed me to one side, placed his hands on the corners and lifted it out in one effortless motion.

'Thief-proof,' he explained, his eyes alight. 'You take that end.'

The damn thing felt like a hollow cardboard box. I laughed. 'You really are quite extraordinary, Vincent.'

'I know,' he said.

I felt the starkness of his breath. It wrapped itself

around my neck as we filed back indoors, and when I was free at last from the playful intentness of his gaze I found my mouth was dry as stone and my arms were trembling.

The chest sat in the middle of the floor on the Baluchi rug. It looked out of place amidst the profusion of Luria's bland landscapes and vast earthenware jugs. She and Vincent were drinking more coffee while George and I explored it.

'It's just an empty box,' said George, holding open the lid.

'No hinges.' Yet the lid swung free.

'What?'

'Look.' I swivelled it round, examined the back. 'There are no hinges between the lid and the body of the chest yet it's . . . how extraordinary.'

'It's connected somehow. They must be hidden.'

'No.' I ran my hand where the hinges ought to be and felt a continuous curve of wood, as pliable as rubber. 'I don't know what kind of wood this is – it doesn't behave like wood at all.'

Then I noticed the edges. 'No joints.'

George peered where my fingertips were probing. Eyes can be deceptive and so I closed mine to trace both sides of each edge, trusting my touch would detect the telltale evidence that even a master craftsman can't conceal. I went over the whole chest, inside and out, felt where plane met plane. Nothing.

I sat back on my heels.

'Maybe it's carved from a solid piece of wood,' George suggested.

'It can't have been, look. The grain is consistent with six flat-cut planes of thin wood. It's . . . impossible.' I laughed at the mystery.

'It's enjoying the scrutiny,' said Vincent suddenly behind me. 'It likes to be admired.'

'Does it talk?' asked George, half prepared to hear that it did.

'It's just a wooden box.'

'A magic box, darlings,' said Luria, shrouded in smoke. 'Show them, Vincent, just one teeny little trick.'

He smiled in mock resignation, opened the lid and drew out a voluminous black cape embroidered with rainbows of arcane inscriptions, gammadions and numbers, slices of melon moon, pentagrams and other strange esoteric symbols. Luria clapped her hands.

'Hey that was empty just now!' exclaimed George.

'Oh, it's never really empty,' said Vincent. 'It just appears that way. OK Georgie.' He pulled me to my feet. 'I need you for this.'

He draped the cape around my shoulders and reached round to close it at the front: his hands so cool, even through the soft warm cloth, and again his breath on my neck.

'Don't be afraid,' he whispered. A disconcerting, theatrical assumption. He asked George to stand a short distance in front of me and Luria against the far wall behind. He himself took up a position against the north-facing window, behind George, so that the whole made up a line. George and I were directed to concentrate on a spot in the other's eyes, which we did with some difficulty, for the day was overcast and the light from the window had thinned and the shadows deepened. Thus we stood for some minutes, quietly staring, focused in patient expectancy.

When George started to fade I blinked, thinking my vision had blurred in the dimness, but only the faintest lines of his silhouette remained, and they too soon dissolved into nothing at all.

I was curiously unalarmed, as though it were somehow a common occurrence for a man to dematerialise, vanish into air. There was only space where George had been and I was staring instead at Vincent, framed in the window, a bemused smile hovering around his lips, his pale grey eyes returning my look. And something else, something I hadn't seen before: his eyes were unimaginably, stunningly beautiful. It was so obvious I couldn't explain to myself how I'd managed until that day to look at him and not feel this unreasonable light-headed surge of yearning, the lure of his gaze. I was transfixed by it now, astounded, almost faint.

'How could you do that to me,' Luria complained. 'It was a dirty trick, turning her into her mother!' Pockets sagging and brightly alive in the middle of the sitting-room floor.

So it had been different for each of us.

'It was wonderful,' she moaned glumly, 'and absolutely awful. A dirty trick.'

George and I spent the rest of the evening buffering her agitation while Vincent remained languidly impatient in the face of accusation. He conceded only to facilitating what he called a meditative trance, but I'm damned if I believe him. He was booked for some club that night and left fairly soon, but he winked at me on his way to the door, reminding me of Lotan. I felt uncomfortably compromised, enfolded in an awkward intimacy. There's something sinister about Vincent. Eyes denser than thought, yet so alluring.

'You must have been hypnotised,' said George. Like me, he pretended to have seen nothing. Presumably, like me, he didn't want to share it, which makes me think it had something to do with Luria.

25

'**H**ow does this sound: "Dear Oscar, Did you murder my mother? Love George."'
    'You can't send that.'
'Why not?'
'Don't be ridiculous.'
'All right . . . "Dear Oscar, Sorry about this but I really must ask, did you murder my mother? Love George."'

She tutted twice and flicked ash. 'You have no subtlety, Georgie.'

'Oscar says that.'

She took the pen and writing block from me, confused the pen with her cigarette several times, then wrote:

Dear Oscar,

    We have a slight problem. I've been showing Georgie my photographs of Maggie: she's been asking lots of questions. My own feeling is that at this time, just as she herself enters womanhood, she is going through a period of late mourning. It's understandable and my friend Dr Walsh says nothing to worry about. But I'm sure you'll agree we must help to ease her through it however we can. It's the finality of death which is difficult to accept, especially in youth, and especially where there's only evidence of past life. Dr Walsh recommends what Georgie needs now is tangible evidence of Maggie's death. The only real possibility is her death certificate, so could you forward it here or, if you prefer to keep the original yourself, let me know where I can get a copy.

Don't worry, she's not traumatised, everything fine otherwise; I'll keep you posted.

Best wishes, Luria

'An ornate construction, Luria, but he won't buy it, I've never mourned.'

'Of course you did.'

'No, I was too young.'

'You're never too young, but in any case it makes mourning now all the more plausible.'

'I bet he won't respond.'

'We're not offering him a choice, Georgie. Pass me an envelope.'

When she went off to make toasted crumpets I wrote the final missive and removed hers from the envelope; she'll never know I replaced it with my own. Unsubtle it may be, but I think it's more effective:

Dear Oscar,

1. *Where is my mother's death certificate? I need to see it.*
2. *If you ignore this, I shall have to assume that you murdered her.*
3. *Before I left I found a letter from my mother to you stuck at the back of the hall table. It accused you of 'sacrificing our child' and of 'not feeling what a father should'. It's been troubling me ever since. Please explain.*

195

4. *I'm sorry about all this. It's not my fault.*

Love George.

P.S.   Please answer a.s.a.p. Exams going well, I think.

It was my most trying week: nine papers in five whirling days, rushing at lunchtime along the back streets between one hall off Tottenham Court Road and another in Tavistock Square, running in the road to avoid the flocks of doctors roving between departments of University College Hospital. If only I'd known. But then George was much more than a handy appendage, I said to myself, wondering what I meant, wondering what empathy really meant when it wasn't with your father.

Running wasn't easy; despite the rising temperature Luria had taken to producing thick crusted fish pies and suet puddings every night, insisting that I needed starch and energy to keep my mental faculties in shape. It is hard to move encumbered by so much well-meaning.

I saw Fanella again at the second history paper, still knee-deep in pens, sucking the ends of her hair, knotting and unknotting her ankles under her seat; distracting.

In the scrum to the toilet afterwards I managed to insert myself next to her in the extended queue and we smiled tired smiles at each other. She was younger-looking without her painted face, prettier.

'What did you think of the paper?' I ventured.

'History?'

'Yes. I saw you at the first, and we met at that café—'

'Oh, yes, I remember. The paper, well, I don't know. I wrote stuff but I'm damned if I know what it was. You?'

'The same. I've done sixteen papers in the past two weeks and I can't remember any of them.'

'Sixteen?' she laughed. 'How many A levels are you doing, then?'

'Two or three more than average . . . I've had a private tutor for years, you see.'

'Ah. Very posh. I only need two to get into the poly, and that's enough for me.'

'What are you hoping to study?'

'Sociology and psychology, joint; they've offered me a place if I can get two Ds: mature student, you know.'

'I hope you don't mind, but I've seen your other work and I'd really like to talk to you about it.'

She stared.

'Fanella . . . ?'

Difficult to say whether she laughed at the idea of me knowing Fanella or of her being her.

'Well don't ask for an autograph because my hand's gone dead. You're not in the business yourself, are you?'

'No, I just wondered . . .'

'What?'

'Well, while the pictures are being taken—'

'Yeah, everybody asks that. There's a bossy prat with a camera tells us what to do, that's all. We talk about what's on telly, the price of bread, ordinary things. Why? Did you think we were—'

'No. I always thought it probably wasn't . . . I just wanted to know.'

We moved up in the queue.

'I've been hornier in the launderette, believe me. But you shouldn't go around asking personal things like that, you know. You should watch it.'

'I didn't mean to pry. Sorry.' I offered my hand. 'My name's Georgie Sondberg. What's yours?'

She stared at me while three doors banged. 'No way,' she said. 'Fuck off.'

*

Mid-week the postman brought a letter addressed in Oscar's florid hand. It contained only a strip of litmus paper on which he'd scrawled: *She gave me a good character but said I could not swim. After exams.*

'What the hell is that supposed to mean?'

'I think he's taking the piss. It's what the White Rabbit reads to the court during Alice's evidence. The Queen's tarts, remember . . .?'

'No . . .'

'They were never really stolen . . .'

She ruffled her forehead. 'Do we wait?'

'Why not; it's only a week. I like the litmus paper.'

Any port in a storm.

Vincent was increasingly on my mind but I felt weighed down by the pressure of events. Words accrued in a jumble, half-thoughts, everything crashing about demanding attention. I wanted to separate it all, to create rooms in my head like those at home, where I could pursue one idea uncluttered by the need to act and feel and come to conclusions about others. There were too many fuzzy connections obscuring the space I wanted for Vincent. These suspicions about Oscar impinged on everything: my past and my future, his work, the trash in the alley, opinions, what I felt about my mother. Everything hung in the wavering balance of . . . ? Even that was veiled. But exams are onerous. I simply got through each day, let it all float around me. I even ignored Luria's cryptic remarks about the age of Vincent's shoes.

My last two exams were practicals, which meant I didn't need to spend the weekend revising, so on Saturday George and I drove up to Oxford. He'd been already; like most innocents abroad he'd been everywhere and seen everything, so he steered me around proudly identifying colleges, most of them incorrectly. It didn't matter; I was only really interested in oné, but it wasn't easy to fit Oscar behind its Cotswold stone. It was cosy rather than cloistered, homely and comfortable, like a sedate but friendly Jacobean manor house. This impression was further reinforced by the informal garden behind the quad, which was dominated by a pert magnolia and a very grand beech tree whose limbs called out for scrambling children, perfect for a swing. There was even a trysting place, a secret bower at the end of a secret path, where lovers in crinolines and powdered wigs could conceal their ardour from Papa. I could see George recognised the potential and pretended a sudden fascination with the variety of shrubs. He's becoming increasingly agitated about sex, frenetic with unfocused aggression. I'm not sure what he's waiting for, but I know now I just want Vincent.

Behind the chapel we found another joke: a statue of a deceased college dean which was legless. The torso merged into a bronze cast chair and to compound the absurdity his heart appeared to be missing, dug out or denied in the concave curves of his chest.

'Just like my dad,' George said, as I posed in the lap for a photograph, the great bronze head hanging dolefully over my shoulder.

We discovered the name of one of Oscar's old colleagues from the servant at the porter's lodge and I left a note explaining who I was and requesting an interview.

I couldn't imagine the introversion and intensity of Oscar's younger more vigorous self contained for a moment by those college walls. It wasn't his style at all. I suppose I expected severity, a more intimidating aloofness perhaps. As it was, it even nestled a pub under its wing. We drank pints of bitter there, sitting under photographs of famous and infamous graduates, then suddenly George seemed to be talking about leaving England. I wasn't ready for that.

'I can't stay here for ever,' he argued.

Leaving. First to visit his sister, then back to the States. He suggested I join him for the visit to Spain and I said anything was possible, thinking it unlikely, thinking that I wasn't organised for loss.

'You'd better do something about Luria soon, then,' I said, poker-faced. He didn't smile either, but he turned to me with a look combining anger and resignation, inscrutable for George.

We rolled back the roof of the car and, following Luria's directions, drove up St Giles to the neo-Gothic pile where my parents had lived. We didn't get out but peered at it from across the street, as though sizing it up for a break-in. It'd been taken over by a language school and a French coquette was dangling from an open window, conducting a minor flirtation with a svelte young man below. She was fair, which allowed me to make her my mother, welcoming hubby home.

'What would you do if it turns out she's living another life somewhere?' said George, reading my mind. 'Not dead at all.'

'She isn't. Luria says it's not possible, she'd have been in touch.'

'I figured not. You don't like your mother, do you?'

'Are you punishing me because of my remark about Luria?'

'I'm on your side, remember . . .'

'I thought I was being . . . sympathetic.'

'Fuck off, I don't care about that. I'm not seriously interested in Luria, whatever you say. Why won't you answer one simple question: do you or don't you like your mother?'

'No.'

'OK, don't spit . . . Why not?'

'Can we leave here? It's like looking through someone's underwear drawers.'

'Why not? I'd like to know. I need to know.'

'Why?'

'I know everything else that turns you on and off. More or less.'

'We shouldn't have come here, it's made you morbid.'

He leaned across and pulled me hard towards him, imprisoning me under his arm, held tight.

'What are you doing, George . . . ? Let me go!'

'I won't. You're OK, I'm holding on here and you're going to take a deep breath and tell me what I want to know and afterwards you're going to feel terrific, believe me. Just say whatever comes to mind, anything . . . I'm not going to be shocked or moral or anything. You can trust me, you know that, so what is it about your mother, Georgie; what is it that's so awful that you can't even talk about her . . .?'

Too absurd. He was nursing suspicions more gruesome than Luria's or mine. Muffled into his sweatshirt, this grappling hold was his way of assuring me of advance absolution, a sort of concession to the psychiatrist's couch and the priest's confessional. I started to laugh, and once I had started I couldn't stop.

'What's so funny?'

He let go but I was already helpless, bunched on his chest, laughing hysterically and making his sweater soggy. I tried to sit up but the sight of his pique set me off again. It annoyed him and he started shaking me. An old gentleman walking his dog stopped and peered suspiciously at the scene in the car. George was a maniac.

'Bloody hell . . . ?'

'Your face . . .'

'Will you get a grip!'

'Stop . . . it hurts . . .'

'I'm just sitting here!'

'You've been reading too many thrillers . . .'

'Huh?'

'You think . . . you think that *I* killed my mother . . .'

He didn't answer but the words when out were sobering. I sat up and blew my nose. 'Don't you?'

'Not really. Maybe. An accident perhaps. It can happen.'

'What . . . an axe-wielding infant? Playing with Daddy's shotgun? How? I was two years old, for goodness' sake. How did you imagine this Oedipal drama unfolding? Oscar presumably has been protecting me? Oh George, you really are ridiculous.' I stroked his arm. 'But I appreciate your intention, really I do.'

'OK so it's crazy. I just thought it might explain your peculiar attitude about all things to do with your mother – it is peculiar, you know. Like you're blocking something out.'

'Ah . . . Matricide and amnesia; it does have a nice Freudian symmetry to recommend it. I suppose my boned Scottish mountains are quite a fitting Gothic landscape.'

'So why don't you like your mother?'

'I don't know. I've never asked myself.'

'It's unnatural.'

'Is it? We're talking about someone I remember only in the vaguest terms, a mere shadow. I don't know her and I don't subscribe to womb worship, that's all.'

'But she's your *mother*!'

'No one expects adopted children to worship their natural parents.'

'That's different.'

'No it isn't. Maggie hasn't been a mother for me. Two and a half years doesn't qualify her as anything. She's just

202

a disjointed letter, an old photograph and a square of embroidery. Can we leave now?'

'Those are pretty formative years. And she has to be more than that.'

'Spare me the Benjamin Spock, George. Please start the car: that house is hurting my eyes.'

When we wheeled out on to the motorway the subject was ostensibly forgotten, but it produced in George an unstated resentment which infuriated me. I frowned at trees and suburbs. Vincent wouldn't goad me with questions, I thought. He didn't ask anything, in fact. He was self-contained, like Oscar, indifferent to the world of lesser mortals.

'I'm sorry, Georgie . . .'

I jumped.

'You were miles away, huh?' He let go of the wheel momentarily to squeeze my hand. 'Look I guess I might have seemed pretty insensitive. I didn't mean to upset you about your mother . . .'

'You didn't, forget it.'

'It's just that . . . well there's all these weird things going on and yet you're not, I don't know . . . disturbed.'

'Why should I be disturbed? It's a stupid mistake, that's all. Oscar will sort it out. It's not as if I don't have other things to think about.'

'Yeah, but why doesn't he just say . . . he must realise you're worried.'

'I am not worried. Luria is worried and you apparently are worried. I'm just trying to get through a day without everybody worrying about things they have no fucking right to!'

'OK OK, sorry I mentioned it, sorry I was concerned, I'm sorry, all right, we'll change the subject. OK, OK . . .'

I nodded and stared at the passing houses. His apology somehow irritated more than his blundering psychology.

I hate feeling guilty.

'I have a friend back home who studied at Oxford, had a really great time, apart from the tea.'

'What tea?'

'Tea and Bath Olivers, he had screwy ideas about immersing himself in English culture and he decided they were it. But tell me, are you really interested in doing physics, or are you just trying to please your father?'

'Christ.'

'What did I say?'

We drew up to some traffic lights in Golders Green and a flock of young Hasidic men in locks and beaver hats drifted across my vision. One turned and looked absently into our car and I was instantly swamped with an irrational compulsion to scream. I was conscious of rising shame, confusion, of the comfortless thought that George was much more astutely perceptive than I'd bargained for.

26

After the last exam Luria was waiting with champagne and bonbons and, encased in a pretty glass box, a pair of antique jet earrings from Stephen Long, beautiful pendulous things, scrolled in a downward spiral. I was glad I need never bump into Fanella again; after our last encounter I couldn't dislodge the idea that she thought me a cheap voyeur. I could see her looking at me, as it were, from the page of her magazine, and the look in her eye disturbed my sense of place. It isn't appropriate to be coldly enthralled by a woman's nudity when you also know her fears. She knows that; also that her posing partners are much more and less than they seem. It makes her collusion with the market even less understandable, whatever Luria says.

I was back in Oxford four days after I'd left my note. Doctor Dance rang up to say there was no one around during the long vacation and he wasn't driving off to his *gîte* yet so I should come and have a chat, since I was my father's daughter. I dressed for comfort and elegance and a singular kill in thin scarlet linen, but I didn't consider the effects of sitting crunched up for an hour in a grimy railway carriage, nor did I allow for the sharp piece of metal edging under my seat which caught a thread of my stockings. It would have been merely a snag, unnoticeable, had I not crossed my legs. As it was, I got out at Oxford station crumpled and cranky and frayed, an inch-wide ladder running from heel to thigh, assaulted by a train. What would Freud make of that, I wondered.

The porter at the lodge directed me to a terse scrawl pinned behind glass on a noticeboard, which read: 'G. Sondberg. 11a.m. Dr Dance's Rooms'. The porter directed me up a corkscrew staircase to a thick oak door. Doctor Dance seemed puzzled to see me. He was wearing a pink nylon shirt, brown trousers, grey running shoes and a strange affair of a sheepskin waistcoat, from the woolly edges of which his limbs and head emerged. A Wildean badly wrapped parcel, overstuffed for the end of June. But there was no heat in the room and I began to regret my linen.

When I'd stirred his memory he ushered me to an ancient marshmallow chair. The windows faced mostly north and were shy of light and Doctor Dance perched on the end of a coffee table, his hands on the balls of his knees, peering from his darkened corner to mine, his mouth tightly shut. I wondered if I should make small talk, volunteer some comment about the weather, perhaps mention my bad luck with stockings. Suddenly he slapped his knees decisively, uttered 'Sherry', and visibly brightened at the prospect of something to do. When he turned, a low pear-shaped tonsure appeared exposing a strangely flat crown. The hair around the edges was mink-brown, hanging over his pink collar in irregular tufts. He must have cut it himself.

'You knew my father then?' I blurted out rashly while he confused his desk with bottles. He was apparently surprised by the fact that I indeed had a father at all.

'Your father . . .?'

'Oscar Sondberg. Professor of Physics here until 1970,' I said.

He swivelled from the hips, turning his body and bending from the knees, eyes on pregnant stalks.

'I'm a mathematician, you know.' Each syllable neatly clipped. 'But of course,' he went on, 'one's mind is not imprisoned by one's discipline, denied the charms of others, such as they are.' He smiled quite kindly as he straightened. 'How are your parents these days?'

'My mother died years ago—'

'Oh. I am sorry, I didn't know.'

'It's all right. I was just an infant, I don't remember her much.'

'Ah. Well, you haven't inherited your mother's looks,' he said, 'but perhaps your father's . . .' He grinned. His teeth matched his hair in colour.

'I wish I had his talent,' I said half-heartedly, accepting the sherry which as sherry goes was rather good.

He remained standing before me, staring down. I felt distinctly silly.

'How interesting,' he said, turning on his heel and resuming his perch at the end of the coffee table.

'Did you know my father well?'

'Oh yes, Oscar was . . . widely known. Do you know algebra?'

I flinched. 'Of course; my father taught me everything.'

He grinned again.

'Charles Dodgson was a mathematician, you know. More familiar to you, I suppose, as Lewis Carroll?'

Interesting coincidence.

'Really?'

'He liked conundrums. Do you like conundrums, Miss Sondberg?'

'I don't em . . .'

'Did your father suggest that you visit?'

I forced myself to stay calm. 'No. It was my own idea
. . . why do you ask?'

Mink teeth again.

'He doesn't know you're here . . .?'

'No, I mean yes.'

'So.' He placed his glass on a pile of books and slapped
his knees again. 'Imagine a twenty-foot wall, Miss Sondberg, over which hangs a forty-foot rope.'

What the hell was this?

'At one end of the rope is a mirror and a weight, and at
the other there is a monkey. Given that the mirror and
weight together weigh precisely the same as the monkey
– what happens when the monkey climbs the rope?'

He waited. I had to think about it. Couldn't. I asked
him to repeat it then thought about it again.

'The monkey . . . will always be level with the weight
and mirror—'

'Yes yes, but what happens at the top of the wall?'

'Why did you find it significant that my coming here
wasn't my father's idea?'

'You haven't answered the question yet.'

'I will when you've answered mine.'

'I'm sorry.' He looked blank, 'what was yours again . . .?'

'Why should my coming here seem odd?'

'I don't recall saying it was.'

'You implied it. You were here when my father left?'

'Yes, of course. I was merely . . . the circumstances in
which your father left were such that one might imagine
him dissuading you to visit, I meant no more than that.'

I pressed myself deeper into my chair.

'Would you mind describing those circumstances to
me, Doctor Dance.'

'Oh.' He rubbed somewhere beneath his waistcoat.
'Oh. I'm not sure . . . that would be at all tactful – I
assumed you knew.'

'Perhaps I do.'

'Well, it is, I believe, common knowledge that television corrupts one's vision.'

My head felt hot, even my eyes.

'And . . .?'

He frowned. 'Your father left when it was clear he could no longer remain.'

'Clear to whom?'

'To everyone.' He smiled. 'But you haven't answered my question yet . . .'

'The monkey meets the mirror.'

'Beautiful!' He smiled seraphically, his fingers spread, crossed on his breast. 'Isn't it beautiful!'

'If you say so.'

'Oh, not me, Miss Sondberg, Dodgson. I like my mathematics in algebraic form. Always.'

'He was disgraced, wasn't he? My father . . .'

'There was . . . something about suspect research, I'm really not sure of the details; so long ago, you know . . .'

I needed air. I couldn't sit there with my head on fire. I struggled out of the stupid chair and thanked the man rather gracelessly for his time. I thought better of it at the door and turned to offer a better goodbye, then found myself crashing towards the floor – tripped by the cast-iron doorstop.

'Oh dear!' He rushed to help. 'I am sorry, are you all right?'

My other stocking was holed at the knee.

'I'm fine, only my dignity . . .'

'Well,' he brushed aside my awkwardness. 'You didn't say what he was doing, old Oscar. Scotland wasn't it?'

'I haven't a clue,' I spluttered, meeting his eyes. 'I live with my godmother in London. We don't keep in touch.'

Fuck you, Oscar.

*

209

I went straight to St Catherine's House from Paddington.

Last ditch.

Within forty minutes I discovered why there was nothing in Scotland: my mother didn't die there. Nor did she drown. She died in London on 1 June 1974. Cause of death: myocardial infarction; a heart attack.

Fuck you, Oscar.

27

My father is a hardened liar, an impenitent fraud, a disreputable cheat. I can't bring myself to think of him without embarrassment and disgust. Even if he's not literally a murderer, he must be insane; why drown your wife in Scotland when she'd died in London? And why a heart attack in one so young; did it happen on the train, was he there, was I? Luria says there must have been some congenital flaw, or extreme hypertension. She's been rabidly drunk and speculating since Thursday but at least she's now satisfied that I've toppled Oscar as God. Small compensation. Mine is certainty: my mother is dead; that doubt, lurking and sly but there all the same, that doubt has gone.

On the Saturday of the party I woke to the sound of Wagner's *Nibelungen* screaming up the stairs and tried to negotiate my first ever hangover headache. Four wine bottles winked emptily on the drainer and Luria was preparing herself for drama and circumstance. I wanted to spend the day wrapped in a blanket but inactivity made me focus on feeling, so I swallowed paracetamol and had thrust upon me a list of last-minute chores which took up most of the day. George helped. We rushed hither and thither collecting crates of booze and cartons of thin cigarettes and Luria's dry-cleaning. We stood in queues for French bread and Swiss cheese, ate lunch on the hoof and met the catering people while Luria swanned about flapping like a butterfly in a diaphanous organdie housecoat. At five everything seemed to be under control so George, smelling of goat, left to ablute and change while Luria and I had a drink which I, at least, as I pointed out, had earned.

It occurred to me that I didn't actually know what one did at a party.

'Get pissed,' Luria said. 'With lots of other people.'

So that was all. And all this fuss.

But Vincent was coming.

It was easy then to settle on that single thought, to vacate my head of everything else and let his name bounce around, the image of his hands, his eyes, a lock of black hair on his forehead. I went off to soak in a bath rich with perfumed oils and fantasy. Well at least that's what I'd intended, but it wasn't the realms of steamy ecstasy I occupied, it was bland romance. I heard phrases such as 'Darling I need you' and 'Darling I want you' accompanied by breathy clinches and tango-style bowed backs. Lips were forever pouting on the edge of tender kisses while his arms caressed like a pussycat. His cock was simply not there.

I've castrated him, I thought, beating my head with the sponge, appalled at my own propensity to create such an anodyne hero. And something else. If Vincent could read my mind, as I half expected he could, he'd see all this slush and abandon me as a silly little girl. I cringed and slithered under the bubbles to plan a strategy to confuse the shape of these errant thoughts.

My dress offered some disguise: a black velvet strappy

number just skimming my crotch and leaving my shoulders bare.

'It fits where it touches,' Luria hissed while adorning my throat with her own rope of jet to accompany my pendulous earrings.

'Stunning,' she approved. 'It's hard to believe that gawky girl from the mountains ever existed now. Your mother would be most impressed and if I wasn't so proud I'd be envious.'

'Stop.'

'No, really, you look beautifully dangerous, darling. I just hope it's all for George,' she said defiantly.

Her own outfit – you couldn't call it a dress – was vaguely Grecian: great swathes of soft white muslin bordered in gold that lit up her copper hair, caught somehow at the ankles and wrists like an Indian's pyjamas. The sheer immensity of fabric on her statuesque frame was overpowering. On anyone else it would have seemed like a tent, but Luria carried it off with magnificent aplomb and great sweeping drama, a slumming Aphrodite. She'd accentuated the whole effect with earrings which were six-inch-long pyramids of mirrored glass, so that with every move she reflected strobed images of light and the world around.

George arrived in a whipped-cream tux and wing-collared shirt and gave both his ladies an orchid corsage. We spun him around to admire his handsome transformation into a movie star while he admired mine into an enigmatic vamp and Luria's to a goddess.

We had a quiet half-hour to ourselves before the first cluster of guests arrived. George and I drank wine but Luria couldn't settle. She fussed about rearranging all the ornamental jokes she'd arranged as proof of her intelligent humour (neurotic, yes?) and regretted too late the indigo tablecloths. Witch-doctor Walsh arrived first with a girlfriend called Frances and Luria instantly blossomed. Her natural *métier* is as hostess, not designing at all. As more guests arrived she insisted on introducing me to everyone in turn, her hands on my shoulders, like something she'd cleverly knocked up on the drawing-board. I grinned inanely and hoped no one would curtsy.

There were numerous clients, fabric designers, wall-paper designers, upholsterers, grandiose extroverts who did things in the media, lawyers and antique dealers who affected a careless air. All terribly cool. The whole atmosphere in fact was one of competitive nonchalance and restraint, with everyone laughing more or less heartily than the next to show their greater advantage.

But no Vincent.

At various stages in the evening I caught sight of George across the room, more often than not trapped in a corner with Sonya, the hat and umbrella thief who wrote to MPs. She was at least forty-three but she was making it pruriently clear what her interest in George was, and judging by his debonair glass he wasn't exactly suffering. I didn't want to meet those other mutual acquaintances Luria and Oscar had talked about, but Luria wouldn't have it. She introduced me to Maxwell, a great wag in cotton tweed and a dicky-bow, glowing amidst the ladies. Ella, the startled girl he'd abandoned his wife for, required a minute description of Geathramh Garbh while her hand-made earrings, like Victorian tools for unblocking a sink, swung to and fro in reverence to nature.

'You must be so bewildered,' she said, 'by London.' But it was actually she who looked nonplussed when I asked where they parked their caravan.

Luria's poetic licence.

Thomas the forger said I was David's *Madame Récamier* and when could I pose? but Luria appeared from nowhere to smack the hand he'd slunk around my waist. His idea of a model's role was apparently considered obscene even in Hong Kong. Rose and Anton the pianist agreed, but while everyone else was thankfully happy only to mention my mother, these two asked after Oscar. However, they were a striking couple and I immediately liked them; he was Aryan fair, much blonder than George, while she was as dark as a gypsy, like identical polarities. They were serene yet bubbly, as though excited by the hubbub of voices but strangely undisturbed, inhabiting their own tranquil centre. She spoke in a flat cockney accent and rejected wine in favour of bottled beer. Anton hailed from Nuremberg, and spoke softly of how he'd always thought Oscar a talented pianist, wasted on science. It was an unambiguous tribute which I couldn't disavow, so I squirmed and escaped their company.

As the night went on I slotted in and out of circles merely to distract myself from the increasing torment of Vincent's absence. I picked up crumbs of anecdote and pointed opinion and offered my own. It wasn't hard; most of the conversation was the type of gossipy chat Luria's magazines are full of: compelling attention to banalities which with alcohol sound almost meaningful. I bumped into George occasionally and we'd compare notes about the property prices and the markets discussed. He was actively interested in all this and handed out little cards embossed by his father. I drank a lot, especially after midnight, by which time I'd given up watching for Vincent's face at the door. Sick with disappointment. Patel I'd been able to allocate to a distant corner marked blighted hopes, but Vincent was different. He ranged too wide.

At 1.30 the crowd was thinner; taxis were being called and people began drifting into the night. My abdomen was knotted and my jaw ached from the tension of grinding teeth. Luria and George, both very well oiled, were in conference with Doctor Walsh and her friend on the other side of the room. I decided to escape upstairs for a quiet huff in privacy, but was surprised to find Sonya sneaking out of the first-floor bathroom with a dishevelled media man in an over-large citrus suit. She grinned, mischievously; Lotan again.

The study light was on. Anticipating another bonking pair, I peered gingerly round the door and there was Vincent, nursing a brandy glass and a small cigar, smiling from the wing-backed chair.

'Vincent! When did you arrive . . .?'

He checked the level of his glass, 'Ten minutes . . .?'

'But where have you been? It's so late – and why are you hiding up here?'

'I'm hiding from the fond farewells below, Georgie.' He patted the arm of his chair for me to join him. 'I've just driven back from Nottingham; roadworks on the motorway.'

'Nottingham?' I perched beside him, conscious of flesh, of breathing.

'Theatre Royal.' He smiled, one finger already stroking my thigh. 'You look ravishing, darling.'

Darling?

'D'you mean you've been working – tonight?'

'While you lot've been swilling the grape,' he nodded, 'I've been pulling rabbits out of hats.' He affected a frown. 'Don't look so cross, it is what I do, you know.'

'But tonight . . . You said you'd be here, not out squandering your talent.'

'I'm here, aren't I, and I'm not squandering anything, my dear. I'm a jobbing magician, part of a small fraternity for whom rabbits in hats are the bread of life. This is our busiest time of year, now and Christmas.'

I stood up, listless, more annoyed than I wanted to admit, confused by the fact that he hadn't been anticipating, as I had, this opportunity. I felt snubbed and needed to distance myself, show him I too could be indifferent.

'I don't believe you could possibly enjoy doing hackneyed tricks like that, not when you can do so much more.'

'Tricks? There are no tricks. Only conjurers and clowns do tricks, children. Real magic,' he said, 'has nothing to do with trickery. It's a science, as exacting and complex as any other.'

'How ironic. My father says physics is a form of alchemy.'

'Perhaps it is.' He got up, loosening his tie, and crossed to where I was standing. His assurance unnerved me. 'Is your boyfriend here?'

'George? Of course. But we're . . .' How not to be obvious?

He laughed, nodded, his eyes roving my body. 'I see.'

Of course he did.

He put his glass on the mantelpiece and slipped his hands under my arms, followed the curve of my breasts, hips. Me? I was paralysed by his power, trembling.

His mouth was not tender but hard and very wide, his breath like a vortex sucking me into him, into his depths. It made me giddy and softened my knees. When I opened my eyes, however, I saw that his had never been closed and I felt strangely stung. He looked at me, steady, unblinking.

'I shall go and talk to Luria,' he said. 'Clarify the sleeping arrangements.'

Just like that.

'I'd better come too, she might be . . . wondering where I am.' I needed another drink.

He raised one eyebrow sceptically and retrieved his brandy, chortled to himself. 'I rather doubt that.'

217

The last of the guests were just leaving and Luria pulled me aside. She was well stewed, slurring her words. 'I want to talk to you, Georgie . . .' Her white muslin had a red wine stain, about knee height, three grapes wide. 'What is all this . . . and what about George?'

'Don't you like the idea?'

She made her eyes small. 'Like it! How could I like it! Vincent is thirty-odd years your senior, for God's sake; he's as old as your father and just as bloody trustworthy. You don't know what you're doing.'

Straightforward jealousy? I didn't want to upset Luria, I wouldn't. I found myself hoping her objections really were based on protectiveness rather than personal affront. She fell against a coffee table and I gripped her arm.

'Tell me honestly, Luria, do you want Vincent or George . . .'

'George!' She tried to look outraged. 'Do you seriously imagine I'd sleep with a boy of twenty!'

'Why not? I'm sure he'd like it, you've been flirting with each other for weeks.'

'That doesn't mean anything, you silly girl, it's just harmless – don't do that with your face, you'll end up with horrible lines. Listen to me, Georgie, listen. I know Vincent, and he is not the slightest bit interested in any kind of romantic attachment . . .'

'Neither am I,' I lied.

'I don't believe you.' She waggled her finger, ridiculous. 'You'll get hurt. And what about George, how d'you think he's going to feel?'

'I told you, he'll feel fine. Where is he anyway?'

'I asked him to walk down the hill with Janie and Frances, to their flat. Vincent is making me coffee.'

'Do you care about Vincent, Luria?'

She shook her head emphatically, her pyramid earrings clunking. 'I don't give a damn about Vincent, we're just

. . . posts for each other, somewhere to lean when we need a rest. I told you before, isn't it obvious. But—'

'I just wanted to assure myself that you weren't after all . . . romantically attached.'

She leaned forward drunkenly. 'Vincent is only attached to himself, he's not capable. He's all right as a post for a woman like me, but nothing else. I know him, he's no good, he's too selfish, too cold, too bloody weird. Now be a sensible girl and forget it. He won't mind, believe me.'

I ignored the tone; she wouldn't use it sober.

'I shall go and invite him into my bed, Luria, and you must do as you wish when George gets back.'

'Don't. You'll feel bloody awful about this in the morning. You're blind if you think George'll like it.'

'It's you George wants, not me.'

'What George wants is his mother – a relationship. That's why he flirts with older women, why he lets you dominate him so much. The point is there's nothing in me that's lactating. And Vincent is another matter.'

'You've got it all worked out, haven't you.'

'Well you don't expect men to think of these things, do you, they're too stupid.'

'Your cynicism is breathtaking.'

'Thanks, I work hard at it and at forty-five I should've achieved some degree of competence. What worries me is that you haven't been working at it at all and Vincent – ' she looked towards the kitchen – 'is using that.'

I'd had enough of her drivel, I spun on my heel and headed for the door. She staggered backwards into a chair but her parting gibe was uncharacteristically vicious, coarse even for Luria. 'He isn't even any good,' she yapped.

The Mirror

28

M uch later, as I brooded into the dark of my bedroom ceiling I reflected that she'd been right. I'd imagined the kind of tenderness assurance brings. I'd imagined unfamiliar avenues, being led by the firmer hand of experience, new vistas and wider horizons, discovery. Ha. I thought about George's pliable limbs and fertile imagination. Luria couldn't have planned for that, she would be surprised.

Vincent had been . . . perfunctory.

Matter of fact.

He had undressed in silence, stripped me in silence, hushing my lips when I tried to speak, got into the bed and fucked me in silence. The whole performance had lasted approximately ten minutes, during which time his eyes remained unblinking open, unmoved by the act. I'd tried not to notice the ridge of uneven brickwork which arose like a ghost in my mind. Then he had patted my shoulder and rolled into sleep. I don't believe he even said goodnight.

I felt distinctly used, like a public convenience, and I couldn't sleep. Over and over I relived each cold-eyed moment, over and over. The alarm on my bedside table counted off the minutes as I thought about his touch, his look, the way he had kissed me, how he'd silenced me then and again in bed, how his eyes had denied me, denied all feeling. And with each passing minute I grew angrier at my own stupid compliance and what I now understood as his utter disregard. At 3.30 I couldn't bear him lying next to me any longer.

Deep in sleep.

Snoring.

Fuck it, I thought, and kicked him.

He didn't stir, so I kicked him again, harder, and caught him behind the knees. He sat bolt upright so fast I flinched into the sheets.

'What the hell . . .?'

'You're a shit, Vincent.'

He stared, still drugged with sleep.

'Wh . . . what are you doing?'

I swung myself out of bed, flicked on the table-lamp, got up and pulled on a robe. 'I've been lying wide awake thinking how little I like being wanked into . . .'

'What?'

'Well that's what you do, isn't it? You don't actually engage in any real sense with women, you just masturbate into their cunts.'

He rubbed at his eyes.

'What do you do for an encore – apart from sleep, that is – wipe her with a sock?'

'Georgie . . .'

'A vibrator would be more considerate, and it wouldn't fucking snore.'

'Oh dear, oh dear.' He was awake now all right. 'What time is it?'

'Three-thirty. Three.'

'Jesus . . .'

'I don't know why you're complaining, at least you've been asleep!'

224

'Will you calm down . . . Look, what do you want, what is this; you want to fuck again? Now, in the middle of the night . . . is that it?'

'Ha! Are you kidding? No thanks.'

'What then?'

What indeed. I wished I smoked. A cigarette would be something to do with my hands.

'You made George disappear, you shit!' What the hell if it wasn't rational. I wanted to shout at him, and I was anyway convinced by now there'd been something sinister in that as well. Absolutely. I'd been duped by a cheap macho con.

'Did I,' he snorted. 'Is that what I did.'

Bastard.

He pulled his hand through his hair, let his head roll back. 'I'm tired, Georgie.'

'So am I, so what? You used me and I don't like it, so tough shit if you're tired. You're a phoney, a lousy phoney. You're transparent. You.'

He laughed wearily, then leaned across the duvet. 'I'll tell you what,' he said, 'if you take that candle from the mantel and place it in the fireplace, I'll organise it so that we can both get some sleep . . . OK?'

???

'Piss off. I'm not interested in another of your pathetic disappearing tricks. Are you mad . . .!'

He tutted, examined the mound of his toes.

'Tiresome for you is it . . .?'

'For God's sake stop screeching, will you,' he said, his palms a shield. 'Look, just take those flowers out and put the candle in the fireplace.'

'Go to hell. In fact I want you out of my room.'

'I'm not going anywhere, it's the middle of the night. And you're wrong you know, I didn't make George disappear, you did.'

225

'That's rich, and how did I do that, pray?'

'I told you. I just create the conditions, not the content.'

'I don't believe a word you say. Not now. I've seen your human form, Vincent, and the content is *all* you. You're an illusionist, nothing more, and passing yourself off as an ardent Casanova was the lowest illusion of all.'

'And you're a bitch,' he said, pushing back the covers, hobbling to the fireplace. 'Just like your feisty mother.'

'Leave my mother out of this, you don't know fuck about my mother – and put those flowers back!'

He moved the basket of lilies and was kneeling to fix the candle on the grate with melted wax. His snort echoed up the chimney. He stood and puffed out the match. 'Silly cow, of course I knew your mother.'

'Liar. You've only known Luria since she got the cats and they're not that old.'

His flesh was blotched where the candle flickered. Fleas.

He laughed. 'You really should get your facts right, Georgie. Those are not the first cats Luria's had, there was an old Siamese queen.' He hopped back into bed and made a tent for his knees. 'I used to come and have a drink with them, Luria and your mother. Your mother was much more entertaining than you are, believe me. They were quite an act.'

What?

'No, not that . . . God you really are green, aren't you. Despite your foul mouth and all your sexy gear, you haven't got a clue. Luria was your mother's bit on the side, sweetheart, her lover . . .'

Oh God. Bloody hell . . .

'Come on, don't pretend you didn't know. Luria doesn't exactly hide it, does she?'

Luria and my mother?

The great love of her life?

Oscar hates Luria most of all . . .

I sank on to my buttocks, literally floored, thinking wildly.

'But you sleep with Luria . . .'

'Sure. So what? She gets lonely sometimes, we both do, and I like her. Now look, I'm going to lie back on my pillow here and whatever happens, remember, I'm just the stage manager – you're the writer, the director, the actor, it's all down to you, understand; it's your need . . .'

I stared at the candle guttering in the fireplace. 'What the hell are you talking about?'

He leaned over and switched off the lamp. I was glad. I wanted to look at my ignorance in the dark.

'Just remember what I said, but wake me at eight, will you. I have to drive down to Exeter in the morning . . .'

Abandoned to the candle, I gulped in lumps of air until the knot in my abdomen loosened. Vincent was muttering low in some incomprehensible vulgar tongue, further and further distant. I wasn't concerned with him any more, I was slotting the pieces together: Luria, my mother, Oscar's jealousy, me. Poor Oscar. Afraid after all of women stealing his power.

Poor Luria.

I let the idea arrange itself and looked at it hard.

What constitutes a 'breakdown'? It would take a very singular jealousy to forfeit friends, career, society . . . for the sake of removing a rival? Quite awesome. But my mother wanted a child, so I'd been a rival too . . . just as I'd suspected. That kind of jealousy was surely destructive. It would make a man capable of all that we mean by anything; rupture, denial, violence, war. Easily murder.

My cheeks burned. I'd surprised myself.

My weight was spread across my hips and thighs and the room seemed darker now, or rather the areas around my peripheral vision had darkened. My room was transformed into a cave, distorting my forward focus. The fireplace had long been unused, it was merely a large empty recess where the candle flickered in the updraught, steadied again. I stared at it vacantly, heard myself breathing, watched the weaving flame.

Shadows inside an altar.

Then where nothing had been, a woman appeared. No, not appeared, became visible. That's wrong too. There was no moment of distinct manifestation, no shifting from ghostly outline to fuzzy form. I had a gut feeling, in fact, that she'd been there all the time, whole and complete, patiently waiting. She had that sort of smile, an 'at last'. A string of black jet and pale curls. My mother.

Her wide-skirted cloak, drawn over her knees, was as dark as old port. I can't explain why, but I was neither shocked nor afraid to find her sitting there in my fireplace, as large as life. Solid. Blood of my blood. Smelling of sea and stone. It was somehow . . . perfectly natural. As familiar as . . . that was the other thing; there was no resemblance whatsoever to the woman in the photograph, none. Luria was right – she was much more the person I saw in my own morning mirror than I would've believed. We looked hard at each other. Just sat, and looked.

Time passed.

When I think of it now, I think of a soft regular pulse between the fontanelles. A warm sensation. Foetal and safe. Nothing else. No other feeling at all.

She opened her lips, very slowly, I thought, to speak. But instead, her tongue ebbed forth from her mouth like a silent wave, a languid, flowing snake. Down it rolled, over her tilted jaw, her breast, gliding down, over her waist, down over her knees and on to the floor. Still I was not afraid yet I watched with frozen horror as her tongue wormed across the carpet, relentlessly towards me.

Somewhere at the back of my mind I was sure that if I blinked this would all disappear. I waited, hung on, reluctant to lose the illusion so soon, but when that diabolical tongue was close enough to touch I took one last look at this woman, my mother, and shut my eyes like a door.

Time passed.

I was dripping sweat. It ran in rivulets between my breasts, down my sides, forming pools in the pit of my navel. Lakes.

When I thought I must be safe I raised my eyelids slowly and the hair on each side of my spine froze in two rigid walls, pulling my body erect. She was sitting there still, watching. And her eyes smelled of yearning. And that diabolical tongue was wrapping itself around my waist and was pulling me towards her. I could not resist. I did not know how to resist. Instinctively I held my arms aloft, knowing without knowledge that were I to touch that tongue it would sizzle and burn like acid. It pulled me closer and closer, not over the floor but somehow above it, gliding on air, until my mother's gaping face was inches from my own. Then the tongue unwound itself and slowly drew back, receded into the cavern of her mouth. I don't recall breathing.

Time passed. The horror had gone. I was warm again, pulsing. Lost in her eyes. Waiting. Time passed.

The anger was sudden and volcanic, and came without warning. One moment I was lost, unconscious of thought, the next, my body had exploded to the ends of every nerve with a wild and savage fury. She reeled from the blast. I needed no movement, no speech, I radiated anger like the forges in hell give off heat. It flowed from me in waves like slabs of molten lava and struck my mother hard in the solar plexus. She reeled with each thundering blow.

I could not control it; it merely was. On and on I burned, exploding all sense of centre, consumed, burning, and still she reeled. I could see her pain. I could see it all. From within the orbit of my fire I could see her writhing and pushing, recoiling, pushing again; her eyes rolling, beseeching; each excruciating moment an interminable agony. I wanted to reach out and wrench it from her, shut myself off from her, shut off the pain, blind myself to the hell in those eyes. I could feel it.

Then I heard the sound – a rumbling groan that tumbled and shook the air. It steadily grew louder and more piercing; it jarred, began to hurt my ears. It was an appalling sound, like the scream of an animal caught by a predatory dog, louder, a siren of fear, anguish. On and on it went, louder and louder, more and more piercing, shrinking my veins, distorting space.

It was drowning my anger.

I had to make it stop, make her stop. Its source was lost in the omnipresent wail and my mother's arms were now raised, crossed before her, shielding her face. My own hands were resting at my sides and I struggled desperately to lift them so that I too could screen my ears from that deafening, grinding wail, but my arms were weighted, numb, anchored to the floor. My anger flowed from me still but was much diminished, thudding like sponge on my mother's heart. But the wail increased. I cringed and skewed my head to the side. I wanted to shrink into myself. Then, in the midst of electric pain I saw Vincent curled into sleep. How could this be? I was horrified, shut out from help, alone and terrified now, my throat thick with panic. I turned again to my racked and convulsive mother. She had to be stopped. I could not understand why she shuddered so, for my anger had paled to an afterglow, a cold blue emanation. The scream had won. I squeezed my eyelids tight and fought to retrieve some sense of my arms. It was vital I should somehow protect myself from that noise, it would surely crack my brain like a crystal. I pulled and pulled and pulled; focused my will on my paralysed limbs. I looked and yes, they were rising, I could see them beneath me, rising like arms from a bog, emerging from sludge, slowly, higher and higher until, at last, I could feel my hands on my neck, then clapped with the joy of relief over my tortured ears.

When I knew that the scream was mine, it stopped. The anger gone. Everything wet. Face, hands, breasts, all soaked, awash with tears.

I looked at my mother. She was smiling again, but her eyes . . . I tried to speak, could not. I could, however, move my lips. I . . . will try . . . mouthed rather than spoken: I could not say the word she wanted to hear. It formed like a nut on my tongue, round and acidic. But I could not say it.

Bang, bang, bang – from somewhere else, from beyond this room, in the real world.

My mother held out her hands to me and opened her palms.

Bang, bang, bang.

In one, a spider the size of a fingernail began to weave its web between her thumb and fingertips.

Bang, bang, bang.

Round and round it scurried until, the web complete, it rushed to the centre and swayed at the core of its spiral.

Bang, bang, bang.

The other hand contained a minute polished stone, black like basalt, a chip of meteor perhaps, a petrified crust from creation. This I took.

'Georgie . . .! I know you're awake, Georgie, I can hear you talking . . .'

Who can he hear?

Bang, bang, bang . . .

'Look forget it, I'll go myself – Luria's still comatose. Come down, will you . . .!'

'. . . Yes.'

I spoke. I heard my voice. Such a normal thing.

But I wasn't on the floor, I was slouched inside the deep wardrobe, both doors almost closed, two dark mirrors reflecting my own startled image.

Bang, bang, bang.

I pushed and the doors swung into clear morning sun, piercing. There was nothing. Only the empty fireplace, the candle long spent. George calling. Vincent asleep . . .

The alarm said 8.47, which meant I'd been lost in that world for hours . . . at least five . . .? And Vincent had slept?

I shook myself, rubbed my eyes, trod over strewn clothes and pressed my face into the window glass. It was cool and hard; I was not dreaming then, had not dreamed, was sure I hadn't been asleep . . .

It didn't matter.

Nothing mattered. I didn't care how or what or why. Outside, sparrows were chattering in the plane trees, a milk-float was clunking from door to door and an elderly neighbour with platinum curls was already busy, spraying the budding growth of her roses. London had roused itself for a morning full of promise and I felt blissfully, euphorically light.

I paused only momentarily at Vincent's still form. Let him wake himself with magic, I decided, laughing at the irony of a Weary Willy wizard, unable to deal with Morpheus. Then I trotted downstairs, conscious of feet and air.

*

232

George was in the kitchen, wrapped like a modern doll in the absurd frilly négligé Luria had left hanging for strategic effect (label showing) in the bathroom. He was chatting, distractedly, to someone just out of sight, behind the tall fridge door. I recognised the bag first, astonished to see it there, dumped by my feet. The fridge door closed, and there was Oscar, a ring of milk pearling the newly grown grey of his whiskers.

29

'What are you doing here?'
He gestured at the debris, 'I gather I'm just too late.'

When I was younger I had at least one revelation a year, usually close to my birthday, small revelations like tide gauges marking the shallower sea of last year's ignorance. I must have been thirteen years old when I stopped saying 'I understand everything now', and believing it.

I only mention this because Oscar's bag, a battered thing in maroon leather, may seem an unlikely source of revelation, yet it was. It was open and my eye slid over the contents: one shirt, one pair of socks, a wallet and a broken-backed novel. Whatever he'd come to say it was too weighty to risk in a letter, but he hadn't come to stay. He was afraid of me.

He volunteered immediately that he'd flown from Inverness, to help me celebrate, he said, and was returning the next morning.

'You shouldn't have bothered,' I said and his eyebrows rose. I could barely look at him. His frame had shrunk somehow, seemed almost slight beneath the mossy mantle of his sweater, his face more gaunt, more sallow. Such an odd and incongruous sight amidst the designer appliances and the congealing chicken thighs, the ornaments and abandoned bottles. Alien. George had moved back to the doorway where he stood awkwardly with the flounced opening of Luria's jade chiffon held tightly across his chest, his long hair unravelled, curling on his shoulder. His chin strangely hard. On my way downstairs I'd noticed the rumpled spare-room bed, and his clothes dumped in a corner. He hadn't slept with Luria. Whatever, I couldn't deal with it now. Not while the world was dislocated and Oscar so small.

Even as we anticipate earthquakes, however, trifles apparently matter. When Oscar stepped back to look at me, searching as though for landmines, there was panic in his eyes.

'What's been happening here?' he demanded.

I was three again, my mouth stained with ink, and the empty bottle beside me. He'd made me vomit with hot soapy water – I can still recall the taste. Of course, I realised, I'd been weeping all night and it showed; I crossed to the window and peered at myself in the mirror on the ledge, encased in sandalwood, herbs and leeks. My eyes were a radius of blood under swollen purple flesh, like something pickled in brine then warmed by a fire.

I needed a more propitious time. Space.

'Nothing, I've just been purging myself of post-exam stress.' I tried to look purged; difficult with hostility.

'Has this young man upset you?'

George's hands moved, a nervous tick, and his frills flew apart offering a nice flash of body. I laughed, but not Oscar and certainly not George.

'No . . . This is my friend, George Gilmour. My father, Oscar Sondberg.'

Oscar ignored the nakedness as far as he could but the

frills were too much. He stared in disbelief while George muttered hello, dragging the chiffon together again.

'Is that ridiculous garment yours?'

'No, sir,' George protested, 'this is Luria's.'

'Luria's . . .!?'

'I just picked it up from the bathroom,' he said, challenging me to clarify.

'To answer the door,' I added.

I deflected the nagging thought of Vincent sleeping upstairs. It was almost nine.

Then Luria padded in, bleary and nursing a headache. 'Well, well!' she exclaimed. 'What a surprise.' Her tone denied it.

She was draped in her organdie again and standing as she was next to George I thought they looked together like a pair of good-time girls in drag.

'Luria,' Oscar nodded, equally restrained.

'I'm afraid you'll have to excuse the mess, we had a party last night. Coffee?' She lurched towards the sink.

'Why don't we go next door,' I suggested to my feet. Apart from anything else I wanted to escape George's weighted stare, but he had other ideas.

'Yes, sir,' he said, 'it sure was an interesting night.' His chin rose defiantly. 'We were just talking about the mess of Georgie's face, Luria, before you came down.'

It was anger he felt.

'What?' She turned from the kettle and squinted, then came for a closer look. Her eyes hardened. 'What did he do?' she hissed.

'Who?' said Oscar, suspicious of George again.

As if on cue, Vincent came thumping downstairs, crashing doors and screeching, 'Look at the time! . . . rotten bitch!' Clearly in a lather. I realised much too late that I didn't want Oscar to know I'd slept with this much older man. The significance was sickening. But it was

236

Luria he turned to as Vincent crashed through the door. Ha. No one moved.

'Hello, who's this . . .' Anger waylaid; pulling on his jacket.

'This is Georgie's father,' said George drily. 'And this,' he sneered, surprising even himself, 'is a bastard called Vincent.'

Vincent merely grinned. 'Pleased to meet you,' he said, instant urbane charm. 'Don't mind the peevish boy,' he nodded at George. 'His horns have slipped.'

'I think you'd better leave.' Luria looked dangerous.

It was all becoming a stupid, distracting farce.

Fuck it, I thought, and dug into my dressing-gown pocket. The stone wasn't there. It had gone. But it had, something had happened.

'You seem rather free with your insults,' said Oscar, exploring implications. 'Just why is that . . .?'

There was another, cooler pause during which Vincent took in the state of my face. Then he shifted his weight and said in a man-to-man matey sort of way, 'Your daughter is quite absurd.'

Fucking audacity.

He brushed his lapel with the back of his hand and added, 'I should've been on the road to Exeter half an hour ago.'

'Unusual, certainly,' Oscar interrupted, 'but why absurd?' His tone remained measured, reasonable. I was surprised he should be so reasonable, especially as George was not. Vincent spread his long hands. 'I need my sleep, you see, and she wanted to talk all night . . . I thought she'd be OK . . .'

No one had heard my cries? Even Vincent in the same room had been oblivious?

'Bugger off, Vincent,' I said quietly. No anger, just contempt. 'We have things to talk about here which don't concern you, so just leave.'

He hesitated only for a second then made for the door much as I imagine him leaving the magician's stage, head erect and mouth fixed in a hopeless icy smile. Only George swayed on his feet. Luria flattened her mouth as the door clunked shut. I didn't know what I was going to say, or how. Some words resist anticipation.

'I met my mother last night. She's not as dead as she used to be.'

All the anger and pain I'd trapped in a nerve was hatred right enough, but I'd neglected to apprise myself of the passion that hatred conceals. We're good at these tricks when the need demands.

So I'd nurtured the symptoms and smothered the cause, and what was that after all but fear, certainly grief.

Forgive – the word I'd failed to utter for my mother's ears – seems trite, so common a word for so much rare import. Even now, saying it beneath my breath, I flinch. What does it mean – forgive? Give up? Pardon? Pardon me for dying. Absurd. How? Loss is just there, a permanent and trenchant reminder of what you once had and don't have now. I don't believe acceptance can fill that hole or make it drift away. We stop looking so hard at the loss, perhaps, but we can't deny it.

And what should I give up? The love? – for that's what lies behind it, of course. Not possible. Not now. I'd shut it out for years and look what happened. I won't do that again.

The anger? It goes with the loss; they're inextricably and irretrievably linked. Sorry, Mother, I can't forgive, whatever that means. But now at least I can say your name without cringing and thinking of Oscar.

Maggie.

30

'He did that to me,' Luria was talking to Oscar. 'It's hypnotism.'

'Don't go, George.' I followed him up to the spare room where he made for his clothes.

'I'm going.'

'You're mad at me.'

'Damn right.'

'I can't talk about it now but please don't leave me with them.'

'What difference does it make?'

'I want to explain about Vincent—'

'I don't give a shit.'

'I hope you don't mean that, George. I made a mistake. I've hurt you but I never intended to do that. I've been wrong about almost everything. I truly am sorry. Please don't hate me, and don't go. I can hardly bear to be in the same room as that man.'

'Your problem. He's your father.'

'Let me just find my feet, please.'

He put on his mirrored sunglasses and looked at me, 'I'm going after breakfast.'

*

I moved about like an imbecile while Oscar and Luria edged around each other like rival dogs. Breakfast was an ordeal. George withdrew his sarcastic remarks but not his black mood. He wouldn't look at me at all and I couldn't look at Oscar, so he and Oscar tried to chat in a normal way, bizarrely enough about skiing. Oscar claimed he'd done a lot in his youth; it might be a lie but he did seem to know the terms. George was quite fooled – unless he too was bluffing?

It was hard to accommodate Oscar. He didn't belong in Luria's grand design; he was like a primitive man just introduced to furniture, but his tacit disapproval got on my nerves. Luria passed me the coffeepot and peered at my face again. 'It's not natural,' she shivered. 'I don't like it at all.'

'So I understand,' said Oscar pompously. 'That's why I'm here.'

'Really . . . I thought you'd just come to exercise the male prerogative. When it's not inconvenient, of course.'

George excused himself immediately and pre-empted any further persuasion to stay by claiming some bogus appointment. He left amidst the scowls.

'You've been pouring poison into my daughter's ears, Luria,' Oscar continued.

'Bullshit. I've been telling her what she bloody well ought to know.'

'What you think you know . . .'

'. . . and that's highly irregular, to say the least.'

'It's a fraction of a story. You've uncovered a fragment of hair and extrapolated, with evident glee, a whole fucking body.'

'And that's fucking tasteless, even from you!'

'You're the authority on tastelessness, dear woman.'

'You say that of me . . .!?'

It was a mistake. Luria might be vulgar but she likes to

think she's always deliberately so. It's her snub to what she sees as punctilious cant and posturing snobbery, as distinct from her own; she wouldn't put up with her sensibilities being sniffed at, especially not by Oscar's withering scorn.

'You puffed-up self-deceiving hypocrite!' she spat. 'Since that girl arrived in this town she has systematically enacted all those tawdry, spiteful little fantasies you spew out from that disfigured pit you call your imagination . . . So don't you talk to me about tasteless, Mister.'

Oscar paled, white against granite.

'Fuck it,' I said. 'You can sort this out yourselves, and when you've finished sniping at each other I want to talk about the more important issue of my mother's "accident". And I want the truth this time, Oscar, not more bloody fiction.'

I stumbled out into the street and didn't turn round when Luria called after me. I just walked. I walked without thinking where I was going, not conscious of walking; not thinking at all. Streets of blankness until I found myself at a corner of the Heath where there were already kites sailing and people strolling on the springy grass. Dogs romping and wagging tails. The sun making silver in trees.

Then I ran – not jogged or trotted, but ran. Like the proverbial bat out of hell. I ran so that my legs were pistons and the warm south-east wind dragged at my wide cotton pants and shirt and tugged at my hair. It felt good pelting along at full speed, breathing hard, concentrated on movement, on the next and the next clump of earth for feet, making rapid decisions which path or not, which hill to take.

I ran like this until I had to submit to my burning lungs

and collapsed, heaving air. Flat on my back puffing at sky. Faces and mythical beasts in the passing clouds.

When I sat up to take my bearings I found I was almost in Hampstead but lower down the hill, quite a way down from the village, closer to Haverstock Hill and the Royal Free Hospital. I could just see its upper floors hovering between the chimney stacks and TV aerials of the nearest houses.

I censored the urge.

In the first place it was Sunday and therefore there would be no clinics. In the second, I couldn't quite pin down my motive. Patel was a million light years away. He was a funny little man with big feet and a rigorously developed conscience. He inhabited another universe, where everyone always did the right thing and thought the right thoughts. I went anyway. Perhaps because of it.

The clinic door held a large cardboard sign reading CLOSED, with a list of opening times underneath. It was exactly as I thought it would be, which made the ache of disappointment seem more self-inflicted and harder to understand. I stood there staring at the notice like Ali Baba, Open Sesame, futility.

I cut through Pond Street and walked up East Heath Road, talking to myself about evasion and ignoring my own advice. I would talk with George, abase myself, ameliorate his anger – this is what I said to myself; but what I felt wasn't so nicely controlled. I wanted to hide, if he'd let me, under the shade of his arm, where the past had no henchmen.

Like everyone else, I enjoy the voyeuristic pleasures of other people's windows, lingering when a particular scene catches my eye. Sometimes I like to get caught, sometimes I don't. It depends what I see. I see that masks have become a fashionable accessory on everyone's walls and coffee tables. So we all exist in a fantasy world masked by the business of living. Occasionally we catch a glimpse of it, crossing a room, talking, in the way we walk perhaps, in a mannerism – sometimes in the middle of a sentence – the look that says I'M NOT WHAT YOU THINK I AM AT ALL, I'M SOMEONE COMPLETELY DIFFERENT.

Luria is really a combination of Mae West and an utterly respectable maiden aunt, a closet Mrs Beeton. If you listen carefully you'll hear she says conventional things in an unconventional way, aware that it frees her to think what she bloody well likes without any difficult pressures.

Oscar . . .?

Oscar just is.

Oscar has always been impulse; for me, the yearning behind the impulse. Oscar is not always the deed, not always the fantasy, but he is most assuredly always the impulse.

I was afraid. Oscar had come to say what he had to say. We all know that. I was afraid because meeting my mother had made it necessary to confront myself with a telescope and, whatever happens, I know that I will still be guided somehow by that impulse and will want to believe, despite myself, despite everything, that my father can read the tides in the wind and the wind in the stars.

Like you, I can't deny the impulse.

But I was afraid.

31

We were in his narrow bunk opposite the skis,
hiding in the rosy light, hanging on to each
other under the duvet for security as much as
comfort – it's easy to fall out of George's bed, in more
ways than one. It was the best place to talk. George had
never seen me cry before and seemed to like the idea. I
cry therefore I feel; sort of reassuring.

'Why can't you just leave things alone?' he said,
hugging my tears.

'What do you mean?'

'First Vincent . . . then setting me up like that with
Luria, I swear – ' he bashed the pillow with the back of
his fist – 'that was the most presumptuous piece of
shit . . .'

'I've said I'm sorry, George. I am. I can't say it enough,
I'm so sorry. Really.' I wiped my face on my shirt and
snivelled. 'What happened there anyway?'

He exhaled through his teeth, sighed then laughed.
'When I got back from Doctor Walsh's place Luria
announced there'd been a coup and we sat around in the
kitchen drinking coffee, eating crumbs of cheesecake . . .
I wasn't – I definitely did not want to jump into bed with
her and—'

'Didn't you?'

'No! You're crazy, neither of us wanted to; it's not that simple, Georgie.'

'Isn't it?'

'You don't consider the emotional baggage that goes with sex, do you? You should. Really. Maybe then you wouldn't get so screwed up by people . . .'

'Perhaps you're right. Other people are never quite what you want them to be, I've discovered.'

'And what is that exactly? What do you expect?'

'I wasn't thinking of you, George.'

'Thanks a lot.'

'No, I mean I wasn't including you in my general disillusion.'

'No . . . But then your expectations of our relationship stop at physical friendship, right . . .?'

Something in his tone made me hesitate. It was true it had always seemed that way, I'd assumed for both of us. We had shared a comfortable intimacy and compatible sex. I'd imagined Vincent would stretch me . . . he was more of a challenge: physically, mentally, emotionally, in every sense. I realised with a jolt that I'd wanted him to want me. Simply that. And he was like Oscar. But George . . .

'What do *you* want George?'

'Come on, you owe me this.'

Perhaps I did.

'I thought I knew what you felt about me, before,' I said. 'I thought there were doubts . . . but you seemed to be bearing those at least with a view to understanding.'

'Hm . . .'

'Now I suspect that Vincent was Gilbert Osmond and you've been Warburton all along. I mean that I want and expect everything, George. A grand affair. Deep and extending and stretching and profoundly felt. Oscar gave

245

me everything, you see, apart from the sex . . . and even then . . . He taught me to want and expect at least the same.'

'You want me to be like your father?'

'I did. Before. And because you weren't like him enough I never saw our relationship as . . . important.'

'And now?'

'Now,' I sighed. 'Now I need to examine what Oscar's "everything" really is.'

'And where does that leave me?'

'I'm not sure. Where do you want to be?'

He paused, shrugged. 'I'm a practical guy, as Luria says. We're young. I won't be in England much longer and the Atlantic's a pretty wide ocean to straddle. Long-term I can't say where I want to be, but like you,' he added with a touch of animosity, 'I expect 100 per cent when I'm there.'

'I wasn't trying to make you jealous.'

'Jealous fuck! You didn't consider me at all.'

'Perhaps not. It seems I have much to be sorry for, not least for limiting the boundaries of legitimate feeling.'

'I like you,' he said suddenly. 'Don't you know that?'

'I like you too, very much.'

We snuggled into this cosy ambience, silent for a while. I thought absently about Oscar and Luria, abandoned to each other's company. What a joke. The celibate pornographer and the moral queen of satin and frills.

George gave me the cash for a taxi and walked with me to the outside door where we leaned against each other and ticked like a clock, back and forth, back and forth. He seemed constrained to say something fertile and reassuring, something to bolster my courage. What he said was,

'When I get back to the States I'm going to furnish you with a whole canteen of personalised cutlery.'

It made me feel brave. We understand each other.

I sat in the back of the cab preparing myself for whatever divulgences waited. Oscar would have to assent to some final name: misfit, manticore, bigot, hypocrite. Malcontent or basilisk.

I saw my mother's spider weaving between her fingertips, then the scuttling rush to the core where all spiders know instinctively they rest on that point of the web where they are most secure, and their power is at its greatest.

32

We sat around the opulent Oppenheim table. Its seamless, perfect finish is of modern design, not antique, though the carved legs, like the legs of a ballerina entwined in foliage, are reminiscent of an age when craftsmen laboured to secure the patronage of kings. It was at present adorned with two silver candlestick branches, lit, which, with the addition of a bottle of Irish whiskey and a bucket of ice, lent the occasion a spurious solemnity. No one had mentioned a conference but there we were setting one up. Oscar was ostentatiously collecting his thoughts, pacing the room with one hand stuffed in a pocket, the other kneading the crop of his beard. Luria was sitting opposite me, sideways on to the table, at her most dignified and sedate, one long leg crossed on the other. Avoiding my eye. I drank. Luria drank. Oscar paced.

We had dined with good wine, talking only of wine and food, like a family conscious of discontent but wary of indigestion; a trio of frauds. They'd made some sort of pact, he and Luria, a truce for a truth no doubt; civilised blackmail is decidedly Oscar's style, and it suited me fine. No one mentioned rape and I held my tongue about Doctor Dance.

Luria was beginning to show signs of impatience: she examined the plaster mouldings on the ceiling and drummed the ends of her fingers. She bites her nails, then grows them again, then bites them. Since I was largely unnoticed, it crossed my mind that I was extraneous to the entire performance; it was just them, their rivalry again, their love for the same woman. I tried to envisage Oscar as a young high-powered academic, doing his TV thing. Out a lot, meeting people for lunch: men in stylish shirts and women with hairstyles. An Oscar who was always busy, writing, on the telephone, entertaining, in demand. Pleased with himself and expecting admiration. Not getting my mother's.

'The great flaw . . .' He was addressing the large china table lamp of a child with a basket of fruit, '. . . in acting on the basis of empirical knowledge is that we cannot ever predict unfolding complications; thesis is axiomatically trapped in the past, its product in the future . . .'

Luria uncrossed her legs aggressively. 'We don't need a philosophical discourse, thank you, just get to the point, and sit down for goodness sake, you're making me nervous.'

He paced. 'The point is, we can only act in good faith and accept that history might subvert our intentions.'

'My mother died of a heart attack, Oscar. Why did you say she had drowned?' I cannot bear palaver.

'How do you know that?'

'St Catherine's House. Why did you lie about it?'

'I didn't.'

'You bloody well did!'

'To you, Luria, I lied, not to George.'

We all sat. Very straight.

'You never told me anything. Considering everything else I have no reason to believe that had I asked, you would have told me the truth. I heard you say my mother's ashes were scattered in the sea.'

'They are.' He leaned on his knees. 'And you're right, I would have lied to you. I lied to you, Luria, because—'

'. . . because you couldn't bear the thought of Maggie coming here, you shit, could you . . .'

'Because I considered it important that George never learn the truth.'

'What!?'

'My own experience determined it; history. I'm sure Maggie told you that I was smuggled out of Hamburg during the war as the child of a Swedish doctor, and from Sweden into England. He was my father's closest friend. It was 1943 and I was two years old. He got me out and delivered me to my father's cousin, who subsequently brought me up. That much is common knowledge. What you can't know . . .' he paused for breath. 'George certainly doesn't because I told her her German grand-parents had died in an air raid. They didn't. It was almost five years before the news reached us that my escape had alerted the authorities; my parents were dragged from their home and herded into a cattle-truck for Dachau.'

He twirled his moustache unconsciously. I saw. Eye flickered.

'They were gassed. For five years I'd lived in a limbo between uncertainty and hope. My aunt and uncle, as I called them, insisted my parents were fine, we'd be reunited soon, so I'd played and grown in ignorance. When I learned the truth, it was a terrible awakening. It was as if they'd died without my grieving; more important, I hadn't even acknowledged their sacrifice.'

'What is this, Oscar?' Luria grimaced.

'Listen. Every moment of those five years, every thought, struck me then as a treacherous dereliction of feeling, a cruel distortion. I was compelled to go over it again and again, there was nothing else, and because of it I grew to despise my own life.'

'This has nothing to do with my mother . . .'

'Stupid people say children are incapable of complex emotion, such as guilt. Absurd. I was suicidal!'

'Get to the point—'

'Maggie almost died having George.'

'What?'

'She developed severe pre-eclampsia in pregnancy. The consultant pressed for termination, because of the risks of coma, the unlikelihood that she'd make it, but she wouldn't even consider it. She spent six months on her back in Lairg hospital and they did an early Caesarean; George was fine but Maggie never fully recovered.'

'The heart attack?'

'. . . was the result. She died in Euston station.'

Luria brushed her mouth with the back of her clenched hand and rolled her eyes. 'I still don't get it. You lied to protect Georgie from the possibility that she'd blame herself for her mother's death? It's fantastic.'

'Perhaps, but I couldn't allow her to nurture such guilt, I knew what it was, remember. I didn't want her to have to cope with that, she'd enough to bear with the loss, was already traumatised, cowering in cupboards in the dark. Think of it. She hid herself in cupboards until she was almost twelve – but never, I'm glad to say, because of self-loathing.'

'But I was rescuing you, I wasn't searching for my mother . . .'

Was I?

'Rescuing him from what?'

'It was . . . just a game.'

'Well I for one am disgusted. It was a deplorable lie – however noble you believe yourself to have been.'

'You would have preferred a murder, perhaps?'

'I would have preferred to have known the truth. I count. Same as you.' She scowled. 'I always did.'

He tushed, resigned to what he saw as the simple fact. 'To hide the truth from George it was necessary to hide it from everyone.'

'I always knew you were twisted, Oscar, but this is the most bone-headed piece of chicanery . . .'

They were instantly engrossed, throwing their hands in the air, stalking each other, my mother a torn thing between them. I wandered across the room, putting distance between them and the riot of twirling moustache in my mind.

I stared at the green of my eyes in the large mirror over the fireplace, as though the colour itself might offer some vital clue to life before the cupboards. My pupils shrank to peppercorns. Behind me, they were still wrangling, but I'd switched off somehow, stopped listening. I watched through the mirror, marvelling at the tenacity of retrospective jealousy, at the fierce defensiveness of Oscar's imagination. How well he hides in secrets. How assiduously he conceals himself in those characters who have no past, no damning secrets of their own. My father's women, my models.

'You two really are making a career out of this, aren't you?'

They turned and met my reflection.

'What?'

'You, Luria, and your personal outrage, Oscar and his long-suffering good deeds. And still the enmity. You're absurd, both of you.'

'I did not want you, George, to grow up thinking—'

'Oh climb down from that martyr's perch, Oscar, I can't absolve you. As far as I'm concerned my mother was just a photograph until last night, someone who got in the way, now she's not. She was a woman as well as a mother. That's what's important.'

'Of course, but you're . . .'

In three strides I was close enough to gauge the movement of every muscle. 'Don't tell me what I am, Oscar. You make mistakes, big ones. I used to think you were all of me until I saw myself in my mother's eyes. Sure, you taught me lots of facts, but you didn't teach me everything. I'd prefer not to shrink from affection.'

And I taught myself to watch. I know when he's cheating.

33

Mid-August.
For ten days I have been walking in the world, officially adult. I have keys. I can drink what I like in bars. I can vote and get into debt. I can gamble and, should I wish, I can emigrate. I can legally drive a car and be imprisoned for crime.

I am eighteen years old.

Addressed by the world as madam.

My birthday present from Luria was the price of George's second-hand car. When I pass the test I shall drive myself off to those sights George says I shouldn't miss. Places of interest, just curious, not desperate. Oscar sent a cheque but I've torn it up. I have a temporary job in a baker's selling cakes; I no longer want his money.

It is ten weeks now since his inventive charade. I've been biding my time, thinking.

Tuesday, 18 August   28,000 ft up

Dearest George,

You were right, flying is less wearing than sitting on trains, but I've given myself up for dead; it's the only way to relax with all that space underneath. To hell with science. This way, if I land at Inverness it will come as a bonus. I can see nothing outside except cloud and mist and occasional patches of dappled grey, but I can just about smell the acrid sea.

Be astonished, George – I have six whole A levels: two As, two Bs, one C and an E - in physics. You could say I'd been distracted by an icon or that I should have studied fine art but you, of course, will understand the slip was purely Freudian. My mind doesn't spin after all for cosmic beginnings but chugs disconsolately, impatient for endings. Oscar said that.

I have driving lessons twice a week with a man whose hand is tattooed with a swallow. Apparently it means he's crossed the Equator twice and lived to tell the tale. An adventurer. During my lessons he offers as a cautionary example descriptions of accidents between larger and smaller cars. He seems to enjoy his work. I've also bought myself one of those yellow Teach Yourself books: Motoring for Beginners by one Dudley Noble. On the flyleaf Mr Noble insists that should the novice secure a grasp of the whys and wherefores of cars, and their use on the Queen's Highway, then his work will have served a useful purpose. You can Teach Youself Conjuring, Mountain Climbing, Indoor Aquaria, Balloom Dancing and Sub-Aqua Swimming, all from your own armchair. I intend to ensure Mr Noble will feel he has done the right thing. I've discovered, for instance, that a block and tackle used for hauling a boat up a beach is similar in principle to a car's gearbox. Luria didn't know this. I cruise around the house practising signals of intent and ask, 'What is the code of behaviour regarding headlamps?' 'Describe the operation known as the Otto Cycle.' Luria can answer nothing. She drives around London quite happy with her ignorance.

Of other things too.

But you misunderstood my last letter; I have every intention of telling her the truth, when I'm sure I know it myself. It doesn't always wear the same recognisable face.

So you've found Oscar in Spanish; the bugger is every-where. How does 'straining bolus' translate? Will you exper-iment in that splendid square in your photograph? Luria has framed you in painted wood and placed you between two reproduction art deco sylphs tossing a ball. I smile at you every day.

Much love, Georgie. XXX

I carted my balsa masks in a sack down to the Kinsaile headland where the cliffs hang over the sea yearning to dive. There was no wind, just a slight breeze, but I shivered as I had done since I'd arrived; London has stolen my resistance to cold.

I sat for a while and stared at the sea while the sun disappeared behind Arkle.

Oscar has been busy in my absence, painting out my colours, tiling roofs, cobbling the dry-stone walls behind the outhouse (not my garden), building his ramparts against guilt with paper and pen and watching his back. I pottered about for two days, meeting myself in the contours of chairs and pathways, gauging myself against what I met. I might be more vulnerable now but I'm taller. Oscar says women grow for longer than men, to help them catch up. He jokes uncomfortably, as with a stranger.

I've decided, amongst other things, that my future lies in wood; carving or sculpture, perhaps even furniture. Oscar raves unconvincingly about the profligate waste of my splendid education.

'Wood isn't worthless.'

'You should go on to university and enter some proper profession.'

'You didn't allow my mother to have a career.'

'That was different, she was my wife. I was her career.'
Paid in unkindness.

Fanella, he insists, has nothing to do with his writing. I didn't agree.

'She only exists in that form because the fantasies she represents, like those of your heroines, disregard her own; she's not thinking them, is she? She didn't find them in herself.'

'I don't know about that. Anyway, it's irrelevant. It would seem that as well as everything else, Luria has turned you into a prude.'

'Not at all. I keep my ear close to the pillow, I hear my own blood. What I notice however, Oscar, is that a woman's fantasies never obliterate the context in which they are felt – the security of knowing one's partner and the freedom to choose. You deny that we need that; the magazines too. You appropriate a basic human impulse and strip its margins of safety. You would even have me fantasise in the process of rape itself, while my mind is screaming.'

'I imagine no such thing!'

'Really? Well that makes it worse. Where is your integrity, then? Not in those books. I've burned all my copies, by the way, Luria and I made a bonfire.'

When I told him I knew he'd lied, he denied it, of course. I knew he would. But his vanity requires my belief and he couldn't easily relinquish that. Eventually we settled down with the brandy and he offered another story. He wiped his forehead and rubbed his eyes because this was an even more tragic tale than the last. My mother was clinically depressed, he said, her letter bore that out. She had slashed her wrists in the toilet at Euston station, a suicide attempt which had failed, but the shock caused her heart attack. He'd lied, he said, because he simply couldn't accept my mother's emphatic abnegation.

So my mother drowned, then I killed her, then she killed herself.

'That's an awful lot of life.'

'Believe what I tell you, George.'

'Too difficult. Even Oedipus rejected the tyranny of the oracle.'

'That was ignorance.'

'Some call it heroism.'

'Is that what you think you're engaged in?'

'I don't know that I'm engaged in anything. I've just come for the truth. This fortress, this temple to your ego just fills me with rage, Oscar, it isn't my home any more.'

'London has taught you insolence!'

'Ha! And to my own father. I expect you'll get over it. I need to know, Oscar. Apart from anything else, should someone ask how my mother died I'd feel rather eccentric offering them multiple versions.'

'How very droll and flippant.'

'I'm sorry, but it was you yourself who established the farcical framework. I don't know how else to talk to you now. This is all too extraordinary and unnerving and not a little lonely. I'm not staying; I doubt that I'll ever come back. You've lost me, just as you lost my mother. What else is there to lose? Please tell me.'

'There is nothing to tell.'

'It would make a difference. To us. Don't you see, I already know. It would make a difference to how I regard you. But then, I don't suppose that really matters much. I'm as expendable as anyone else. Tell me anyway.'

'I've told you—'

'. . . two nasty little fairy tales. Three, with the slashed wrists.'

'Why didn't you believe me? Luria believed me.'

'Perhaps. But I've lived with you and I learned to recognise the lie. Your body betrays you, and so does your castle: that tragic story about your own parents, for example . . .'

'What?'

'It was a pious façade, Oscar. What did you think I was doing all those years I was growing up? After I found your book I searched this house for the others; I know every crevice, every corner, I've explored every drawer and every scrap of paper. I've seen birth certificates, marriage certificates, death certificates: your father's, not your mother's. But then he wasn't Jewish, was he? Sondberg was your mother's name. Your father was German. Very . . .'

'And if he was . . .'

'Oh I'm sure it means something, all right. Something very nasty, some other secret truth that would no doubt explain why he, in fact, survived long after the war whereas my grandmother didn't. It hardly bears thinking about. Perhaps it was your father before you who taught you to sacrifice women? Tell me what really happened, Oscar.'

We looked at each other across shadow and light. He leaned down and threw a log on the fire. It flared up and crackled.

'Nineteen seventy-four.'

He sighed. 'I've told you how she died.'

'Your first book had just been published. *Lucas*. My mother didn't know you were writing them, did she?'

He wove his fingers together and attempted a scoff. 'Of course she knew.'

'She approved, did she, encouraged you even? Really? You forget I didn't know myself until I stumbled across that book – because you write like a thief in the night, Oscar. My mother mentioned your nocturnal prowling. I bet she hadn't a clue what you were doing while she slept.'

'These are wild, absurd speculations, George . . .' He reached towards me but I flinched when he pressed my shoulder.

'Did she stumble on the truth in the station – buying a novel or a magazine for Luria? Is that what happened? I've no doubt that her heart was dicky, Oscar, but you knew that. I think your books killed her, the shock of discovering you'd been writing them behind her back, and using her name . . .'

'Good God, George, a foolish conspiracy theory . . .?'

'You underestimate me and deceive yourself.'

'This is juvenile thinking!'

'I suppose it's comforting for you to dismiss it as such; conspiracy theories aren't attended by thinking at all, are they, they're symptoms of acquiescence and complacency. I feel neither.'

'You would blame me for your own disillusionment, your own guilt about the past.'

'I feel no guilt, only regret that I've never known my mother. I regret my blindness but I don't hate myself because of it. I was a child, your child, and you chose – chose – to exploit your power and influence over me to satisfy your ego, your implacable self-evasion. The responsibility lies at your feet; you encouraged every avenue of thought, every feeling.'

'I exploited nothing, and even if it were true, there's a saying about horses and water.'

'How cynical. Do you really think you can regain control with a superficial chat about liability? I'm not just your daughter any more, adoring or otherwise, and you'll never be simply my father. It's over. Your pedestal is dust and I can't stop myself from analysing your motives.'

'I was not responsible for your mother's death.'

I looked at him from inside a strange calm, somewhere behind defeated, beyond anger, recrimination.

'I only wonder, Oscar, that you're such an insomniac.'

There were twenty-seven masks, twenty-seven empty hooks on my bedroom wall. I'd carved them long before I'd seen that first dress, over many long evenings. They were feather-light and floated like corks in the savage Atlantic currents. I tossed the last one out over the cliff and it swung in a wide arc over the edge, down into the sea. Then I sat again and hugged my knees as I watched. The loose chain of pale wooden faces, each of them something of Oscar, drifted out into the ocean, so many sleepless eyes fixed on the moon.

Also of interest from Virago

AQUAMARINE
Carol Anshaw

'Startling and vibrant . . . The writing of this novel has the swift ease of flowing water. Surreal in structure, it is a dream of a novel, but always earthed in real emotion and the hope for what might have been' – *TheTimes*

With stiking ingenuity, *Aquamarine* explores the intricate ways early choices, made impulsively or agonizingly, reverberate throughout a life. Jesse Austin, on the verge of turning forty in 1990, is inhabiting three equally plausible lives: married, pregnant, living in her home town of New Jerusalem, Missouri and having an illicit affair with a maverick skywriter almost half her age; lesbian English professor in New York bringing her lover back to Missouri on a visit; divorced mother of two, running a down-and-out swimming academy in Venus Beach, Florida. Each is haunted by the moment she can't get back to, the moment hidden behind the aquamarine, when she lost the gold medal for the hundred-metre free-style at the 1968 Olympics to a fatally seductive Australian swimmer named Marty Finch.

With wit and wry affection, Carol Anshaw explores the unlived lives running parallel to the ones we have chosen.

THEREAFTER JOHNNIE
Carolivia Herron

'This first novel comes close to perfection of voice and vision
. . . a detached but intimate story of power and passion'
– *Sunday Times*

Thereafter Johnnie is a bold and brilliant novel which tells of the
fall of a family, the discovery of incest, and the birth of a child.
Johnnie is the daughter of an incestuous union between her
mother and her grandfather. More boldly still, it turns their
tormented union into a strand within a larger tapestry of abuse
whose origins are as old as slavery, and whose consequences are
nothing less than apocalyptic, Johnnie's is a story passed down
through generations, 'a swirling and terrifying epic . . . stunning
and incandescent . . . luminous and visionary' (*Los Angeles
Times Book Review*).

Carolivia Herron lives in Massachusetts. She has completed a
second novel and is at work on a third.